TWISTED CIRCLES

CLAIRE

NEW YORK TIMES BESTSELLING AUTHOR

CONTRERAS

TWISTED CIRCLES

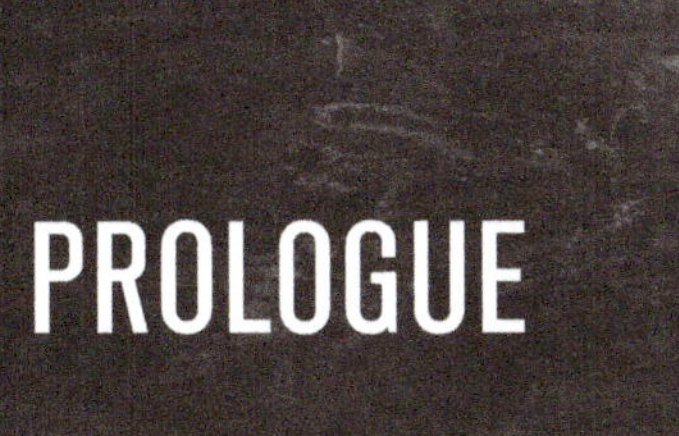

PROLOGUE

T HEY WERE FORGING A FIRE BETWEEN US, AS IF TO MAKE SURE WE knew our place.

It was the first time in my life that I stood still. Probably because it was the first time that I truly felt the weight of responsibility resting on my shoulders. My last name carried integrity, honor. It was one of the reasons I was the president of the secret society. When they asked me to do something, I did it. I wasn't compelled by a moral compass that others seemed to have. I only knew facts and calculations and those were the things I used to ensure I could do whatever was asked without getting caught.

It was what the men before me would have done. I followed a lineage of men who had led and fought in revolutions. Skilled workers who made money long before I was born. Plaques, busts, and photographs adorned my homes growing up. Reminders of what I should aspire to be like, of what others who came before me accomplished. Some would say that that in itself was a responsibility. The knowledge that not meeting certain requirements by a certain age meant failure. It was the sum of all of those things that drove me to try harder, to be better, to push myself to beat my twin in all things academia, since my brother had me beat in contact sports and other things.

But, as I stood there, my gaze on the licks of the flame, I realized I didn't know a thing about responsibility. And worse, I didn't want it. If being responsible for someone was going to make me feel this helpless, I'd rather not have it, because as she stepped toward the fire and stood still on the other side of it, my heart leaped into my throat. I knew that there were only two things I could do and both ensured the same outcome: we were all doomed.

CHAPTER ONE

T HEY SAY WE'RE ALL CUT FROM THE SAME CLOTH. THAT, IF WE EXAMINE the photographs that depict our lives, tilt them a certain way, maybe squint hard enough, we can see how similar we all are. People love to analyze every fiber of a person's existence in an effort to understand them better. As if breaking down our stories and magnifying the faults in their paths will bring us answers as to why we end up the way we do. Maybe they're on to something. Maybe others should be held accountable for our truths, our faults, and our actions. The problem is when the things we do don't add up to the person they would like us to be, they stake us.

I was told that my life started in a prison cell, so it should come as no surprise that twenty years later, a prison holding cell is the very place it began to unravel. I'd been brought in two hours ago. No one had even bothered to glance in my direction, regardless of how loudly I demanded answers, because that cloth we're all cut from shows no similarities in this lighting. I closed my eyes and thought back to two hours prior to this, when I was minding my own business and walking to my car before I was picked up by the police officer. My mind was so foggy, I could barely remember how that even happened. Had I argued with them? Was that why they'd arrested me? At the sound of dress shoes, I sat up straighter, and looked up when I saw the detective come full stop in front of the cage I was in.

"Miss Guerra, I'm Detective Barry, and I have a few questions for you." He unlocked the door and held it open.

I stood, my joints complaining about the movement after the lack of it for so long, and walked over to him, following him as he led me into a room I knew for a fact was being recorded. It had a glass wall, a table, and two chairs. I may not remember much about last night or the night before, but I remembered watching enough docuseries to know I was being interrogated and I had no idea why. A prickle ran through me.

"Am I in trouble? I didn't do anything." I froze at the door. At least I didn't think I did.

"Really?" His gaze swept to mine quickly, eyebrow arched. "I was told you were resisting an officer."

"Because the officer had no right to arrest me. I was walking home. I'd done nothing."

"Let me be the judge of that."

My grip tightened on the doorknob. "I need a lawyer."

"We're just talking, Miss Guerra. You won't need a lawyer for this."

"That's what they all say."

"You've been arrested before. Trespassing." He read off the papers in his hand and looked up at me.

"I was sixteen." I'd been alone and hungry and temporarily homeless after Karen kicked me out, and yes, I'd squatted in an empty house. I wasn't proud of it, but the beds were still in there and it was between owners.

"Still on your record." He waved the papers in his hand.

They seemed endless. I wondered what else he had on me. Did he have my entire life story written on those pages? Was it as hopeless as the real story? As pathetic? I let go of the doorknob and walked inside, taking the side across from him at the table. He pulled out his chair and signaled me to sit in mine. I signaled him to sit first. He shook his head and took a seat. I followed suit. He seemed like the kind of man who let his daughters walk all over him. The kind of father Aisha had—stern but fair, and completely bendable.

"Are you going to tell me what I'm doing here now?"

"How do you know Chris?"

"Who's Chris?"

"Chris Ryan. You were in his house last night."

"Oh." I felt myself frown. I was in someone's house last night? That must have been before I ended up in The Institute.

"So, Chris Ryan," Detective Barry prompted.

"I don't know him."

"You don't know him?"

"This is going to sound extremely convenient." I ran my hands over my face and exhaled. "But I have no memory of what happened last night. I woke up in The Institute this morning and checked myself out and I don't even know how that happened either."

"Chris says you met him on Tinder."

I searched Detective Barry's clear blue eyes. "Did something happen to Chris?"

"No. He's fine."

"So, why are we talking about some random guy I met on Tinder?"

"He called us about you."

"Why?" I blinked. "Did he also drive me to The Institute?"

"No. He says you left in a Lyft and he didn't know where you were going." He flipped through his stack of pages and brought out a picture, sliding it over to me and tapping it twice. "Do you know this woman?"

I picked up the picture and stared at it, then looked at him, and at the picture again. "It's . . . me."

"Is it?"

"I mean, it must be." The girl in the picture had my long, wavy, brown hair, brown eyes, caramel skin. She was wearing makeup, which I rarely wore, and a fancy-looking blouse I'd never seen before, but she looked just like me. I set the photo down. "Is someone trying to frame me for something?"

"Why would they do that?"

"I don't know. Why does anyone do anything? Why did I wake up in a mental institution this morning with no memory of how my night went?"

"Do you have enemies? Someone who would try to frame you?"

"No. Of course not."

"Who do you live with, Miss Guerra?"

"Alone and I keep to myself for the most part. My friend Aisha can attest to that."

"What do you do on a regular basis, besides meet guys on Tinder and go to their homes? Hang out with Aisha?"

"I'm a teacher's assistant at a small parish school and I'm studying elementary education. I hang out with my friends and drink occasionally."

"Drink?" he raised an eyebrow. "That's not legal."

"I guess you have reason to arrest me then."

"You clearly have no issues being arrested even though it'll go on your record, and I don't know about you, but I don't know many teachers with records."

"So, what's up with this?" I nodded at the picture, ignoring his analysis of me.

"This is a missing girl." He raised the picture up. "I just spent the last two hours trying to grasp what the possibilities could be and the only one I can come up with is that you're sisters."

"Yeah right." I scoffed. "I don't have a sister."

"You were both adopted on the same day from the same place, St. Nicolas' Orphanage. You have the same birthday. You both attend Ellis University. She lives a block away from campus, you live a few blocks down. Have you ever looked into who your birth parents were?"

I let myself process his words before nodding, unable to form words over the knot in my throat. Of course I'd tried to look for my birth parents. Tried and failed. I didn't have the kind of money I needed to hire an investigator or lawyer who would actually fight with me against the orphanage I'd come from, especially since it was funded by the Catholic Church. Even Karen, who was a devout Catholic and had donated half of her measly paychecks to the church most of her life, had no pull in that department. I glanced at the picture again. A sister. A twin sister. Hope bloomed inside me. It was the kind of hope life had repeatedly squashed until I no longer believed it existed, yet there it was again, rearing its head and trying to seep through.

"Miss Guerra," he said.

"The orphanage told us that it was a closed adoption. My mother—my adoptive mother—helped me once. She said they were pretty clear about not going back and asking more questions."

"Are you close to her?"

"To Karen?" I pursed my lips. "I guess. Life has kicked her down a lot, to the point that she's decided to self-medicate, but it's okay since she's drinking Jesus's blood all day until she passes out."

"I'm sorry to hear that."

"That's life." I shrugged again, then looked at the picture of the girl who wasn't me. "So, she's missing?"

"She was last seen leaving her apartment and headed to The Manor. Have you heard of The Manor?"

"Ummm . . . " I paused, rummaging through my memory bank, which remains nearly blank. "I don't think so. Is it a club?"

"It's a house, actually."

"Oh. I definitely haven't heard of it."

"Are you familiar with the secret societies at Ellis?"

"You mean the weirdos in cloaks? Yeah, who isn't."

"Well, the red cloaks, they live in The Manor. Or have parties there. I'm not really sure what else goes on there."

"So, she's part of the secret society?"

"We're not sure. We know she got an invitation from them before she disappeared."

"When was this?"

"On Friday."

"It's Sunday."

"Yes."

"And you're already this deep into this?" I felt my brows rise. "What's her name?"

"Who?"

"My sister."

"Stella."

"Stella," I repeated. "Is she rich?"

"What?"

"My sister. Is she rich?"

"Why would you ask that?"

"Why else would the police be so heavily involved in the disappearance of a brown girl who's only been gone a day, maybe two?"

He stayed quiet for a moment. "Let's just say her father is very important, and besides the fact that he wants to find his daughter, he can't have this happening now."

"So, she's rich."

"We would do it for anyone."

"Sure. What about her mother? What does she do?"

"Her mother isn't in the picture."

"She died?"

"No, she's just not in the picture."

"Hm."

"Her father has a proposal for you."

"Her father knows about me?"

"He does now. He knows we picked you up. He's watching from the other room." Detective Barry nodded his head toward the glass. I looked over and stared, wishing I could see the man on the other side.

"What's the proposal?"

"He wants you to go to The Manor as Stella."

"What?" I looked between Detective Barry and the mirror. "Did you already go to The Manor? Did you look around and ask and do your job?"

"Of course we did. They claim she never showed up there."

"That sounds like bullshit."

"It's our word against theirs."

"So you want me to pretend I'm her and show up there?"

"That's the only plan we have right now."

"Are you serious? What kind of a cop are you? If she really did disappear there or if they did something to her or whatever, they'd never buy it."

"No, but they'd be spooked enough to talk." The voice came from the overhead speaker and made me jump in my seat.

"With as much money and connections as you probably have, I'm sure you can think of another way to break them down." I looked at the glass.

"This isn't the first time someone has gone missing," Detective Barry said.

"No shit. I know that. Didn't a girl die last year because of one of the secret societies?"

"That was an unfortunate circumstance and nothing like this one." That was the dad's voice again.

"Why doesn't he just come into the room?"

"Legalities," Detective Barry said. "You can always just be yourself and go to The Manor and say you're looking for her. I'll drive you there myself."

"Don't you want a chance at having a sister?" the voice in the other room asked.

"Of course I do." I shot the glass a pointed look and hoped the glare made its way to the other side. "But this is crazy and doesn't make sense and I don't want to die."

"We'd wipe your records," he said. "No school is going to hire someone with a record. We'll pay off your student debt."

"You're just going to give me money, just like that?" I raised an eyebrow. "What if I don't find her? What if she's . . . " I inhale the word before it spills out of my mouth.

"She's not dead. As far as the money, you keep it and do whatever you want with it," the man said.

"And the secret society pays fifty grand for joining," Detective Barry added.

"What the . . . ? Fifty grand, just like that?"

"Just like that."

"How do you know that?" I narrowed my eyes at Barry.

"We hear things."

"But you can't question for shit."

"We questioned. We searched. We found nothing. We need answers and we need them fast and this is going nowhere quick."

"And you can't have another death on your hands less than a year after that Ly girl died."

No one said a thing about that, which I took as confirmation. Fifty grand plus whatever Stella's father was willing to give me and I'd come out with a sister and answers. I looked at the glass again.

"Do you know who our birth parents are?"

"We also tried and hit a wall, but if you do this, I'll turn every stone and find out, since it's important to both of you," the man behind the glass said.

"I don't know anything about her. I wouldn't know where to start."

"They don't know much about her either, not really. I'll give you her clothes, her apartment, her car, and you can go from there." He paused. "They're having a party tonight. She would have gone to that."

"And you want me to go as her."

"Please. The only way to find out what really happens in these societies is to join one of them. Detective Barry can't do it. I can't do it. You're the only one who can. Stella needs you."

"Stella," I repeated.

"Stella Thompson," he said.

"Stella Thompson." I tried it on, then again. The third time I repeated it, I tripped over the last name. "Thompson as in the neuroscientist? Aren't you running for office?"

"You're up to date with current events." Detective Barry raised an eyebrow.

"The signs are hard to miss. And he treated my father after he had a stroke," I said, looking toward the glass. I'd been too young but Karen never let me forget that name. She'd felt indebted to him for working pro bono.

"I hope he's well," Dr. Thompson said.

"He's dead."

"I'm sorry to hear that." He paused for a beat before asking, "Will you do this? Will you help us find my daughter?"

"I have another question."

"Ask."

"If people know she's missing and the cops alerted the people in The Manor, wouldn't it be a little strange for me . . . or her . . . to show up?"

"No one else knows she's missing. The reason I do is because she didn't show up for breakfast yesterday and we always have breakfast together. And her phone stopped tracking the minute she got near that house."

"You track her phone?" I balked at the mirror.

"Yes and I'll track yours if you're going to do this."

"Seriously?" I blinked. "Are you going to pay for my phone bill too?"

"Sure, why not?"

"Oh. Okay then. I guess you can track it."

"You'll do this?" That was Detective Barry, who almost looked like he wanted me to turn it down, but wasn't at the liberty to say that.

"That's what I'm saying."

Stella Thompson was a far cry from Eva Guerra, but then again, so was everything else about her life, it seemed. It didn't matter though. She was my sister and I'd accept her for whoever she was, as I'm sure she'd do the same for me.

CHAPTER TWO

O n our way to The Manor, Dr. Thompson filled me in on a few things—Stella's major and schedule. He drove his fancy Audi as I stared straight ahead, trying to memorize the roads we were on. I'd placed my backpack by my feet, but Dr. Thompson had reached to the backseat and given me a brown leather MCM backpack that belonged to Stella.

"So everything will be consistent," he said, eyeing my hair. "Maybe I should take you to the hair salon first."

And he did. Without even calling ahead, we showed up at Ellis's most prestigious salon, and were seated and treated within five minutes. I'd never been to a hair salon before. Not like that. They'd given me champagne, and unlike Detective Barry, no one batted an eyelash at whether or not I was of age. A nice man with purple and pink locks, trimmed my ends and conditioned my hair before styling it into pretty loose waves. My hair had been a cross between curly and beach waves from relaxing treatments and a perpetual wash-and-go routine, and this was a far cry from that. A nice girl that couldn't have been much older than me did light makeup after waxing my eyebrows and then took me into a back room to wax other parts of me. The entire experience was excruciatingly amazing. By the time I stepped out of the salon and back into Dr. Thompson's car, I felt like a brand-new person. His eyes looked haunted when he saw me, and I was reminded what my purpose here was to begin with.

"I have a suitcase in the trunk with her things in it. You'll take it with you to The Manor and use it. You'll also have access to her apartment, but by the time you run out of clothes I fully expect this nightmare to be over," he said as he drove.

"What is she like?" I looked over in time to catch his slight smile.

"She's funny, smart, kind. She's reserved. Extremely devout in her faith."

"Really?" I looked over at him quickly, feeling myself smile. "I am too, despite the arrest record."

"She wanted to become a nun." He met my eyes briefly. "Her brother and I talked her out of it. It would be a waste to have such a brilliant mind and beautiful face in a convent for the rest of her life."

"She has a brother?"

"Gilbert. He's seventeen and studying abroad right now. Good kid."

"Abroad where? Is he also adopted?"

"No." Dr. Thompson smiled as he shook his head. "His mother and I were colleagues. We were never together. We co-parent pretty well though. He's in Ireland at the moment finishing up his senior year. He goes to an international school in the city that allows those opportunities."

"Wow."

"Stella did the same. She chose Spain. Barcelona."

"I've never even left the state." I laughed lightly.

"You will." He glanced over at me as he slowed down the car. "Once this is over, you'll have plenty of opportunities to travel."

We both looked at the iron gates ahead of us. There was an S written on both sides of it. Beyond the gates, there were two long rows of trees that led the path to whatever lay ahead.

"This is like Bruce Wayne's house," I said.

"Please be careful, Eva. Report anything you hear." He handed me a brand-new cell phone, still in the box. "I'm going out of town for a conference, but I'm one phone call away. If you ever feel like you're in danger, Detective Barry's number is also saved there for you."

I took the phone and finished shoving all of my belongings into Stella's MCM backpack. I took a deep breath as the gates opened before us and Dr. Thompson began to drive his car toward the house, my lungs stalling as I took in the magnitude of it.

The Manor wasn't a house. It was a castle. It must have had at least twenty bedrooms and I couldn't begin to imagine how many acres accompanied it. Karen had a friend who had a big house and growing up it was my favorite place to go. I'd spend the day there sometimes running around in their yard and splashing in their pool. Their house looked miniature in comparison to this. It wasn't a far-fetched idea that Stella could have gotten lost in there.

The question was, would I? Would I be able to find her and save myself at the same time? I unlocked the car and stepped out, walking to the trunk upon hearing it click and open. After getting the suitcase out, I waved at Dr. Thompson and walked up to the door. Even those were massive, larger than life, as I stood before them. They were iron, just like the gates, and just like the gates, their maker had bent the iron and willed it to intertwine and create a masterpiece. There was a gold S scripted in the middle of each of them. I took a deep breath and rang the door-bell and looked back as I heard a car retreating. Dr. Thompson was driving away, slowly, but still, driving away. I rang the bell again, then tried the handle, which was locked. I wasn't sure how much time had gone by before I remembered the key in my backpack. Surely, I wouldn't have a key to this place though. I'd woken up with that key in my own backpack, not Stella's, but as I reached into her backpack, which still smelled of new leather, I found two keychains. I brought them out and looked at them. They had the same S on them and looked like the same key. My hands shook.

With my heart lodged in my throat, I brought one of the keys to the lock and slid it in. It fit perfectly, but I knew from experience sometimes that didn't mean much. Once, Karen had tossed me out of the house and changed the locks on me. When I returned home, the key fit the lock, but wouldn't turn. After pounding and calling and threatening to call the cops, I ended up having to sneak into my bedroom that night. It was that memory that made me pause before turning the key, and the thought that, if it didn't turn and unlock, I wasn't sure what I would do. Would I run home with my tail between my legs and pretend none of this happened? Would I go to my therapist with this? I didn't want to. That was probably what happened last night. It was probably how I ended up sleeping at The Institute in the first place. I shuddered. The Manor was where a secret society resided and even though I didn't know much about the societies, I knew they handpicked wealthy students with connections to join. There was no way facing a bunch of rich kids would be worse than dealing with the staff at The Institute.

On that thought, I turned the key.

CHAPTER THREE

ANTICIPATION ROLLED THROUGH ME AS I STEPPED INTO THE DARK house and shut the door quietly behind me, instantly feeling like I'd been transported to another century, a foreign place unlike anything I'd ever known. The walls on either side of me were covered in some kind of wallpaper and wood panel. On every panel was a sconce holding a flickering candle. On every piece of wallpaper, a portrait. Classical music was playing loudly, seemingly making the candles flicker more with each touch of the piano and stroke of the violin. I began to walk quietly, slowly, taking in every portrait, which had men in military suits, archbishops or cardinals or whoever wore those fancy hats, doctors in their white lab coats, all with eyes that seemed to move as I moved past them. All watching, waiting, judging. I swallowed my nerves and moved forward, finding the place oddly familiar, wondering if I'd been here before, but no, it was impossible. I may not remember what happened to me these last two days, but that didn't mean I had no memory prior and I knew I hadn't been here.

Once I reached the end of the long hall, the house seemed to open up. There was a large round table in the center with a large glass vase that contained red roses. So many roses. It must've cost a fortune just to fill this vase regularly. Just past the table, there were two grand wooden staircases covered in dark red carpet. To either side of me, there were two endless hallways, but unlike the one I was in, light from outside shone in and basked both sides with the natural, dim light that the setting sun provided.

"Hello?" I followed the music, rolling the suitcase behind me.

To my left, there was an open space, a sitting area with fancy sofas I wouldn't dare to dirty. Beyond it, there were windows that looked over the back of the house. The only things I could see were woods and more woods. I kept walking. The music grew louder still. My grip tightened on the handle of the suitcase as I opened my mouth to call out again, but stopped when I reached the next open area—a vast room with a black grand piano in the corner, three large white couches surrounding it, and four guys wearing different color polos. One of the guys was sitting behind the piano, his fingers moving deftly on the keys as he seemingly played along to the song blasting on the speakers. The other three were sitting on the couches looking relaxed with glasses in their hands. One was passing a joint to the guy beside him when I did a little wave to catch their attention. Then, the one passing the joint, hit a button on the control beside him, putting a stop to the music on the speakers, but the pianist didn't seem to notice as he continued playing along, a beautiful, haunting melody that seemed impossibly difficult to play.

"Um. Hi." I licked my lips. My voice was small in comparison to my surroundings.

The pianist stopped playing instantly and stood in one swift motion. He was tall and lean and when his eyes met mine I felt a jolt of lightning strike through me. He kept his expression guarded, so I couldn't be sure he'd felt it too, but at least as I stood there, the air felt charged and my words seemed to be stuck in the back of my throat, unable to make their way out of my mouth.

"Are you Stella?" the pianist asked after a moment.

"Yes." I cleared my throat, tilting my chin up a little, wondering if the real Stella Thompson would feel small or like she fit in just fine with the likes of them. "Stella Thompson."

"You were supposed to be here yesterday," he said.

"I got caught up in something." I took a deep breath. "But I'm here now."

The three guys on the couches looked over at the pianist as if waiting for him to comment on how to handle the situation. I looked at him as well, even though the scrutiny in his eyes made me feel like I was shrinking by the second. I'd never enjoyed being in a room with rich people. Once, I'd had a job in the country club by my house as a hostess, and I never felt like I belonged. They were never outright mean to me, but the judgment they cast was enough for me to know I wasn't worthy of sitting at their tables, only cleaning up after them. It was fine. I wasn't like my friend Aisha, who always felt the urge to fit in. At the end of the day, the demons I carried were enough to remind me that I was an island all on my own. I studied the faces of each of the guys in the room, who all seemed surprised by my presence, and fought the urge to turn away. These specific kinds of rich people were the worst—entitled and unforgiving.

"She's a woman," one of them said.

"Well, now that we got that out of the way, can you tell me what I'm doing here?" I looked at him and back at the pianist.

"You've been hand-selected to potentially join our society, The Swords," the pianist said.

"Potentially?"

"There's a test you have to pass before we officially invite you in."

"A test?"

"A test," the pianist said. "Will is going to show you to your chambers now."

I tore my gaze from him to look at Will, the joint passer, as he set his glass down and stood, walking over to me. The closer he got, the bigger he got and the more he reeked of weed. He smiled a little as he stopped in front of me and it reached his brown eyes, setting me at ease, at least momentarily.

"Right this way." He signaled toward where I'd just come from.

"Stella Thompson," the pianist called out just as we began walking away. Will and I stopped walking. That was another thing I hated about rich people. It was as if they rehearsed the exact moment in which they'd call the room's attention back to their target. I met his gaze again. "The party is at nine. Be ready by then. We'll have food brought up to your room in the meantime."

"Okay."

"Your outfit is in your closet, as well as your robe. Wear both."

I nodded and looked away. I needed to work on holding his gaze longer, but unlike Will's, the pianist's eyes were cold and his expression was hard and it made me feel things I wasn't entirely prepared for. I held my head high as we began to walk again. I could be cold too. Will stopped at the foot of the second set of stairs.

"I'll take your bag." He set his hand beside mine on the handle.

"You don't have to."

"My mother would kill me if I let a lady carry her bag up these stairs." He raised a dark eyebrow. "I insist."

"Well, at least one of your mothers raised you well." I let go of the bag and began walking upstairs beside him.

"They're all pretty okay." He smiled, looking over at me. "Adam takes a little while to warm up."

"Adam's the pianist?"

"Yep."

"Is he the leader of this cult?"

"Cult." Will chuckled. "Yeah, you can say that. He's the president."

"That's exactly how self-important people stay self-important, because people keep throwing fancy titles at them."

"Well, he's an Astor. He was born with a self-important air and a fancy title." He winked. I exhaled when we reached the top of the steps, grateful he'd carried the bag after all.

"I believe it." I looked down at the middle of the stairwell and noticed how high we'd climbed, then shuddered and stepped away from the rail.

"Scared of heights?"

"Scared of death."

"Hm." He nodded as if taking note.

"What's on the other side of the hall?"

"More rooms." He nodded that way. "Guy's wing." He nodded this way. "Girl's wing."

"How many girls?"

"So far? One."

"Where is she?"

"Standing right in front of me."

"Me?" My brows rose. "Where are the rest?"

"Didn't show," he said. "Honestly, I'm surprised you're even here."

"Why? Because I was crazy enough to receive an invitation and report to the address alone without doing my research?"

"When you put it that way, you make all of us sound crazy." He laughed.

"Aren't you?"

"Depends on the time of day."

"Right." I stopped walking in front of the door he stopped walking at. "Second door to the right then."

"This one is yours."

"And the other three girls will stay in the other three rooms? If they were to show up, I mean." I glanced at each door. "Why am I number two and not number one?"

"That's the way it was written."

"Where?"

"In the instructions we received."

"From Adam the self-important pianist?"

"No." Will's eyes twinkled. "From the Chancellor."

"Sounds important." I felt my lips twitch. "And self-important."

"He is both and he has a God complex." Will took a key out of his pocket and handed it to me. It was on the same red keychain as the ones I had in my backpack, but this keychain had a number 2 written in the front and ABA written on the back.

"What's ABA?"

"Adam Barnaby Astor."

"Barnaby?" I frowned. "And why do I have his key?"

"He's in charge of your initiation, which means he's in charge of you."

"Says who?"

"That's the way it's written."

"Jesus." I breathed out. "I would love to see that book."

"You will, assuming you make it out of the initiation."

"Initiation? What does that mean?"

"It means you're in for an interesting next few days." Will shot me a kind smile. "Just remember, you chose to be here." With that, he turned and walked away.

"I chose to be here." I put the key up and unlocked yet another door.

CHAPTER FOUR

THE BACKPACK HANGING OFF MY SHOULDER DROPPED WITH A thump, along with my jaw as I switched the lights on and took in the room. Huge would have been one way of describing it, but that word seemed insufficient to what I was looking at. It was bigger than my apartment. I left my bags by the door and walked the entirety of it, wondering who in the world would need this much space. Like the rest of the house, it seemed like it belonged in an old European castle. The wallpaper was white and pink, the bed was a queen four-post cherry wood bed with white sheets. The dresser was cherry wood to match the bed. In the corner of the room, there was a sitting area and vanity. It looked like something a queen would have in her room. I pushed the door to the left of the bed open and found a bathroom with white tile and white walls with gold details. There was a large white clawfoot tub in the center of it with gold feet that looked like lion's and a gold faucet that sat on the back side of it, closest to one of the walls. Surrounding it were four white see-through curtains that were currently tied to four gold, thin poles. It looked like a dream. On the other side, a sink that looked like a small version of the tub, an ornate gold mirror over it, and a see-through shower that looked like it had recently been installed.

I walked out of the bathroom and into the room again, past the bed, dresser, and sitting area, and opened the two doors there, which led to a walk-in closet the same size as the bathroom. Hanging in the closet were three black garment bags and sitting beneath, one pair of black heels and white, fluffy slippers. I unzipped the first garment bag and found a black sequin dress with a modest neckline that would hit me right at the collarbone. When I turned it over, I found the entire back was exposed and also hanging from the hanger was a black mask that I knew wouldn't cover my face fully. The next garment bag had a white robe. The other, a red robe. I remembered the first on-campus party I'd attended with Aisha and how we'd been spooked by people wearing red robes and hoods. I zipped the bag back up, unpacked the clothes in the suitcase, and set up the phone Dr. Thompson had given me.

As promised, Dr. Thompson's number was saved under "Dr. Russel Thompson," as well as Detective Barry's number and Stella Thompson's. My heart skipped a beat at the sight of her name. I pushed the number and dialed. It went straight to voicemail, but upon hearing her voice, my own breath held.

"Hey, this is Stella. Don't leave a message. I won't get it. Please text me. Spanx!"

I called again and played it again. It didn't sound like my voice. I hated my voice. Hers sounded nice. She enunciated every letter in every word the way a proper lady would. I practiced it.

"Hey, this is Stella."

"Hey, this is Stella."

"This is Stella."

I said it over and over, until I thought there was a chance I might convince myself of the fact that I was no longer Eva Guerra, but Stella Thompson. Then, I stood and practiced it in front of the floor-length mirror. There was a knock at the door, which interrupted my rehearsal. When I opened it, I saw an older lady who looked like she could be someone's grandmother, wearing blue scrubs.

"Um. Hi?"

"Your dinner, Miss Thompson."

"Sure." I opened the door wider and let her come in with the tray in her hands. "Do you want me to get that for you?"

"Do no such thing." Her tone made me shut my mouth.

She was short, with wide hips and dark eyes that looked like they'd lost their light long ago. It killed me to see that in older people. Karen wasn't as old as this woman, but her eyes were like that too. Faraway looks that made me wonder what this was all for. All of this life and experience we gain through the years that seem to amount to the loss we bear.

"You may shut the door," she said, setting the tray down on the table in the sitting area.

"Oh." I did as I was told and shut the door quietly.

"You may approach." Her eyebrow rose. "I don't bite."

I laughed lightly, walking over to her and taking a seat on one of the two chairs. She sat in the other. I didn't know what was underneath the silver bowl, but I was starving and whatever it was smelled good.

"Grilled cheese and tomato bisque." She nodded at the tray. "It'll get cold if you don't start eating. I'm only here because I don't like it when people eat alone."

"Oh." I uncovered the plate and began eating, then stopped mid-chew and raised the plate, with the other half of the grilled cheese to offer it to her.

"I'm fine." She smiled. "Thank you."

I kept eating, too hungry to speak; I dipped the grilled cheese into the soup and devoured the meal as if it was my last, and then it hit me, I couldn't remember the last time I ate. Had Dr. Thompson fed me? I didn't think so. I had water and champagne at the hair salon, but that was it. They definitely didn't feed me at the jail. I couldn't remember anything prior to that so it was no use. I thought hard, squeezed my eyes shut as I chewed to try to remember the last time I had something in my stomach, but it was no use.

"Slow down," she said. "You'll get a stomachache."

I slowed my chewing and swallowed. "So you work here?"

"I do. Otherwise, these boys would starve, though I will say a few of them know their way around a kitchen."

"How long have you been working here?"

"Forty-three years."

"Forty . . . what?" I blinked. "How old are you, if you don't mind me asking?"

"Sixty-five and it's a rude question." She shot me a pointed look. "I feel fifty-five most days."

"You look younger than sixty-five." I continued eating.

"That's why I keep working. It keeps my mind sharp and my muscles tight." She flexed her arm.

"What's your name?"

"Marie. What's yours?"

"E . . . Stella."

"Estella?"

"No." I cleared my throat. "Just Stella."

"Hm." She eyed me funnily. "Do you know what they do to girls around here?"

"No." I lowered the bite of sandwich I had left and held my breath. "What?"

"I don't know. I'm asking you."

"I've been here a few hours. You've been here forty-three years. You'd know more than me."

"Well, there are rumors." She glanced toward the bathroom. "But I don't believe rumors."

"What are the rumors?"

"Nope. I don't gossip either." She met my gaze again. "God frowns upon gossip."

"True." I finished the sandwich.

"There's a chapel. If you're interested. In the mouth of the woods, you can't miss it." She picked up the tray. "They have services every Sunday at eight in the morning. We also need help cleaning it, so if you'd like to busy yourself with something in your time off I can put in a word."

"And that's part of . . . this?" I waved a hand around the room. "The cleaning the chapel, I mean."

"No. The Swords aren't allowed in the chapel, so you shouldn't tell them."

"But they know about it," I said. "Right?"

"Yes." She set the tray on her hip as if carrying a baby. "They don't wake up early enough for Sunday service, but if you want to come, you're welcome to."

"Who attends the Masses then?" I stood slowly.

"Let's just say, it's a women's Mass. For women, by women."

"What denomination?" I asked. She looked at me like I was going too far, so I added, "I only ask because women aren't allowed to give Catholic Masses and I'm Catholic and you called it a chapel, so . . ."

"Join us next Sunday and find out."

"Maybe I will."

"Good. See you there." She started leaving, but took a step back into the room and glanced over at me. "And girl, don't trust anyone in here, you hear?"

I nodded, suddenly a lot more frightened than I was when I walked in here.

Where the hell was I?

CHAPTER FIVE

I LOOKED AT THE CARDSTOCK AND READ IT AGAIN. I THOUGHT about Marie's words. *Don't trust anyone in here.* It shouldn't be an issue considering that I didn't trust anyone outside of here either, but hearing it aloud from someone who worked here as long as she said she had was different. I started to pace the room, hitting my hand with the cardstock as I did. I'd checked Stella's computer and found nothing of note. She seemed to only use her computer for academic purposes, which I couldn't relate to. She didn't have social media, but then again, neither did I.

Debbie Maslow hated social media. She said it was a breeding ground for bullies and I didn't need any outside factors affecting my mental health, and because I'd known Dr. Maslow for as long as I could remember and she treated me more like family than a patient, I listened dutifully. Besides, the one month I had downloaded Snapchat I thought it was incredibly dumb, and I didn't have enough cute outfits for Instagram. Stella obviously did though. I stopped in front of the closet and looked at the clothes I'd hung up. She had an eclectic style, which I liked. I was more of a jeans and T-shirt girl. I wore my Converse until I could feel the pavement against my socks. To work, I usually wore jeans and pretty blouses or conservative dresses I found at Goodwill. I was the best bargain shopper by far, according to Aisha. I stopped walking at the thought of Aisha and called her.

"Hello?"

"Hey." I smiled at the sound of her voice.

"Why are you calling me?"

"What do you mean?" Her tone wiped the smile off my face. "Why wouldn't I call?"

"I meant it when I said I no longer wanted to be your friend."

"What? Why?" My chest squeezed.

"Eva. I can't. I don't have time for this shit right now. What you did was messed up and I'm not going to stand here and take that kind of treatment from you."

"What are you . . . ? I don't know what you're talking about. I don't remember what happened the last couple of days and I just need you to explain—"

"Look, I'm not the one who has to explain anything to you." With that, she hung up.

I felt instantly bereft. Aisha had been a part of my life for as long as I could remember. How could she just hang up on me right now? And say she wasn't my friend? It made no sense. There was no Eva without Aisha. I stumbled as I tried to find the edge of the bed, to look for the pills in my bag I knew would set me right again. My vision began to spot before I could reach them. The bedroom door opened and I saw a flash of red walking in. A cloak. A red cloak. As he stepped forward, lowering the hood from his head, I lost my battle with my eyes and they shut completely.

"Stella."

Slap.

"Stella."

Slap.

"Ste—"

"Jesus Christ. What is wrong with you?" My eyes popped open and I sat up straight, batting the hand away, my head woozy as I focused on my surroundings. I didn't know where I was, but I could make out Adam's face too close to mine. "Is slapping women your kink?"

"You passed out."

"I had a spell." I shimmied my body and pushed myself away from him.

"A spell? You faint often?"

"Sometimes." I shook my head and waved a hand. "It's not a big deal."

"Depends where you get them I guess." He frowned. "Have you been to a doctor for these?"

"I take a thousand pills for a thousand ailments. Yes, I've been to the doctor. No, they don't help." I got a better look at him. "Why are you wearing that ridiculous red cape?"

"Cloak. It's part of the first night of initiation." He flung it behind him to reveal the tuxedo he wore beneath. I definitely wouldn't admit it aloud, but Adam was hot.

"Right. Initiation. What are you doing in my room anyway?"

"I was making sure you were getting ready. I kept knocking,

you didn't answer; I figured we had a case of a runaway, so I decided to come in and check."

"Right. Since you have the key." I eyed the key in his hand. He tucked it in his pocket.

"Exactly."

"Are you going to use that key to come in here in the middle of the night?"

"Are you inviting me to?" He cocked an eyebrow, but his hazel eyes were twinkling.

"No." Even as I snapped the word I knew I wouldn't throw him out if he did show up. Adam broke whatever was brewing between us by standing up.

"You're due downstairs in half an hour." He glanced at his watch. "Twenty-five minutes now."

"How did you just dock five minutes from me?" I stood with the help of the nightstand beside me.

"You were passed out for five."

"Five whole minutes?" My jaw dropped. "And what exactly were you doing, Prince Charming, staring at me?"

"What was I supposed to do? Kiss you?"

"I guess that would have been slightly creepy, being that you're wearing a red cape and all."

"So if I'd taken the cape off it wouldn't have been creepy?"

"Still creepy, just slightly less." I brought a hand up and used my thumb and forefinger to measure an inch. "I just think it's beyond creepy that you stared at me for five minutes."

"I also measured your pulse."

"Oh, you measured my pulse while you slapped me. Well, thank you, Adam." I placed a hand on my heart. "You have revived me. You can go now."

"Twenty minutes." He turned around and closed the door behind him.

I ran over and locked it for good measure, not that it would keep him out. I needed to figure out a way to move the dresser in front of the door tonight. There was no way I'd get any sleep knowing someone had access to this room.

"Eighteen minutes," he said from the other side of the door. I jumped.

"Are you going to stand there the whole time?"

"Yep."

I grunted out my disapproval loud enough so he'd hear me and marched over to the bathroom.

CHAPTER SIX

WHEN I OPENED THE DOOR, TWENTY-FIVE MINUTES LATER, ADAM was indeed standing on the other side of it, waiting for me. His eyes didn't even move past my face to see how I looked. He just shot me an exasperated look, as if to tell me I took too long. I shrugged and raised the mask in my hand.

"Am I supposed to wear this?"

"Was it with your dress?"

"Yes."

"Then, the answer is yes."

I put it on over my hair, which I'd managed not to mess up while I showered and changed. There was no way in hell I could recreate salon hair on a time restriction.

"Have any of the other girls gotten here?"

"I wouldn't know. I've been standing outside of your room for the last hour."

"I didn't even take an hour."

"Sure felt like it."

"Aren't you the president? Shouldn't you know who's arrived?" I held on to the rail as we started going down the stairs.

"I'm glad William decided to fill you in on all things Adam."

"All things Adam." I glanced up at him. He was still taller

than me even in the four-inch heels I wore. "Do you even hear yourself talk?"

"Yep. Same as everyone else."

"Normal people don't talk like you."

"Good thing I don't like normal." He winked.

I shook my head and looked away. "So, this party, am I your date or something?"

He chuckled. "Don't you wish."

"Um, excuse me, sir." I looked up at him, pausing mid-step. "Don't *you* wish. I'm just asking so I can act accordingly. I don't know how this whole initiation thing works."

"I wouldn't worry about it if I were you. I've never initiated a woman before, but something tells me you're going to do a lot better than all of the guys who have come before you."

"What's up with that anyway? Me being the only girl and all?"

"I don't make the rules. I just follow them." He waved a hand for me to hurry it up and keep walking. "The Chancellor said he'd explain it. Apparently, it's in our manual."

"You haven't read the manual?"

"Not all of it. It's seven-hundred pages of antiquated information." He raised an eyebrow. "Do you want to read the manual?"

"No, thanks."

We went down the main hallway and took a left. Like the entranceway, this hallway was filled with portraits, busts, and sconces illuminating the way. The dim flicker of the candles didn't make it easy to make out the faces on each portrait, but it definitely made them look creepy, and maybe that was the point of it all.

"How old is this place?"

"As old as time." He glanced at me when I shot him a look

that I wasn't sure he could make out until he said, "That's what they told us when we first got here. *This place is as old as time itself.*"

"The Chancellor said that?"

"He and the benefactors."

"Am I meeting them as well?"

"In due time. They're not around much this time of year." He reached into his pocket and brought out a mask, securing it on his face as we reached a door that looked like it led to a dungeon. Instead of opening the door, he knocked ten times in a sequence that sounded familiar.

"Is that the Imperial March?"

"Will's idea." He shook his head.

"You guys are total nerds." I shook my head.

Hot nerds, but nerds nonetheless. There was a loud click and I found myself holding my breath as the door opened with a slow creaking sound. A masked tall guy was standing on the other side.

"Sixty-seven people have arrived." Will closed the door slowly behind us.

I tried not to react when I heard the heavy thump and the obvious lock that followed. It wasn't that I was claustrophobic, but being enclosed in a dark space with two guys I didn't know, who could overpower me, wasn't necessarily ideal. I didn't even have a weapon on me that I could use to defend myself.

"Let's go." Adam offered me his hand to take.

"I thought you said this wasn't a date."

"You're wearing six-inch heels. You want to fall to your death, that's fine, but you won't be doing it on my watch. Grab onto my arm."

I did as instructed because he wasn't wrong. I gripped his arm tighter when my dress caught on my left heel.

"See?"

"They're four-inch heels, not six."

He shook his head, but remained silent as we continued to walk slowly down. The only thing I could make out was the cobblestone walls on either side of us that most likely matched the steps we were taking. There were lit candles in sconces here as well. Maybe he wasn't wrong about this place being as old as time itself. It sure looked like it. I couldn't even imagine how many people it would take to keep this place clean. I thought about Marie and what she'd said about needing help in the chapel.

"What's in the woods?" I asked as we reached the last step.

"Bears."

"I'm serious. Is there anything out there? It's a big property."

"Yes, there are things out there. All of the houses in Blood Point share one common perimeter of the woods," he said. "So if you see anything out there, it doesn't necessarily have to be ours."

"You didn't answer me. What's in the woods?"

"Some abandoned buildings close to our property, but we're not allowed."

"Not even you?"

"Not even me."

"Why?"

"You ask too many questions." He sighed heavily and stopped walking when we reached a circle.

"I don't like going into things blindly."

"Yet you showed up because of a simple, mysterious card."

My mouth opened and shut quickly. My first instinct in any situation was to argue, set up a parameter of defenses, but he was right. I showed up. We stood in the middle of two dungeon doors. I felt myself shiver with anticipation. Adam noticed. I was sure there wasn't much Adam *didn't* notice. He eyed me but didn't say anything. He didn't reassure me that I'd be fine or warn me about what was to come. He just stepped forward and opened the door to the left and led me inside. Loud EDM music blared, a shocking difference from the muted sounds in the hall. The walls and doors must have been thicker than I thought for the sound to not travel. In here, strobe lights whirled around dancing people. It was a full-blown party, and we were inside of a cave.

They must have been here forever for them to have built the mansion on top of it. The rocked wall looked like something you'd find in the Parisian catacombs, which was a low-key obsession of mine. I stuck a hand out and touched it as we walked, the tips of my fingers grazing over each bump and groove. The DJ booth was set up smack in the center of the room, on top of a rock that overlooked everything, but not even the thumping of the music moved these walls. I continued my perusal as Adam led me toward the back. Not everyone in here was wearing a cloak. There were women in flapper dresses and sequin dresses similar to mine. Men in tuxedos, some in red cloaks, but their hoods weren't covering their faces. Everyone had a mask on. My hand was still in Adam's, I noticed, when I tried to turn around to take in the rest of the room. He looked at me over his shoulder as I slipped my hand out of his grasp when we reached the bar.

"Whiskey," I said loudly. "Whiskey on the rocks. Please. Make it a triple."

"A double." The bartender raised an eyebrow as he lifted a bottle of Blue Label and poured, handing it to me. He looked at Adam. "For you?"

"I'll have the same."

"Is this an open bar?" I asked as Adam got his drink and turned around, leaning against the bar.

"You think we're going to invite people to a party and charge them for the alcohol they consume?"

"I mean, isn't that what most people who throw a party like this do?"

"Not unless they're trying to raise funds for a good cause."

He looked like he wanted to ask me something, but thought better of it, and I decided I needed to get my rich girl lingo together before I made statements like that again. It was just foreign to me. I mean, what kind of life did an Astor live? What kind of life did a Thompson live? Where I was from, people charged five dollars to get into a regular house party and you were supposed to bring your own booze. Bringing the glass up to my mouth, I took a sip of whiskey and nearly orgasmed. I usually stuck to Jameson. It was what Karen kept in the house. It was cheap, but I liked it. This, however, was unlike anything I'd ever savored.

We both looked at the dance floor as we stood there sipping our drinks and I wondered where in the world the real Stella Thompson could have been. If she'd really been dropped off here, how had she not made it inside the house? It seemed impossible, yet I had her key. She'd left it behind in her backpack. I had two red keys that opened the front door, which meant I had also been given a key to come here. My blood ran cold. I'd been so distracted with the house and the party and moving forward and getting this over with, that I completely forgot to go back to my own backpack. I glanced up at Adam.

"Do the other girls have names?"

"What?" He leaned in.

"Do the other girls you're expecting to come have names?"

"Of course."

"Do you know what they look like?"

"No."

"So the president doesn't know everything."

"Neither of you have social media, which is pretty ridiculous." He shot me a pointed look. "How do you show off about your life?"

I hid my laugh behind the glass as I took another sip. I had no life to show off about, so even if Dr. Maslow hadn't insisted from early on that social media was bad, I probably wouldn't have caved. Aisha was obsessed with Instagram and TikTok. Sometimes, when I was feeling extra lonely, I understood the value of the platforms. You couldn't feel like you were alone in the world if you were scrolling endless content with proof that there were others out there. I also wasn't as desperate for attention. I lowered my glass and nodded toward the dance floor.

"There are a lot of girls here."

"An all-guy party wouldn't be very fun." His mouth tilted.

"Are you going to dance?"

"No."

"So you're just going to stand here all night and watch everyone dance?"

"You're free to do whatever you want." He shrugged a shoulder.

I drained the rest of my whiskey, set the glass down, and made my way to the dance floor. There was no way my hips could ever resist a song, and I definitely wanted to talk to someone besides Adam. When I reached the side of the dance floor opposite of him, I looked back up and saw him watching me.

"You here alone?"

"Maybe." I looked up at the guy beside me. He was wearing a black cloak and mask. His lips pulled into a wide, slow grin at my answer.

"I'm assuming the black cloak means you're part of a different secret society?"

"The best one."

"Really?" I let out a laugh. "What's so special about it?"

"Aside from the fact that I'm in it?" He glanced around the room. "I guess the same thing that goes along with most of the other societies."

"Ah, I thought you were going to try to convince me to jump ship and join yours instead."

"I wouldn't dare." He smiled and eyed me again. "That white cloak means trouble."

"Trouble how?" I glanced around the room quickly and realized I was the only one wearing one. Shit. How had I not noticed that before?

"It means you're off-limits."

"Yet you decided to saddle up and come talk to me."

"I have a thing about rules."

"Interesting." I raised an eyebrow. "So do I."

"What's your name, Lamb?"

"Stella." I fought back a shiver. "What's yours?"

"Nolan." He cocked his head. "Stella what?"

"Thompson." I mimicked his movement. "Nolan what?"

"Astor."

"Well, shit." I shook my head and looked in the direction I'd left Adam, finding he was still staring at me.

I couldn't say exactly how, but I could tell he was brooding. Maybe in the way his jaw ticked or the way his glass seemed to be frozen mid-air, as if he was holding his breath in anticipation of how this would play out.

"My reputation precedes me," Nolan said. "I used to think that was a good thing. These days, I'm not so sure."

"Does it matter to you if it's a bad thing?"

"I guess it depends on what they're saying." He shrugged a shoulder, stirring his nearly empty glass.

"What about your brother?"

"What about him?" When he met my gaze this time, his expression was serious.

"What's his reputation?"

"With him, what you see is what you get."

"And with you?"

"I rarely let anyone see me."

"Must be lonely."

"I'll live." His lip twitched. It struck me that his mouth and chin and jaw were eerily similar to Adam's.

"Who's older? You or Adam?"

"Him." He set the glass down behind him. "By one minute."

"You're twins." My brows rose. My heart felt like it had leaped twenty steps with the knowledge. *What were the chances?* "Your hair is long."

"Most people focus on the scar." He grabbed my hand. I jolted at the movement. And brought it up to his mouth, letting the tips of my fingers brush over his soft lips and the scar he was pointing out.

"How'd you get it?" I managed over roaring ears.

"Hockey."

"Oh." I pulled my hand away and grabbed onto the side of the cloak I wore.

"So you and my brother are a thing."

"No." I frowned. "Why would you say that?"

"Just a guess."

"Wrong guess."

"So, if I ask you to leave this party with me, you'd do it?"

My eyes flicked up to his, heart slamming against its cage. *Why was I hesitating?* It was unlike me in a situation like this. I thought of Karen, who had a theory on moral code and how that feeling deep within our gut is what drives it. I'd always rolled my eyes at the theory, told her the only thing rumbling in my gut was whiskey and Taco Bell. As I held Nolan's gaze through our masks, I wondered if this was my limit. My moral code. Because I'd have to see Adam in the forthcoming days. I'd need him to answer questions for me if I wanted to find out where the real Stella was. If I wanted to meet her. People did things for their families all the time—bad things, good things, and whatever seeped into the cracks in between. For the first time in my life, I felt like I was up for that challenge. I didn't know Stella yet, but she was coursing through my veins and I needed to find her.

"I wouldn't," I said, finally.

Nolan smiled and gave a nod.

"Why would you ask a girl you think is involved with your brother to go home with you?"

"Why would I not?" He tilted his head slightly.

"It's wrong." I frowned.

"All the more reason for the invite." He chuckled, straightening. "Well, it was nice talking to you, Stella Thompson. Good luck at the burial?"

"What burial?"

"Yours."

With that, he walked off.

My heart roared so loudly, it drowned out the music. A bartender walked by with a tray and paused, lifting it as if to offer me a drink. I looked at the tray, which had nine glasses on it. Each row was labeled: tequila, vodka, whiskey. I grabbed the whiskey and began drinking it quickly, but stopped midway. If I kept at it, I'd get drunk and I couldn't, wouldn't, let my guard down in here. I looked up and Adam was no longer upstairs. The music switched to rap. There were guys rapping along loudly, everyone seemed to be bobbing in sync, the way I normally would have been but my feet were lead, rooted to the ground.

Burial.

Mine.

What?

It took me the length of the song to shake it off as hyperbole. He was trying to spook me, trying to make me second-guess my decision to choose this society over any other. He had a competitive nature. One five-minute conversation with him and I knew that. Another black cloak stood beside me. I sighed heavily.

"What's the deal with you black cloaks? You walk around trying to size up the opponent?" I said before the tall guy beside me had a chance to.

"I would hardly call The Swords opponents." He smiled. "Besides, my cloak isn't black, it's navy."

"Navy." I looked at it again, but it was too dark to tell the difference. "And what secret society do you belong to?"

"Quill."

"You're the ones who publish the members' names in the paper the first week of every semester."

"We have no use for anonymity." He shrugged a shoulder.

"Interesting."

"We could use more women though." He turned toward me and even with the mask around his eyes I could see him checking me out.

Before I could answer him, someone pulled me away and I turned to see Adam standing there.

"Let's dance."

"What?" I pulled away slightly, on the border of the dance floor, in that place where I had to make a choice—in or out.

I looked at the guy I was talking to, but he was now looking at Adam as if they were having some sort of standoff. I couldn't be sure if that was the case, but the guy walked away, and I got the indication that Adam won.

"I thought you didn't dance." I turned back to Adam, who was bobbing to the beat of the song.

"I didn't say I didn't dance. I said I wasn't planning on it."

"And?" I stepped closer. He put a hand on my waist as I began to move to the rhythm.

"I changed my mind."

"Because too many people were coming onto me?"

"Maybe."

"I would accuse you of being jealous, but you don't know me, so it can't be that."

"Jealousy is an emotion. Like love and hate. It's beyond reason." He winked.

Winked. My heart slammed, full stop. Maybe I hadn't been paying attention, but I was pretty sure no one had ever winked at me. As we danced, I continued sipping on my whiskey and decided to worry about the real Stella and what was happening inside of this place tomorrow. So far, cloaks aside, it seemed like a college frat house. The comment about the burial wasn't far out of my mind, even though for now I was choosing to ignore it.

The pocket of my cloak vibrated halfway through the next song, and I set down my drink on the nearest rock and took it out.

Dr. Thompson: anything?

Me: Nothing yet.

Dr. Thompson: search the property

Me: I'm trying

I silenced the phone and tucked it back into the pocket,

leaning into Adam to tell him I was going to step outside for a second. He looked like he wanted to come with, but I walked away too quickly for him to offer. *Search the property.* How exactly was I supposed to do that? Once I stepped outside and shut the door, my ears rang loudly, as if I was still standing beside the speaker system. Suddenly, I felt hot and annoyed by the white cloak and mask. I took the cloak off and held it in my arm, leaving the mask on for anonymity. Before I could talk myself out of it, I opened the door to the right and let myself inside. The first thing that hit me was the smell of incense. It smelled like the church I'd grown up in and I was instantly reminded of Father Murray, walking around with that silver thurible and swinging it throughout. The second thing I noticed was the darkness. With the door slightly shut behind me, I could barely see anything. Unlike next door, there were no strobe lights, only the glow of candles. *Maybe they'd illuminated this area so people knew they were in the wrong place and wouldn't get lost.* I turned around, thinking about the couple days of blank memory in my head that I still needed to account for myself. I didn't even remember getting the key to this place. I didn't remember getting an invitation or opening it. Nothing. *Blank.* Just as I reached the door, I heard something. Voices. Multiple voices. They were quiet at first, and grew louder. I turned around and walked back. Beyond the large rock that seemed to serve as a wall of separation, there were ten people in cloaks. They were chanting something I couldn't understand but somehow felt familiar, as if I'd heard it in my sleep and my consciousness had evaporated the memory.

The cloaks weren't red, but brown. Brown cloaks with a rope tied at the hip. My heart stopped beating. The only other place I'd ever seen those was . . . but no. I shook my head. No way. I inched closer to the edge of the wall and crouched down to see if I could make out what they were walking around. It was some sort of surface made of rock, a bench of sorts, but I couldn't tell if anything was on it, until they made way for a second and I saw a person.

A naked person. *A woman?* They held hands in the midst of the chant and shifted once more. A naked woman. I brought my hand up to my mouth to keep in any sound. If I was discovered, who knew what would happen. They suddenly came to a halt. The chants stopped. I moved my head slightly to try to make out who the woman was, but one of them was blocking her face. I couldn't tell whether she was dead or alive. She remained unmoved. They began to chant again, this time a very familiar prayer, and I felt myself grow dizzy. They were monks. If I had any doubt before, that solidified it for me. The one at the foot of the table began disrobing and climbed up to the table to join the naked woman. Dread crawled up my spine. My hand tightened over my mouth. I couldn't find the strength in my legs to stand up now and get out of this room before anything else went down. I couldn't look away. The only thoughts I could summon were: *Was nothing truly sacred? Should I do something? Should I come out from the shadows and help her? Did she sign up for this? Who were these people?* I felt water rolling over the hand I had over my mouth and realized with surprise, that I was crying.

Suddenly, I felt a presence behind me, and froze. I'd been caught. I'd been caught and my brain wasn't switching on my flight response. A hand came over mine over my mouth and another hauled me up. I began to kick and scream beneath our hands. I wiggled to try to get the person to drop me. It was no use. Whoever had gotten a hold of me was stronger than me by a lot. The door opened and closed and suddenly I was back in the round hall between the two doors, still cradled in someone's arms and fighting to be let go.

"Stop fucking moving. I'm going to let go of your mouth now and set you down. Don't panic." It was Adam.

Don't panic? I was hyperventilating, my air coming into my lungs quicker than it could get out. My tears continued to fall, blurring my vision, as if I knew the person on that table. I didn't. I didn't have to. I knew those monks. Not those monks, but, thanks to Karen, I knew monks. I'd known monks and nuns and clergy and that was not something they'd approve of. Instead of setting me down, Adam carried me up the dark, winding cobble stairwell. He opened the dungeon door and kept walking down the hall until he made a left, or right, I wasn't sure with the disorientation and wooziness in my head I was experiencing, and finally, in there, he let go of my mouth and deposited me on some kind of couch.

"You okay?" he asked. "Breathe. Deep breaths. Focus on your breaths." He positioned me so that I was sitting down, even going as far as placing my elbows on my legs and holding my arms there so they wouldn't wobble off. "Breathe."

I did. I focused. Breathed in, breathed out. I thought of Dr. Maslow, who had always instructed that I *"Breathe in the good things, expel the bullshit."* In my head, I said those words as I breathed. When I finally felt like I'd gotten a grip, I wiped my tears quickly with my palms and looked up at Adam, who was kneeling between my legs.

"What the hell did I just see?" My voice was hoarse, the screams I'd contained ripping the tone from it.

"I don't know."

"What do you . . . " I shook my head, covering my face. "You're not going to tell me. You wouldn't tell me. You're the president of this freakish cult. Of course you wouldn't tell me."

"I don't know." His voice carried and brought my gaze back to his. "I really don't know."

"I don't believe you."

"That's too bad." He shook his head. "It doesn't change the fact that I'm not lying."

"I should have left with your brother."

"My brother?" His expression turned serious. He glanced away for a long moment, staring at the portrait beside us. I had no idea who it was, but it was a man wearing a black little hat and a cross. A priest of sorts. Adam looked at me again. "My brother can't help you."

"And you can?" I nodded toward the back of the room. "You won't even tell me why I just saw a group of monks potentially raping a woman."

"I don't know the answer to that." His jaw set.

"Your brother said you were going to bury me."

"What else did Nolan decide to tell you?"

"Not much."

"He shouldn't have spoken to you. He knows better."

"Free country and all."

"Not in here." Adam's lip tilted. "You're under our command in here."

"Are you going to do to me what they're doing to that woman?"

"No."

"Are you going to bury me?" I swallowed, waiting.

"Yes."

Yes. No hesitation.

"Are . . . are you going to kill me?"

"No."

"You're going to bury me alive?"

"Yes."

Again, no hesitation. My heart skipped. Where was I and who were these people? I realized that I could scream, I could punch him, I could try to run, but I wouldn't get very far.

"Is that part of the initiation?" I licked my lips, mentally preparing myself.

"Yes."

"Were you buried?"

"We all were."

"Has anyone died?" My lip quivered again. I blinked my eyes, more tears fell. I wiped them quickly.

He didn't answer, but with the way his lips set into a hard line, he didn't have to.

CHAPTER SEVEN

IT WAS A CHILLY NIGHT. I WAS GRATEFUL I'D PUT THE CLOAK BACK around my shoulders. It was hiding my nervous shiver as we walked outside. People from the party had spilled out into the front lawn, still wearing masks, seemingly unaware of the activities happening in the room beside where they were partying. Adam was standing close to me and I wondered if it was to ensure that I wouldn't take off running. I turned to ask him just that, when we heard the unmistakable sound of sirens and tires crunching the gravel of the front of the house.

All of our heads turned in that direction. Adam grabbed my hand so I stayed put. Partygoers were no longer smiling or laughing. Some ran to the nearest temporary trash can and tossed their cups in them. Others ran toward the front. A few ran to the side of the house and disappeared into the yard next door. It all happened fast, but my attention was everywhere. Will walked over to us, mask off, and cloak down, looking bewildered.

"What the hell?"

"Your guess is as good as mine," Adam said.

"Second time this weekend." Will shook his head, frowning as he looked toward the side of the house, where Detective

Barry and a couple of police officers appeared. They were walking over in our direction.

"Second time they've been here? What did they want the first time?" I asked, ears roaring.

"They never say anymore. We assume it's protocol after what happened last year." Will shrugged and focused on the officer approaching. "Evening, Officer."

"We heard there was a party." The police officer's gaze swept over the yard. "Not many people here."

"Hey, Riley," Adam said, letting go of my hand. "Did someone call it in?"

"Someone called," Detective Barry said. "Would you mind taking off the mask?"

I reached up and took it off. I hadn't realized it was still on my face.

"What's your name?" He flashed a light in my face, making me squint.

"Stella." My eyes darted from him to Adam to Will and back. "Stella Thompson."

"We received a call from Stella Thompson." That was the officer beside him, the man Adam called Riley. "Are you in danger?"

"No." I shook my head quickly, hoping the cloak was still able to hide my shivers.

I felt like I was under a microscope with Adam and Will looking at me in disbelief and Detective Barry seemingly trying to figure out who I was. My chest started to pound harder.

"You called them?" Will asked unnecessarily. "How are you in danger?"

"I didn't call," I argued. "I'm fine."

"We should bring her with us," Officer Riley suggested.

"On what basis?" Adam asked. "She just said she didn't call."

"Did you call us?" the third officer, a woman, asked.

"No. I didn't. I don't even have my phone on me."

"Do you mind if we take a look around?" Detective Barry asked.

"Go right ahead. It's not your first rodeo." Adam signaled toward the house.

Detective Barry went inside with Officer Riley. The woman in front of me stayed put. Adam and Will followed Detective Barry inside.

"You sure you're fine?" she asked.

"I'm fine." I looked inside quickly and back at her. "She said her name was Stella Thompson?"

"Yes."

"And she gave you this address?"

"I was on patrol. Drove right over and called it in." She squinted out into the distance. There must have been at least an acre of land between us and the area where the woods started, but somewhere far into the distance there was a dim light. "What's out there?"

"I have no idea. I just got here today."

"And you didn't call us?" She looked at me again.

"I swear I didn't call."

The doors behind us opened again and Detective Barry stepped out with Officer Riley and Will and Adam following closely behind.

"She says she didn't call," the officer beside me said.

"Do you believe her?" Detective Barry kept his eyes on me.

"I do."

"Well, then, I guess it was a false alarm." Detective Barry walked in the direction they'd come from. "We'll just have to keep coming back until we find something."

"As long as I'm here, I guarantee your searches will be futile," Adam said. "There's nothing to find."

"We'll see about that, Mr. Astor." Detective Barry glanced over at me. "Good night, Miss Thompson."

I waved a hand and walked inside. The burn of Will and Adam's gazes followed me as they stepped in behind me. Will said good night and went deeper into the house. Adam and I stood in the hall, in front of the piano room where I'd first seen him earlier. Gone was the palpable connection between us, replaced by hesitation and wariness. I wished I could say I welcomed it, but I didn't. For some crazy, strange reason, I liked Adam. Maybe it was like he said, beyond reason.

"You lied to them," he said after a moment.

"About what?"

"You had your phone on you. You stepped out of the party after you got a call or text."

"I didn't call." I searched his eyes. "You don't believe me."

"I don't, but I guess that doesn't matter yet."

"Yet?"

"By the end of the initiation, I'm going to know everything about you, whether you like it or not."

"What if you don't? What if I don't tell you everything?"

"You will."

"What if I do and you still don't believe me?"

"For your sake, you better hope that's not the case."

It was with those words that he left me standing there. He went inside the piano room and even though he didn't shut the door between us, I didn't dare step inside. I just stood there, in the hall, listening to the haunting melody he played, and thinking about how apt it was for all of this.

CHAPTER EIGHT

I LEFT THE MANOR AT DAWN, CALLING AN UBER AND TAKING IT BACK to my apartment. I needed some semblance of normalcy before I headed to Stella's classes today, even if I didn't know what normalcy was to me right now. I knew Aisha. Or thought I did. I knew Karen. But I still didn't know what happened to me and I had no clues as to what happened to Stella. As I unlocked my apartment and walked inside, shutting the door behind me, I felt my new Stella phone vibrate in my bag. I took it out and saw a text from Dr. Thompson.

Dr. Thompson: Stella has an appointment with her therapist today at 3 p.m.

Me: Okay?

Dr. Thompson: I need you to go in her place. I'll send a driver to your apartment at 2:30 p.m.

Me: You want me to pretend I'm her?

Dr. Thompson: Don't be late. Stella is never late. Getting on a plane now. Talk later.

Wait. He wanted me to pretend I was my twin sister at a session with her therapist? I decided to call him. This wasn't exactly something I could talk about via text. The call went straight to voicemail. I had to assume that was exactly what he wanted me to do, but I couldn't. Besides, if he went to the cops about her supposed disappearance, wouldn't telling her therapist be the next step?

I thought being in my apartment would give me a little peace, but it didn't feel right. I walked around and looked for things to jog my memory, but the only thing I found was stale bread and dusty countertops. As I walked out of my apartment, dressed in Stella's clothes that I'd brought along with me to change into, I called Karen. The line rang, and rang, and rang, until the operator told me to leave a message. I hung up without one. The uneasy feeling crept back as I walked toward my car. I looked around as I turned it on, making sure I wasn't being followed. Once I convinced myself that I wasn't, I drove the seven minutes to the building I needed to get to. Ellis was impossible to walk in its entirety.

Aisha and I tried it once and made it a quarter of the way before deciding it wasn't worth it. We ditched the attempt and went to a little bar we knew would serve us alcohol instead. As I got out of the car and locked it, I considered calling Aisha again to remind her that I couldn't remember what I'd done a few days ago. I remembered the anguish in her voice, the distrust, and shook the thought away. I'd have to get by without her for now.

Opening the door to the classroom, I was grateful to find that it was large enough that I could probably get by without calling too much attention to myself. I beelined toward the back.

"That's a sight," a pretty blonde said, smiling straight at me.

"What?"

"You sitting in the back of the class."

"Oh." I glanced around quickly. "I'm tired this morning."

"Do you want me to send you the notes?" She was still smiling.

I considered the sincerity behind the question. The blonde was the kind of pretty and had the kind of smile that made her unattainable and sure to be popular throughout her life. The fact that she was being nice to me was inconceivable, even though I knew it was Stella Thompson she was being nice to, not me.

"I think I got it. Thank you though." I smiled and continued walking to the back of the room, taking a seat there. The blonde stood and walked over to me, taking a seat beside me.

"I went by your place the other night," she whispered, leaning in. "I know you said you're not ready for . . . this, but I wanted to explain myself."

My heart launched to my throat. Stella was a lesbian? As the blonde leaned in closer still, I felt the weight of an impossible responsibility. As much as I wanted to do right by Stella, I couldn't pretend to like this girl, *like that.* Potentially I could trick her brother, her teachers, even her therapist, but not a person she was attracted to.

"I really like you and I had fun with you last week," she said. "If you want to do casual, I can do casual."

"I . . ." I cleared my throat. "Can we talk about this another time?"

"Sure." Her expression fell. I set my hand on hers before she walked away and she met my eyes, hope flaring in them.

"I have a lot going on and it has nothing to do with you or me or us. Please give me time."

"Okay." She squeezed my hand and walked away with a smile.

I let out a long, deep breath.

"I didn't see that coming." The voice came from my other side.

I jumped. It was Nolan. He didn't have a mask on and in the light, he looked eerily similar to his brother, but the long hair gave him away. I could also see the scar on his lip that he pointed out last night.

"What didn't you see coming?"

"You being a lesbian. I didn't get those vibes."

"We met once."

"A few times." He raised an eyebrow. "But yeah, I guess I only invited you back to my place once. Does my brother know you're a lesbian?"

"That is none of your business. Or your brother's," I whisper-shouted. "And what do you mean we met a few times?"

"Dude, we did a group project together last year." He looked at me like I was crazy.

"Oh yeah." I nodded as if just remembering, though I knew it wasn't me he was in the group project with.

"So, does my brother know?"

"About what?"

"You being a lesbian."

"Oh my God, will you drop it." I turned fully in my seat and faced forward, hoping the blush on my face wasn't obvious.

"Speaking of." Nolan looked up, grinning. I followed his gaze and spotted Adam walking toward us.

"What the hell," I said under my breath.

"What the hell indeed," Nolan said, still grinning as Adam drew near.

Dropping his backpack on the floor, he took the seat in front of his brother's and looked at me. "Where were you this morning?"

"Gone. Obviously."

"Gone where?"

"I'm sorry to be the one to break this to you, but she's a lesbian," Nolan whispered, leaning in so that only Adam and I could hear.

"Shut up already. I'm not."

"You're not?" Nolan raised an eyebrow. "Cameron thinks you are."

Adam looked at me for a long moment before shrugging and facing the front of the classroom. I didn't like that and that was as unexpected as the new information on my sister. I wanted to punch Nolan and shake Adam and tell him that I was completely attracted to him, not Cameron, but that I couldn't do anything about it because I was pretending to be someone I wasn't. Nolan stretched his legs, taking over his space, mine, and Adam's. Adam didn't move. He was probably used to his brother being all up in his shit. Well, obviously, they'd shared a womb.

I tripped over that thought. I'd shared a womb with someone as well. *A stranger*, I thought as I looked at the back of Cameron's perfect blonde hair. It wasn't that I thought all twins were exactly alike, but I didn't realize how different they could be. I looked at Adam and Nolan again. They shared the same athletic body composition—lean muscle, rigid jawline, wide back—but Nolan was obviously the more athletic of the two. Or maybe it was that he was a different kind of athlete. Where Adam looked like he could play baseball, maybe pitch, Nolan looked like he belonged on a football field.

"Maybe you swing both ways?" Nolan asked. He was looking at his phone and hadn't looked up at all, but must have sensed me staring.

"Maybe." I glanced away. "I'm surprised you even come to class."

"It's my last year here. I kind of want to graduate."

"What's your major?"

"Business and Art History." He glanced at me. "Our father owns galleries. My parents are into art."

"That sounds like fun."

"What's your major?"

"Psychology."

"Hm." He nodded at the professor, who had just walked in. "My mom is a retired psychologist."

"Is that her?" I looked at the professor. She looked too young to be his mother.

"No." He chuckled. "I was just letting you know the professor was here."

"Oh." I looked at the professor again. She was writing something on the board behind her. *Genes.* "Why'd your mom retire? She must be young."

"She is. She says she wanted to help dad with the galleries."

"Really?"

"Yeah. I think she got tired of hearing people's shit all day when she had her own shit going on at home."

"Her own shit meaning fielding phone calls from Nolan's teachers every five seconds," Adam said without turning around. Nolan flicked him in the back of the head, making him rub the spot and glare at his brother. "Don't start."

"I'm not." Nolan put his hands up in surrender. He glanced at me and whispered, "He might look all clean-cut, but he's a savage. I hate to admit it, but he's kicked my ass before."

"Twice," Adam said, without turning around. Nolan shrugged a shoulder in admission.

At that, I laughed.

The professor began to speak and everyone cut their conversations short. The class was Genealogy. The topic of conversation, which apparently was left over from last class, was a twin study they were conducting at The Institute.

"Did any of you do more research on the matter?" the professor asked.

A lot of people nodded and said yes.

"Did you find anything interesting you want to share?"

Cameron raised her hand. "They say any two strangers can share 99.5% of their gene sequence."

I sat up straighter, then looked at Nolan. "Are we talking about twins or strangers?"

"The Twin Study that The Institute did a few years back," he said. "Strangers who look alike. Doppelgangers."

"Doppelgangers? So, completely unrelated twins?"

"Pretty much."

"Hm."

"Have you noticed how many twins there are at Ellis?" A student asked. "Not kidding, I'm taking four classes and there are two sets in each class."

"You're welcome," Nolan hollered, making everyone fall into a fit of laughter.

"That is interesting," the professor said. "Did you know, and please, correct me if I'm wrong, Astor brothers, that twins get a discount here?"

"No." Someone gasped. "Why?"

"Ah, that is one of the gifts The Institute makes to the university. The second twin gets a scholarship."

"Just for being born?" I asked.

"Just for being born." The professor smiled. "We're getting off-course. Back to doppelgangers."

They continued talking about people who look eerily similar but come from different parents.

Doppelgangers.

Could that be what Stella and I were?

CHAPTER NINE

"H EY, WAIT UP."

I turned around to see Adam jogging up to me. "What? You want to bury me in broad daylight?"

"No." He exhaled, looking around briefly. "Are you going back to The Manor?"

"Now? No. I have Spanish."

"You don't know Spanish?"

"It's an easy elective, besides, I'm rusty." I shot him a look. "Stop judging me."

"Okay." He cocked his head and squinted his eyes like he was really trying. "But you are coming back to The Manor, right? In general?"

"Maybe."

"You're going to give up?" He straightened.

"What does it matter?"

"This is the chance of a lifetime. Limitless doors open for you if you're a part of The Swords."

"If that's true, why doesn't your brother join?"

"He's in another society. Ours is scientific. It's about finding the best version of yourself and building bonds that last a lifetime."

"That's exactly what all the sororities say on rush week."

"This isn't a sorority."

"Obviously. I'm the only woman there and the only other woman I saw there outside of the ones at the party was being raped. Or something."

"Don't say that." His eyes narrowed. "Don't throw that word around unless you know for certain."

"There were monks in that dungeon and they may have been raping a woman." I pointed outward, though I wasn't sure what direction The Manor was to where we stood. "You know it and I know it. I can't trust you or go back there if you can't even say it's a possibility."

"I need you to go back there."

"Why?"

"Because you were chosen."

"Where are the other women invited?

"I don't know."

"What are their names?"

"I don't know. I don't have that information."

"Yet you knew my name. You knew who I was from the moment I walked in there."

"Of course I did. You're under my care."

"Whose care are the other women under?"

"They never showed, so technically, no one."

"You don't think it's weird that this chancellor or whatever, his highness, person, hasn't given you the names of the other women so you guys could go look for them?"

"We have to initiate you, then maybe they'll give us the other names."

"Doctor . . ." I started over. "Was my father a Sword?"

Adam shook his head. "From what I heard, he wanted to be, but the society didn't approve. Things were different back then."

"Different how?"

"Different. Not everyone was accepted everywhere."

"They didn't let him in because he's black?" My brows rose.

"I don't know." Adam frowned as he mulled that over. "God, I hope that wasn't the reason."

"So you don't know the reason?"

"I don't, but I know enough to know that if they're inviting his daughter it's because they regret turning him away."

"Maybe." I looked at the time on my phone. I still had a few hours before Dr. Thompson's driver would pick me up, but during that time, I wanted to do some digging in Stella's apartment. "I have to go."

"Did you really not call the cops last night?"

"I really didn't." I looked up at him and shook my head.

"Who else knows you were there?"

"No one."

No one knew aside from Detective Barry and Dr. Thompson, yet someone had supposedly called from the premises to say she was in danger and her name was Stella. If that was the case, was she there? Were they hiding her? The memory of the naked woman on the rock flashed through my mind. *Would she be next?*

I looked at Adam. "I have to go. I'll see you later."

I reached into my back pocket and unlocked the door to her apartment, walking in quickly before shutting it behind me. I'd tried to be as quiet as a mouse when walking the hall to not alert any neighbors by my presence. Just because Dr. Thompson said Stella didn't have any friends, didn't mean it was true. He obviously didn't know about her and Cameron. I wondered if he knew about that side of her life at all. I switched the light on and let the backpack slide down my right arm before setting it down on the floor by the kitchen counter.

The place was immaculate. It even smelled like the lavender *Fabuloso* I used on my floors often. It didn't look like anyone lived here at all—with the pristine pillows on the living room couch and the squeaky clean full-length mirror placed at an incline by the entrance table. I stood there for a moment and gave myself a once-over. I was wearing skinny jeans, a frilly white blouse, and white wedges to match. My hair was glossy from being freshly straightened this morning and my olive skin was glowing from the body mousse I'd taken from The Manor. *Was this what Stella saw when she looked in the mirror every day before she left the apartment?* A shiver ran through me as I looked at the girl who was me but didn't feel quite like myself. I blinked away from my reflection and continued my assessment of the place, stepping into the bedroom, where a queen-size bed with a white, fluffy comforter and oversized, white pillows sat untouched by wrinkles.

I walked up to the bed and sat down, then lay on my side and inhaled. It smelled like my body soap. Olay Deep Conditioning. My eyes popped open. *We use the same soap?* I hopped out of bed and walked into her bathroom. It was all white—white cabinets, white tile, white grout. The shower was glass and looked like it had never been used. I picked up her toothbrush and swiped the bristles. It was dry. The toothpaste was the only thing that gave any indication that someone lived here at all, with the end rolled up to squeeze out whatever bit it had left.

I set out to look for clues as to who Stella Thompson was and found very little to go on. She was girly, liked to dress in cute summer dresses, and had bright coats for the winter. She liked designer heels and sneakers. I felt like I already knew those things based on the suitcase Dr. Thompson had given me. Stella had a collection of handbags on the top rack of her closet, all in dusters, from designers I'd never dreamed of even looking at. From the back of the closet, I took out high school yearbooks and journals that had been scribbled on from beginning to end. She was voted Most Likely to Succeed, Kindest Smile, and Most Athletic. The dedications from high school friends were all generic—stay in touch and I'll miss you, but nothing that screamed intimacy. I wondered why she brought them with her. That seemed odd to me. Looking at the time, I realized I needed to get a move on if I was going to make it back to my apartment in time for the driver.

When I got back to my place, I took a Valium. Dr. Maslow would not approve. She was always completely against taking it right before I met with her because she wanted to assess the situation fully, but I was the one who had to meet with Stella's therapist and pretend I was someone else.

With a refreshed mind and looser limbs, I grabbed my things and walked outside to meet the driver.

CHAPTER TEN

"**H**EY."

"Hey." I was shocked to find the driver was a woman.

A young woman. She wore a suit and tie, her straight brown hair pulled back into a high ponytail. There was little makeup on her pretty face and I wondered if she preferred it that way or if she was trying to blend in with the men who had her job. She opened the back door of the black town car and waited until I was seated before closing it and getting into the driver's seat. I pulled my phone out and texted Aisha. I couldn't handle this anymore.

Me: I know you're mad at me but we really need to talk

I waited, watching for three little dots to appear on the screen. They didn't. What the hell had I done to her? I closed my eyes and pressed my head to the headrest as I rummaged through recent memories, but came up blank. It was interesting that I could remember high school and Karen, but nothing recent. I thought about Ellis and remembered my first day of school there, how walking up to the first few buildings felt like the most daunting thing in the world. Aisha's parents were with us for orientation. Karen was too drunk to get out of bed that morning. I remembered the animosity I felt toward her and how I'd taken it out on Aisha when she told me she chose a stranger as a roommate over me. My eyes popped open. I was so mean to her that day. She'd accused me of lacking empathy. I'd said empathy was for kids who had grown up in perfect homes. It was a lie and a low blow, two things I was skilled at, and it happened two years ago, and even though we'd spoken since, things definitely hadn't been the same for a while.

"Have you decided?" the driver asked.

"Decided what?" Our eyes met through the rearview.

"Whether or not you're going to tell Dr. Maslow that you think you found your twin."

There was no way to hide the shock on my face, no way to think fast and come up with an answer as to why I'd suddenly gone mute. *Dr. Maslow was Stella's therapist?* If so, which one? Neil or Debbie? It didn't matter. How was I supposed to lie to either one of them? They'd both been there for me from the beginning—when my temper tantrums went from impertinent toddler to "we may have a problem on our hands." Dr. Debbie Maslow had come to the rescue, going as far as to send people to our house once a month to record my progress. Neil and Debbie became like family to us, and Karen, who rarely showed appreciation, used to cry at their feet sometimes when they arrived. So, presenting myself as Stella Thompson was definitely something I was not looking forward to. They both knew me and that meant they'd been hiding the fact that I had a sister all along. And secondly, *Stella knew about me?*

"You okay?" The driver frowned.

"Yeah, I just . . . " My heart was beating too quickly. *Stella knew about me.*

"Last time we saw each other you were panicked and said you found a sister." She looked between the street and the mirror as she spoke. Each time she looked in the mirror, she looked more concerned. "Your dad didn't believe you, but I do."

"I'm scared to tell Dr. Maslow," I said finally.

It wasn't a lie.

They were serial prescription givers and constantly looking for new forms of therapy to whip our brains into shape. If I told them this, I wouldn't see the light of day. They'd lock me in the white room and start tweaking my brain until I surrendered and said I was fine.

"I'm sorry," the driver said, and I could tell she meant it. "I didn't tell anyone what you told me, but it's weighed heavily on me. I can't imagine what he would do to you if you said anything to him, especially after trying to cure your being gay."

So Neil is her therapist.

I licked my lips, unable to speak. My heart hurt for Stella. I'd pictured her in this perfect life, with a doting father and deep pockets, but that didn't mean she was exempt from worries. They'd tried a lot of different forms of therapy on me, but never anything extreme. I wondered how they tried to cure my poor sister of something she couldn't help. I glanced outside the window and focused on the trees as we drove into the iron gates of The Institute. *The Maslow Institute* was what was written everywhere. It was the official name for the four-hundred-acre mental institution. Sometimes, when I was still in the stages of driving up and hadn't been here in a while, I could trick myself into thinking I was pulling up to the Ritz. Everything from valet drivers to world-class pools made up The Institute. The chefs were James Beard contenders and the bedrooms rivaled a five-star hotel's. Everything about The Institute was made for appearances. Everything except the white rooms. Those were their dirty little secret, and if they weren't, they should be. Everyone who walked out of the white rooms walked out different. Sometimes, it was a good different. Jayson Melvin had been cured of his fear of flying. Once he left, he was able to travel.

Sometimes, the results were devastating. Katrina Skulski had been forced to remember the grueling rapes she suffered as a kid and left defeated. She hanged herself as soon as she went home. I knew them both from group therapy sessions I'd attended as a teenager. When the people from church suggested that maybe my anger issue was just a teenage thing, Karen began to question everything Debbie told her, and in turn, question my feelings. Despite that, Karen stuck to the sentiment that therapy sessions were the only things keeping her from kicking me out. I had a feeling it had more to do with the fact that therapy actually kept me out of the house four hours a week. Whatever the case was, I never resented therapy or Dr. Maslow. Debbie had been a saving grace for me. If not for her, I wouldn't have survived life.

The driver stopped in front of the building and waved off the valet who was running toward the car.

"I'm going to the café." She drove past the valet and parked the car on the right side of the circular driveway. Once she parked, she came around the car, but I was already halfway out the door. "I hate that you always do that."

Stella did that? I smiled. "I'm perfectly capable of opening my own doors."

"So you've said."

So *I've* said. I walked in the doors and went straight to the elevator, taking it to the fifth floor, where Dr. Neil Maslow's office was. I usually got off on the fourth floor, where Dr. Deb was, but I tried not to think about that or fixate on the fact that I was about to try to trick a person I knew. Dr. Maslow's secretary let me into his office just as he was finishing up his lunch.

"Well, don't you look well-rested today." He smiled wide as he stood up and waved at me to have a seat on the sofa in the sitting area across from his desk. "How were your classes?"

"Good." I sat down, setting my backpack on the floor, my mind on his comment. If I looked well-rested, Stella must really get no sleep. "We talked about the Twin Study."

"That's nice. Dr. Nichols?"

"Yes." I smiled. "Was she one of your interns?"

"Yes, years ago. She did her internship here." He glanced at his watch. "I have a new one starting today."

"Another intern?"

"Meredith dropped out of the program." His eyebrows rose. "She decided to switch majors."

"To what?"

"General practice. She was in the teen wing here and couldn't handle it. You know not everyone can." He winked.

"Yep." I knew from experience because I'd been one of those teenagers.

I got the feeling Stella was as well. How had I never seen her here? God, I wanted to yell that question out into the universe, into Neil's face, even if just to see the shock on it.

"Enough about that. What's going on with you? How are you sleeping? Better?"

"Yes." I cleared my throat and thought of the driver. "I just . . ."

"What?" He crossed his legs, twirling the iPad pen in his hand and clicking the iPad so it was on. "What's going on?"

"I saw someone who looks exactly like me." I bit my lip, pausing to gauge his reaction. He gave nothing away, but jotted it down. "It was at a party on campus."

"Were you drinking?"

"No, of course not."

"And?"

"And it was like looking in a mirror."

"Stella." He sighed heavily, setting the iPad and pen down on the table between us. "Not this again."

"She looked just like me."

"We've been down this road before." He stood up and went over to his desk, picking up his keys and unlocking the drawer to his right. He brought a folder out and opened it. "There was one time at the mall, a girl wearing the same shirt as you. The girl at your new church who sat too far away for you to truly see her, but was definitely your twin. So on and so forth."

He stared at the folder for a second before looking up at me. "It's completely understandable for you to want a sister, or a mother, or someone out there with your blood. I understand it, Sweet Pea, I do, but I'm sorry. We're all you've got."

My pulse roared in my ears. Sweet Pea was what his wife called me, what he called me on the occasion the three of us met outside of sessions, which wasn't often, but had happened. Once when Karen was at the hospital for pneumonia and once when I ended up at the hospital with a broken leg. The Maslows were more than just therapists. To me, they were family. I knew I got treated differently than some of the other people in here and I always chalked it up to the fact that I'd been with them long before The Institute became what it is today. The Maslows had always had my back. She'd said I was an unbearable child, a bad seed, but The Maslows disagreed. They said seeds were only as good as the nurture they received. Karen didn't outright disagree. She wasn't one to speak against people with a title in front of their name, but she made comments at the dinner table every once in a while that told me she didn't understand their thought process.

"Stella?" Dr. Maslow prompted. I blinked.

"So you think I'm making it up?"

"This isn't the first time this has happened." He walked back over and picked up the iPad again, tapping it quickly. "I just sent you a new prescription. Please pick it up and start taking it today."

"The cops took me down to the station." I cleared my throat.

"What? Did you get in trouble? Why didn't you call?" That made him sit up straighter.

"I didn't. They thought I was someone else." I watched him closely.

"A lot of people look alike. Hell, Dr. Nichols is teaching you about it right now." Neil sighed heavily. "If you had a twin, a real twin, we would have found her by now. You know Deb and I have worked with the orphanage and looked extensively into your past in hopes of finding answers for you about your mother. It's difficult to trace these things in other countries."

Debbie always told me my mother gave birth to me in prison and when I'd questioned why she'd been in prison, to begin with, she gave few answers and fell back into the same old "she doesn't want to be found" excuse.

"But if I was born in another country, maybe we were separated upon our arrival—"

"Stella, we have your birth certificate and your mother's birth certificate. Our guy spoke to everyone in that village. If you had a twin, we'd know it."

I bit my lip. This was the same spiel Debbie gave me when I'd asked her about my birth mother. The Institute sent doctors to small villages in the Dominican Republic all the time, not for mental health purposes, but to provide vaccines and clothing items. I knew because they'd enlisted the help of our church from time to time, and I'd spent a lot of time collecting and sorting through clothing items and boxes of crayons and coloring books they took over there. Sometimes, I'd write little notes and stuff them into the pockets of the jeans we were sending, a way to let someone know they weren't alone, that even though I'd been gone from the island for the entirety of my life and didn't remember it, I still felt connected to them.

"Stella?"

"Yeah." I blinked. "Sorry."

"Hey, it's okay." He spoke calmly, his blue eyes compassionate. "Has anything else happened since I last saw you? Any new adventures or clubs you've joined?"

"No." I thought about The Swords, but there was no way I'd bring them up here. Besides, I hadn't passed their requirements yet.

"Any boys?"

"No."

He took a breath. "Girls?"

"No."

He let out the breath. I thought of the driver. Stella trusted her enough to tell her things, maybe I should too. I needed to tell someone all of this, or else it would drive me crazy. My mind went to Karen, then Aisha. If I wasn't on speaking terms with Aisha, I wondered how my relationship with Karen was holding up. We'd always had a tumultuous one, to say the least. I looked up at Neil, who was watching me closely, waiting.

"Have you ever forgotten chunks of your life?" I asked.

"No. Have you?"

"No."

This was useless. Lying to your therapist was like lying in your diary. Neil knew I was lying, too. I could tell by the way he just stared at me, waiting for me to retract my statements, but I wasn't Stella, the good girl who actually admitted her real feelings. I was Eva, the one who guarded my heart and held my thoughts closely. After all, Karen taught me that those were the things people could turn and use against you. *If you give them your heart, you might as well lie down and wave your white flag. It's over after that.*

"Listen," Neil spoke again. I looked at him. "Grab your medication on your way home. I want to see you back here next week."

I nodded and said goodbye as I picked up my backpack and walked out of the office. In the elevator, I stared at the four. If it stopped there, I'd get out and go see Debbie. Otherwise, I'd go home. If it didn't, I'd chalk it up to destiny and go about my day, trying to figure out what the hell was happening. The elevator stopped at floor four. My heart quickened as the doors opened before me. I braced myself to get out, but when they opened fully, I saw Adam Astor standing on the other side. He frowned when he saw me, seemingly as surprised as I was. He stepped in and I couldn't find it in me to step out. Destiny? Maybe. Chickenshit? Definitely.

"Fancy meeting you here." He waited until we were outside of the building to say that.

"I was thinking the same about you." I stopped walking between the valet and the town car that was waiting for me. "What are you doing here?"

"I'm doing an internship here." He pointed a thumb in the direction behind him. "I was just dropping off some paperwork for Dr. T."

"Here." My voice was flat as I looked between him and the building behind him. I didn't know why this turn of events made my skin crawl, but there I was. "You're a psych major?"

"Pre-med. Future neurologist, I hope."

"So you're not interning with the psych department?" I said. "Why were you on the fourth floor?"

"That's where your father's office is." Adam frowned. "I thought that was why you were here."

"No. My therapist works here."

"Oh." He eyed me a little closer as if he'd missed something the first few times we'd interacted.

I'd never been one to hide my need for therapy. Maybe it was because I'd been seeing one for as long as I could remember. Karen always hid it and it irked me. I hated when people made excuses for mental health, as if one-hundred-percent of people weren't completely unraveling on their own. My eyes drifted to the car waiting for me; I caught the driver's eye through the rearview and put a hand up to let her know I'd be there soon.

"I'm headed out for lunch," he said when he spoke again.

"So I guess I'll see you later?"

"Initiation tonight."

"Right. The burial."

"Stop thinking about it as a burial," he said. "Think about it as an existential awakening."

"Oh. Wow. Of course. Who wouldn't want to be buried in order to find the meaning of their own existence?"

Adam chuckled. The sound hit me between the ribs. My mouth opened to make a flirty remark, but I shut it quickly, reminding myself of who I was, or who I was pretending to be.

I wasn't sure I knew the difference anymore.

CHAPTER ELEVEN

ADAM

Because Dr. Thompson had gone out of town, I was working with Dr. Maslow. Working with Dr. Thompson had its perks. I was able to sit in actual neurosurgeries and shadow him when patients came in. The last few weeks, I'd been jotting notes as Dr. Thompson examined patients who were recovering from strokes. It was the job I'd signed up for, the one I'd been after for as long as I could remember, but working in The Institute awakened a curiosity I didn't have before.

And so, when Dr. Thompson left on his trip and told me to report to Dr. Maslow's office in the morning, my excitement bubbled. I'd finally see the rest of The Institute, the areas that had been off-limits to me until that point, and to top it off, I'd get a tour from the boss himself. We were walking through the corridors of what everyone referred to as *The Hotel*, and I could see why. It looked like a swanky five-star, with white-glove service and everything.

"It's like you dropped The Ritz in the middle of Ellis."

Dr. Maslow chuckled. "We definitely took inspiration from The Ritz."

"With a place like this, I wouldn't mind taking a mental vacation."

Normally, the connotations that came with mental institutions were negative—people strapped to beds, fighting their meds, getting electric shock treatments that would set their brainwaves into submission. They were all things I only knew of secondhand, due to a bipolar grandmother who spent more time in a mental institution than her own home while I was a teenager. My grandmother was one of the reasons I'd become so interested in the human mind. I figured, if I could help come up with a map for the brain and provide a solution that wasn't as invasive as the ones I'd seen her endure growing up, I could make a real difference in the world. My family said I took after my mother, while my brother took after our father, but I wasn't sure. I wasn't straitlaced or perfect, but I did appreciate structure, which was something Nolan hated.

"This is where you'll be working this week." Dr. Maslow stopped walking in front of an office and led me in. It was a small office, all white, the only pop of color coming from the plush navy blue lounge couch in the corner. "There's a questionnaire on the iPad that you'll use whenever a patient comes in, you'll ask the questions, press the answer, and that's it. Simple. It's connected to my server, so I'll get the answers automatically and be prepared when I see the patients."

"Sounds simple enough." I nodded once, looking from the iPad on the desk to the large window behind it. "I'm surprised you have glass windows."

"Hurricane impact," Dr. Maslow said. "No way anyone can jump through them."

"Oh."

I'd never heard of anyone who had hurricane impact windows. We were so inland that the only thing we ever got was severe snowstorms during winter. The chance of Ellis ever being hit by a hurricane was precisely zero, but the forethought of someone here trying to break through it and jump to their death was pretty smart. Of course, when I paused to think about it, I wondered if anyone would try that. Even in movies jumpers sought the roof, but people couldn't be underestimated.

"Come. I'll show you the rest of it."

I followed Dr. Maslow out of the office and down the hall again. The spaces opened into large, open areas, where people sat and watched television. Some were knitting, others were reading books, and some were talking amongst themselves. They all wore sweatpants and T-shirts or sweatpants and sweatshirts and even though their sneakers had no laces, they were still clean Nikes. Everyone was definitely under thirty and they all looked like they were here willingly, which, I knew couldn't be the case for all. As we walked, Dr. Maslow pointed out things along the way—cafeteria, which looked like the five-star restaurant it was, two game rooms, where I saw even more people who looked like they could be enrolled in Ellis University, playing air hockey and table tennis. By the end of the tour, I was convinced The Institute was indeed the best hospital, mental or otherwise, that existed in the entire U.S.

When Dr. Maslow left, I walked back to the office, and waited for my first patient. The questions were simple, but they took their time answering them, as if they were scared there was another part to all of this. It gave me pause, but not enough to question them. Besides, that wasn't the job I was here to do. I was cleaning the iPad and clicking back to the beginning of a new questionnaire when there was a knock on the already open door. I signaled for them to come inside without looking up; the damn iPad was frozen on the last person's signature. Still not glancing up, I sighed.

"Give me a second please." I jabbed on the screen, trying

to get a response and set it down while picking up a pen to jot things down with my other hand. While the technology sorted itself out, I'd have to write everything down freehand, the way Freud would have. The way Maslow would have.

"Name?" I asked.

"Stella," the voice said. My entire body went cold, then hot, as I glanced up and looked at the girl sitting across from me. "Stella Thompson."

"Hey." I was still frowning and felt it deepen when I took in her appearance.

"Um. Hey." She frowned back slightly.

I had always been intuitive. It was something my brother and closest friends relied on me for. Nolan had been burned too many times by friends that I hadn't approved of from the get-go, so he'd made it a thing to bring over new friends and get my okay on them first. I'd always been intuitive, but I'd be the first to tell you I didn't believe in gut feelings or otherworldly things. I may be in a secret society that was headed by men devoted to the Catholic Church, but they were also devoted to science, and that was what I appreciated. I didn't react based on emotions, but facts. When others reacted, I waited. It was why my intuition was rarely wrong. It was why I was good at poker. Looking at Stella, sitting across from me, I felt . . . confused, my intuition absent. I'd seen her, what, an hour ago? Maybe two? And she hadn't been wearing a gray hoodie and her hair had been straight, not short and in tight curls, like this.

"What are you doing here?"

"What do you mean?" She rolled her neck left to right, then right to left. "What are you doing here? What are any of us doing here?"

My pulse roared as I set my pen down. "Why did you say that?"

"Say what?"

"What you just said."

"I . . . I don't know. It's just something I say." She frowned again.

"Yeah, right." I shook my head. She was trying to play head games with me. I didn't know why or when or how she'd changed her appearance so suddenly, but she wasn't going to get under my skin. "So, Stella Thompson, how are you feeling today?"

"Fine. Same as yesterday. They changed my pillows though, so my neck hurts a little less."

"Your neck was hurting because of your pillow?"

"Seriously?" She shot me a look, then looked at the blank iPad in front of me. "Why is that thing off? Shouldn't you have all the notes on me by now? I was in a car accident last week— or that's what they told me—and my neck has been stiff since."

"When did this car accident take place?" I lifted the iPad and shook it. "Technical difficulties. I'm writing this by hand."

"Last Friday." She yawned, stretching. As the sleeve of her hoodie pulled, he caught a glimpse of a tattoo. A small, thin cross.

I wasn't sure what my expression looked like, but I hoped it remained passive as I took in all of this information. Stella didn't have a tattoo. She showed up at The Manor last Sunday, but she was supposed to get there Friday night.

"Where were you going?" I asked after a moment.

"Huh?"

"When the accident happened. Where were you going?"

"I don't know." She looked around the room for a long moment, her knee bouncing as she took all of the blank spaces in.

"What do you mean you don't know?"

"Geez, are you going to get that thing up and running or what?" She nodded at the iPad. "I don't remember. I have no memory of last Friday. I think I went to see my mom? A lady. I called her mom." Her frown deepened. "But I don't have a mom. I mean, I did, everyone has a mom, but mine left when I was two. Anyway, I woke up here after my accident."

I tried to turn the iPad on again. This time, it worked. I waited until it was ready and scrolled through the names of the patients. I stopped short when I nearly scrolled past a very familiar face. I clicked on the image. My heart stopped. *Eva Guerra*. I looked up at the stranger in front of me that didn't look like a stranger, but definitely acted like one. I looked at the restricted file in my hand and stared at Eva's familiar face. She looked a few years younger in the photo, but was just as striking, her big brown eyes and long dark lashes prominent on her caramel skin. The only thing I could see was her birth date.

"You still haven't found my file?" Stella's scoff lifted my attention back to her.

"One minute." I closed out of Eva's file and looked for Stella Thompson, finding it quickly.

The photographs were different, but the faces were identical. I thought about myself and Nolan. About Will and Nora, who were also twins. Will and Nora, who no one on earth would have assumed were even related—he was black, and she was white, and they looked like they may as well be from entirely different families, and yet, they shared a womb and were born minutes apart from each other. There was only one explanation for all of this. Finally, I set the iPad down and looked straight at the girl who claimed she was Stella Thompson.

"Do you have a sister?"

She looked thrown by the question, sitting straighter and swallowing quickly, not quite meeting my eyes. When she finally did, it was after taking a deep breath and straightening her shoulders.

"No, I don't. Why do you ask?"

"You look familiar."

"Oh. Well, I don't." She evaded my eyes again.

My intuition was never wrong, never faltered, and I knew without a doubt that she was lying.

I just didn't understand why.

Before leaving The Institute, I saw Stella one last time, in the common living room area, curled up reading a book. As I walked out of the wing, I spotted a nurse who was headed in the opposite direction.

"Hey. Do you interact with her?" I pointed at Stella.

"Miss Thompson? Of course." The nurse smiled, shaking the cup of pills in her hand. "These are hers."

"What are they for? What is she here for?"

"I'm sorry, who are you?" She looked at my name tag.

"Adam Astor. I work for Dr. Maslow."

"Which one?"

"Neil Maslow."

"Oh. Okay." She raised an eyebrow. "Well, Miss Thompson seems to have suffered a panic attack of sorts last week. We're just keeping her comfortable and relaxed until she's ready to go."

"Does she come often?"

"I'm new here." The nurse shrugged a shoulder. "I wouldn't know. They say she's always in this wing though. She's one of the doctor's daughters." She whispered that last part.

"Yeah. I know." I looked at Stella again.

"Poor girl. She keeps crying out for her sister and Dr. Maz keeps telling her she doesn't have one."

Blood roared in my ears. "Dr. Maz?"

"Yeah, Neil." The nurse blushed. "He told me to keep a close eye on her. I don't think she'll hurt herself or anything. I think he just doesn't want her to leave until she's ready."

"Probably."

With that information, I said goodbye and turned around. As I walked toward the exit, I pulled up the email with Stella Thompson's schedule. It was given to me a few weeks ago when The Swords informed me that this hunting season would be different than the last. Instead of going after men who showed promise or were from prestigious backgrounds, I'd go after Stella. Once I found the schedule in the mass of junk mail and student center emails, I took a screenshot and held my phone in a firm grip.

I wasn't sure who was lying, but I'd get to the bottom of it one way or another.

CHAPTER TWELVE

EVA

Karen never envisioned herself with a daughter like me. Even though her late husband, Esteban Guerra, was a hardworking, dark, Dominican man, in Karen's daydreams, her daughter would be blonde, like her, and laugh emphatically at her mom jokes. Instead, the church parishioner, who was helping her with finding a baby girl to adopt, found me. An olive-skinned, curly-haired baby with brown almond eyes that were so large they would only later be rivaled by her poor attitude. Karen said I never slept. Not as a baby, not as a toddler, and not as a teenager. My restlessness kept her awake at night. Karen, who was an avid ID Channel watcher, told me she thought she saw me in her room in the dead of night once, just staring at her. I told her she was imagining things. She told me I was crazy and had me committed the following morning.

Dr. Maslow never gave me any inclination of what she thought was happening in my house, nor did she seem concerned when I told her the reason my anger couldn't be managed was that Karen was constantly trying to control me. Dr. Maslow's job wasn't to coddle Karen or me. It was to assess the situation and do what she could to help, which in my case was welcome me in The Institute and give me drugs to numb my emotions. She hated when I said that about my meds, but it was the truth. As I got older, I began to realize just how difficult it must have been for Karen to raise someone like me. I realized that it wasn't because I wasn't blonde or looked like her that we didn't get along. Some people just don't mesh, and that was true for me and Karen. These days, we gave each other ample space, but reached out every few days of not speaking just to make sure the other was doing okay.

As I pulled up to Karen's small, faded yellow house, I noticed the grass had been freshly mowed. Probably by Peter from down the street. Around here, teenagers still went around knocking and asking what needed to be done as a way to earn an extra buck or two. I took a deep breath and closed my eyes on the exhale as I stepped out of the car. As much as I hated to admit it, this felt like home. I'd only been back a handful of times once I'd been accepted to Ellis, and I hadn't planned on coming back for a long time, but this felt important. Maybe I'd find some kind of answers from her. Besides, it was unlike Karen to continuously ignore my calls. I brought the key up to the lock.

"How is she doing?"

I looked at the neighbor calling out to me. "Who?"

"Your mother. Is she still in the hospital?"

"What?" I lowered my key and turned to face her, confused.

"Can you come over? I can't stand this hollering."

I walked over our grass and then hers and stood at the bottom of the steps of her porch.

"You were here Friday." She frowned at me. "You called the ambulance."

"I'm sorry. What is your name again?"

"Mercedes." She blinked. "Your new neighbor. We met Friday night."

"I'm sorry. I am so . . . " I took a breath. "I . . . I have no memory of Friday night."

"You don't remember being here?"

"No." My shoulders slumped. "Is there any way you can tell me what happened?"

"Well, I don't know what happened." Her lips pursed as she scrutinized me, her eyes bouncing between me and the house and back to me. "I heard people screaming, so I looked out the kitchen window to see what all the fuss was about. You were leaving and your mother was screaming at you. She went inside and shut the door and you got in your car." She shrugged. "I thought that was the end of it and went about my business, but then I heard a gunshot and saw you running toward the house again. By the time I went outside the paramedics were here."

"Did they say what happened?" I held my breath.

"No, but you did. You said Karen got her gun and fired into the air and collapsed so you called 911."

"What did I do? Did I leave in my car?"

"You did. The paramedics took your mom." Mercedes shut her mouth into a thin line. "It looked bad." She shot me a sympathetic look. "And once you were done talking to the officers, you sped off."

"I sped off?"

"You sure did. I almost yelled for you to slow down, but you wouldn't have heard me."

The cops had been here Friday? I'd argued with Karen, then left, presumably trying to chase the paramedics down, and then . . . what? I had a date Saturday night according to Detective Barry. I felt myself frown as I tried and failed to piece everything together. It was an impossible task, but maybe the police officers had information on where the paramedics had taken Karen. I glanced up at Mercedes again.

"Did any of the police officers leave any information with you by any chance?"

"One of them left a card. Hold on." She turned around. Her screen door creaked open and shut as she disappeared into the house. I looked at the house next door, at my bedroom window, which faced Mercedes's kitchen window. I remembered that much at least. The door creaked again, and I looked up as she handed over a white card. I stared at the card, feeling the color drain from my face.

Detective Barry.

"This man was here on Friday night?" I handed her the card again.

"He was here Saturday morning," she said. "He asked a couple of questions about what happened. I assumed he was trying to make sure you hadn't tried to kill your mother." At my wide eyes, she smiled slightly. "Don't worry. I told him you looked completely distraught."

"Did I look distraught?" I asked tentatively, figuring I might. Karen and I had our differences, but she did raise me.

"I was a social worker for many years." Mercedes leaned in closer. "I saw a lot of shit I wish I could forget. Heard a lot of stories." She looked far off into the distance as she spoke, as if remembering, and then looked back at me again. "You didn't look distraught. You looked relieved."

CHAPTER THIRTEEN

Calling the hospitals around town proved to be futile. Karen Guerra was in none. I kept thinking about Mercedes' account of what happened on Friday night. It didn't add up to what Detective Barry told me in the wee hours of Sunday morning. He said some guy named Chris called him and I went with the story because I couldn't remember anything else. He didn't say he'd seen me on Friday night. He didn't say he came back and questioned my neighbors. The only thing that made sense was Karen and I getting into an argument. My memory may be shit, but I knew an argument between us was a possibility. Our relationship was rocky at best and Karen must have been out of her mind drunk on Friday when she rushed inside to get a gun I didn't even know she owned.

The driver dropped me off back at my apartment and I decided that I was done pretending. I was going to drive my own car to The Manor and own up to all of it. I would tell Adam and Will who I was and what I was sent there to do. I would tell them what I knew about Stella Thompson, which wasn't much, and find a way to uncover more. One thing I couldn't do was continue to lose myself in someone else's identity. Not when I was on the verge of losing my own.

That was what I thought I was going to do, but then the gates creaked open and I drove in, my tires bumping against the gravel, and I fell back into the trance. Eva Guerra didn't belong here—at least as far as they knew. If I told them who I was, they'd kick me out. If they kicked me out, I may never find out the truth about Stella or what happened the night she disappeared, though the more I found out about her, the more I wondered if maybe Stella hadn't gone missing at all. Maybe she just didn't want to be found. Whatever the case, I needed to find her, not for Dr. Thompson, but for myself. I mulled over what I knew for certain happened these last few days: I'd ended up in The Institute, I'd ended up at the police station, I'd been told to pretend I was Stella, someone called the cops saying they were Stella and they were in trouble. It wasn't much to go on, but I'd use it.

I drove beneath a sycamore tree and set my car in park, my gaze on the back of the house, on the endless land that led to an endless forest. I thought about the woman who invited me to the chapel out there in the mouth of the woods. Maybe that was where Stella was. Maybe they were holding her captive. Maybe she'd be next in the disgusting display the monks had planned. A shiver rolled through me as I got out of the car and walked toward the front of the manor, the key in my hand to unlock the door. When I reached it, I noticed it was slightly opened. I pushed it open a little more, peeking my head in without committing to walking inside.

The hall was darker today, only the light from the setting sun behind me illuminating the wood-paneled walls and creepy paintings on them. I stepped inside, shutting the door quietly behind me. *Should I lock it? Should I leave it?* It had been open, after all. I left it and kept walking. I was halfway down the hall when I heard the faint music of the piano and decided to head in that direction. When I reached the room, the doors were shut, but the music was vibrant behind it. I turned the knob and entered without knocking. Unlike the other doors I'd encountered in the house, this one didn't creak when it opened. Behind the piano sat Adam, his back straight and his hands gliding along the keys in a fury.

Pressing my back against the door, I watched him. He seemed like he was in a trance, his expression serious, brows furrowed, jaw clenched. His hands seemed to carry the weight of whatever wrongdoings he was trying to exorcise, like he was at the mercy of the keys beneath his fingers as they jumped to punctuate each note of the hauntingly beautiful song. His hands stopped moving suddenly and he looked up to flip the page of the book in front of him, starting a new song. This one was upbeat and made me feel like I was in the ballet. His hands sped across the keys, his brows furrowing slightly as he continued to play. I was completely riveted by the performance. The piece seemed to go on forever and I found myself not wanting to move out of fear that he might ever stop playing. When it did come to an end, he hit the keys with a *bang, bang,* like it was a grand finale.

"I hope you enjoyed yourself." He was still looking at the book in front of him.

"You knew I was here?" I peeled myself from the door and walked over, sitting on the armrest of the couch closest to him.

"Not much escapes me."

"Interesting fact." I licked my lips. "Your brother says you're very—what you see is what you get."

"My brother said that?"

"Yup. You guys are close."

"We are." He closed the keys and rested his elbows on it, watching me closely. "You have a brother. Are you close?"

"Not really." I glanced away because Adam was looking at me like he was trying to read way into me and I wasn't sure how to feel about it.

This would be the perfect opportunity for me to tell him who I was, yet I wasn't sure I could. Could I trust him? For all I knew, he was in cahoots with Barry and Thompson and whoever else knew about this charade.

"What were you playing?" I nodded at the piano.

"Which time?"

"Both times."

"*Rage Over a Lost Penny* and *500-Year-Old Melody*."

"I loved them both. I could watch you play all day." I looked away quickly as soon as the words were out of my mouth.

"You're welcome to." He looked like he was on the cusp of smiling again. I wished he would, but then he stood up, and as he walked toward the door, said, "If you stay."

And I decided I would.

All it would take was being buried alive and after everything I'd been through in my life, in The Institute, how bad could that be?

"What's next?"

"Meet me outside in thirty minutes and you'll find out."

"Okay."

"Do you have black jeans?"

"Yeah."

"Black T-shirt?"

"I think so."

"I'll leave one outside your door. Wear all black tonight."

I felt like he was dismissing me, so I left, rushed upstairs to what I considered my room, unlocked it, and shut the door behind me. I changed quickly into the ripped black jeans I had and looked outside to find a black T-shirt hanging from the door. I pulled it over my head. It was huge and smelled like Adam, which I liked. I tied it at the side to give myself some semblance of shape and picked up my phone to dial Karen again. This time, I left a message.

"Hey, it's me. I went by the house and called around town to try to find you but no one knows where you are. Give me a call . . . or shoot me a text. I just want to know you're okay." I hung up. I couldn't remember the last time I left her a message. She'd never been one of those mothers who worried much when her kid went out, though whenever I went over curfew, I always got an earful, and because it was the only time she seemed like she truly cared, I missed curfew a lot. I tucked my phone into the back pocket of my jeans and my keys in the other. As I walked by my backpack by the door, I remembered the bottle of whiskey I'd brought. I took it out, uncapped it, brought it to my lips, and took three shots.

Then, I headed downstairs. Adam was standing right there, at the foot of the steps, wearing black jeans and a black T-shirt. We looked like we belonged in the Addams Family.

"What's so funny?"

"I was thinking that we look like we belong in The Addams Family, and your name is Adam, so it was funny."

"It would be hilarious if Blake Roberts hadn't made it a never-ending joke in elementary school."

"Oh, man. What'd you do?"

"Nothing. Not for a while anyway." Adam shrugged a shoulder. "I was a puny kid and was in like the twentieth percentile for height."

"So you got beat up a lot?"

"Not really, just made fun of." He started walking toward the door. I followed.

"You said not for a while," I said as we got in his black sports car. "I'm assuming you got revenge at some point."

"I wouldn't call it revenge. It's not like I was lying awake at night thinking of ways to get back at him." He switched on the ignition. "But I did date the girl he was pining over throughout all of elementary and middle school."

"That seems fair." I laughed. "I bet she was more than happy to play the girlfriend role."

He was quiet for a moment. It occurred to me that I hadn't even asked where we were going. I opened my mouth to ask, and he spoke before I got my question out. "So, was my brother telling the truth? You like women?"

"No." I bit my lip hard and looked out the window.

"Is there anything you're not telling me that I should know?"

I bit my lip harder. This was my chance. My knee started bouncing. What if I told him and he flipped it on me? What if he was reporting to Dr. Maslow or Detective Barry or Dr. Thompson? The list was endless. And worse, I didn't know why any of this was happening. I took a deep breath and let it out.

"No."

"Hm." He continued to drive. "We're going to make a stop before we start tonight's task."

"What's the task?"

"You'll see when we get there."

CHAPTER FOURTEEN

"So, tell me about yourself. Your upbringing," I said, trying to fill in the gaps of silence as I drove to my parents' condo.

I couldn't stop thinking about what happened at The Institute. I couldn't get Eva Guerra out of my head and I was torn between thinking that there were two different women—one named Stella and one named Eva—or that she was both, and if she was I didn't know what to do or think.

"I was adopted; my dad raised me and my little brother alone. The end."

"What's your background?"

"Dominican. Well, my birth mom's Dominican. I don't think they'd consider me Dominican if I went back there now." She laughed a little.

"And your mother?"

"She's never been in the picture."

"I'm sorry to hear that."

Her phone vibrated on her lap and she gasped loudly as I parked the car on the sidewalk across the street from my parents' condo. She answered the phone using a high-pitched tone.

"Where are you?" She seemed on edge as she awaited the response, and then, "Why would you go to Florida without letting me know?" Then a frown. "No. Absolutely not." Followed by a heavy sigh as she brought a hand up to her face, rubbing the bridge of her nose. "I don't remember that. I'm so sorry. I called all the hospitals. No. What? What do you mean?" Her hand dropped and she sat up straight suddenly. "Are you sure? When are you coming back? Will you let me know the minute you're home?"

By the time she hung up the phone, it looked like a hundred things were racing through her mind and I found myself leaning in a little closer, as if those things would spill out of her brain and into mine. She glanced up at me and stared for a moment, as if her eyes were having a difficult time focusing on me.

"Where are we?"

I wasn't sure if she was asking because I hadn't said or because she'd blacked out just now. Either was a possibility, after all, especially if what I thought was happening was actually happening. I stayed quiet for a moment, waiting for her to speak again.

"Adam, where are we?"

"I need to make a quick stop before we go where we need to go. Are you okay?"

"Sure. I'll wait for you here." She nodded slowly.

"No. I want you to come with me."

"I just need a moment. Are you going to take long? I don't mind waiting."

"I'd rather you come."

If she didn't go inside, I'd never know what my mother thought about her and her situation. Worse, I wanted her to go with me, because despite the fact that I thought she was certifi-able, I genuinely liked her and wanted to help her.

"Okay. Is this where you live?" She glanced over at the mid-rise building across from us.

"My parents own a condo here. I live a little closer to south campus. Let's go."

As we stepped out of the car and looked both ways to cross the street, she looked over at me. "Are your parents here now?"

"Yes. They're here for the weekend." I looked at her as I opened the lobby door for her. "My brother has a game. They usually try to go to those."

"You don't?"

"I'm not a huge fan of hockey." I let the door close behind us and waved at the security guard behind the front desk. He waved back as we continued walking toward the elevator. "I do go sometimes. Moral support and all."

"Do you think he'll go pro?" she asked. Her mind seemed occupied, but she continued making small talk regardless. I re-alized she was probably nervous. About meeting my parents? About the phone call?

"What was the phone call about?" I asked finally, now that we were trapped in a slow-moving elevator and she had no-where to run.

"Nothing."

"It didn't seem like nothing."

"I don't want to talk about it right now, especially not right before I meet your mom." She squinted. "What do you call her? Mommy? You seem like a mommy's boy."

"What if I am?" I felt my lips twitch.

"I knew it." Eva grinned suddenly, her entire face trans-forming with that one movement, and I felt the air between us crackle.

Damn that air and damn that crackle.

She was always pretty, but she was stunning when she smiled like that. My body inched toward hers. It was automatic, magnetic, something that couldn't be helped. She tilted her head up slightly, her big brown eyes searching mine.

"Just do it," she whispered.

"Do what?"

"Stop thinking about it and kiss me."

Somehow, during our exchange, I'd lowered my face closer to hers, my lips closer to hers. I was a sucker for the impossible. It was one of the things my brother and I had in common. We both liked the challenge, the rush, the prize. Without warning, she grabbed a fistful of the black T-shirt I wore and pulled me until my lips were on hers.

I didn't know who I was kissing. I didn't care. The only thing I could concentrate on was her mouth moving against mine and her tongue finding mine. She reached up and tugged the ends of my hair as she deepened the kiss, making all of the blood in my body rush to my nether region. I pushed her against the wall of the elevator, my head dizzy as my hands began exploring her body. As if on cue, the elevator dinged and rocked as it came to a full stop, and I was forced to pull away. Through hazy eyes, I found that she looked just as taken aback as I was. Her lips were slightly parted and looked so soft; the only thing I could think about was having them on mine again. She'd lowered her hands from my hair.

"I guess we should go." She dragged her eyes from mine and looked outside of the elevator. I already knew what awaited. The code made the elevator open up smack in the center of my parents' condo.

"Yeah. Let's go." I breathed out and without even thinking about it, grabbed her hand in mine as we walked.

"Well, I can't say this isn't unexpected." Nolan walked out of the kitchen and into our line of vision as we walked down the hall. He was wearing sweatpants and a gray Ellis Athletics T-shirt. He looked at the two of us. "Damn, look at you two matching and shit. Taking this dating thing to a new level, huh?"

"Shouldn't you be at practice?" I let go of Eva's hand and punched my brother in the shoulder when he went to hug me.

"Does Mom know you brought a guest?" he asked.

"Nope."

I hadn't wanted to tell my mother that I was bringing someone because I knew she'd start asking questions and making assumptions. With our parents, it was always best to just surprise them. Besides, it wasn't like we were dating. I didn't even know if she was Stella or Eva or both, for God's sake, yet there I was, wishing like hell those elevator doors hadn't opened at all.

"Welcome, Stella," Nolan said, turning to her, and I remembered once again why this was all so complicated.

Stella.

I'd keep rolling with Stella for now.

"Hey." Nolan turned around. "Mom's on the phone. Dad's getting dressed."

When we entered the kitchen, our mother set the phone down and looked up with a huge smile on her face as she stood.

"I didn't know you were bringing someone." She walked over, arms wide as she hugged me. She was a foot shorter than me, but still held me as tight as she did when I was little. When she pulled away, she looked at Stella. "I'm Leah. Nice to meet you."

"Stella." She smiled and held her hand out, but my mother pulled her into a hug instead.

"I'm sorry. I get so excited when I see my boys that I start hugging everyone without asking." Mom pulled away.

"I'm not much of a hugger." Stella's face heated. "Sorry."

"No worries." Mom batted away her apology. "I should really ask."

"I should really get used to hugs."

"Why don't you like them?" Mom tilted her head slightly.

I walked back over to where Nolan was standing and left my mother speaking to Stella slash Eva.

"What's going on?" Nolan whispered.

"I met her twin. I think."

"What do you mean *twin*?"

"Well, I don't know if she's a twin or if she has multiple personalities."

"What?" Nolan blinked. "One of them is a lesbian though."

"Seriously, dude? Focus on the issue at hand."

"Right. What's the issue?"

"I don't know what to believe. Is she a twin or is she one person pretending to be two?"

"Ah." His brow arched. "I mean, look at the bright side, it'll be like being with a different woman every night."

"Nolan."

He chuckled. "Sorry."

"I saw her at The Institute. I saw her walk out of there and leave with a driver, then I saw her back inside saying her name was Stella. The file was restricted but there were a few visible notes. It said she suffered from delusions. She's been known to talk about a twin she thought she had. What are the chances?"

"And she says she was adopted?" Nolan looked behind me. "This one, I mean."

"Yes."

Nolan stayed quiet for a long moment. "Was she invited into The Swords?"

"Stella was."

"But Eva wasn't?"

"No telling. I don't have the names of the other people invited."

"Dude." Nolan's eyes widened on mine as he glanced back over to Stella slash Eva and our mother. This time, I looked as well, my gaze finding hers. She flashed a small smile and I felt myself return it. When I looked at my brother, he looked troubled. "Have you told Will? Wolf?"

"No. No." I shook my head. I didn't want to bring attention to this. Not yet. Not until I knew.

"Why?"

"I don't know."

"Those are your brothers." Nolan searched my eyes. "You pledged loyalty to them, not her."

"I know." That was eating away at me. I'd pledged my loyalty to them, but she seemed to need it more than they did. She needed someone in her corner. "She'll be a Sword tomorrow."

"Well, then." Nolan exhaled. "I guess you've made your choice."

"There's nothing to choose."

"Sounds to me like you're choosing your girl over your brothers."

"She's not my girl."

"Isn't she though?" He crossed his arms. Adam felt his jaw tense.

"Drop it."

"Why'd you bring her here anyway?"

I scratched my head. It didn't itch, but I didn't want to answer and I figured if my hand was busy scratching my head it wouldn't end up on my brother's face.

"Jesus, Adam. You brought her so Mom could psychoanalyze her?" Nolan chuckled, shaking his head. "Does Mom even know?"

"No."

"Not that it matters. You've been here five minutes and she hasn't stopped asking her questions. If I had to guess, she's making her uncomfortable."

I glanced over. Sure enough, Eva was shifting her weight between both feet. My mother was smiling, that kind smile of hers she used to trick patients into divulging things they'd normally only say to their priests.

"Why'd she join your cult anyway?"

"Cult?"

"We have a legitimate organization. What you have over there is creepy and weird."

"Really? A legitimate organization? How many shell companies are linked to The Eight currently? I seem to remember it being at least four."

Nolan scowled. I was right. Last year, The Eight had a major issue involving a member who'd been buried alive in hopes she wouldn't be found. I would know. I'd been the one to find poor Mae deep in that hole. The memory of it still haunted me sometimes. The *"what if"* of it. I looked at Stella again and walked over. My father stepped into the kitchen wearing jeans and the same gray Ellis Athletics shirt Nolan had on as I closed the distance between me and Stella.

"Adam. I didn't know you were coming." Dad walked over and pulled me into a hug. "And you brought someone with you. Who is this pretty face?"

"Stella Thompson," my mother said, smiling as she looked at me. It was different from her sympathetic smile. This one was a smile of approval. I wanted to tell her there was nothing to approve of.

"It's a pleasure to meet you." Dad walked over and pulled her into a hug. This time, she laughed, even though her shoulders stiffened.

"You guys sure love hugs," Stella said.

"She doesn't like hugs, Avett."

"So sorry." Dad pulled away quickly. "It's just, Adam and Nolan's friends are our friends as well." Dad winked at me. "When they bring them over. Which, they rarely do these days."

"You see my friends all the time," Nolan argued.

"I meant friends who are women."

"Oh." Nolan shook his head. "In that case, don't hold your breath."

I rolled my eyes. Freshman year, after Nolan's high school girlfriend broke up with him, he decided he wouldn't date seriously at all during college. It didn't matter if he met the girl of his dreams, he said, he wouldn't settle down. Not until after he had his diploma in his hands.

"Well, you'll have that diploma in your hands next semester." Mom winked at Nolan. "Can I speak to you for a second, Adam? I need you to be honest about your father's birthday present and your brother seems to be in a joking mood today." She turned to Stella. "I hope it's okay that I steal him for a moment."

"Totally fine." She waved a hand.

"I'll get you a drink." That was my dad as he turned to the fridge. "Water? Soda? Juice?"

"Water is fine." She smiled at me and only then did I feel like it was okay to walk away and follow my mother toward the master bedroom.

Nolan was busy texting someone. No doubt one of the members of The Eight to fill them in on what I hadn't even filled The Swords in on yet. My mother closed the door behind us and turned to me.

"Is this serious or a fling?"

"We're not together." I ran a hand through my hair and exhaled. "We're friends."

"Friends." Mom pursed her lips. "Adam. Please. You won't quit looking at the girl."

"We're not together."

"You don't bring girls around unless you think there's something more there." She shot me a pointed look.

"Well, this is the exception. Sort of."

"Sort of?"

"I wanted you to meet her. I need to . . . I need you to tell me what you think of her mental state."

"You brought her here so I could provide you with my professional insight on the mental state of a potential girlfriend?" His mother crossed her arms and I got the feeling it was her way of scratching her head. "Is this the trend now?"

"I think she suffers from multiple personality disorder or something."

"Really, Dr. Adam? When did you get a title?"

"This is serious. I think she thinks she's two different people."

"That's definitely not something I could tell you from ten minutes of talking to her, but she seems fine to me. A little rigid, but there could be a multitude of reasons for that. She said she's adopted and her adoptive mother was always a little distant, but she also said she knows she loved her." Mom shrugged. "We all have a story. We all have our issues."

"This is more than that, Mom."

There was a knock on the door followed by Nolan walking in and shutting it behind him.

"We're busy," I said.

"This is important." Nolan walked over, waving his cellphone. "I just got a text from Max. You know, Paper Boy."

"I didn't even know you were friends with him."

"Yeah. Logan wanted me to befriend him and . . . it's a long story." Nolan shook his head. "Max did a quick search for Eva Guerra and Stella Thompson." Nolan paused. He loved to pause for dramatic effect.

"Spit it out already."

"So, Max actually knows Stella. They went to high school together, she's a real person. And she is a lesbian." Nolan raised an eyebrow.

I felt my eyes roll. "You need to lay off the porn sites, bro."

"Eva Guerra, also a real person. She was working at an elementary school not far from here." Nolan clicked on a link. "Parents: Karen Guerra and Esteban Guerra."

"What the fuck." My chest tightened. I reached for my brother's phone and read quickly.

Eva Guerra had been arrested last week and released, but not before they took her fingerprints. There was more information on past arrests, but you had to pay to get it and I didn't care about her past right now. I looked at the date of the fingerprints again.

"That was the day she went to The Manor." I handed Nolan back his phone. "Text that to me."

"I hope this teaches you to stop labeling people," our mother said.

"He's not completely wrong to question her, Mom. She has a record." Nolan flashed the screen at her. "If I find anything else, I'll let you know. You sure you don't want to come to my game tomorrow night? You can bring her."

"I don't think so. Maybe next time."

"I gotta go. Love you guys." He gave each of us a hug and Mom a kiss on the head before walking out.

"So you don't think there's anything crazy about her?" I looked at my mother again.

"I don't like that word." She shot me a look. "But if we're going to use it, then we have to say that we're all a little crazy." She walked over and squeezed my arm. "I like her. She's one of the good ones."

"I thought you couldn't determine much from a ten-minute conversation?"

"Light expels from the good ones. You don't have to dig very deep to find it."

CHAPTER FIFTEEN

"WHAT IS YOUR PROBLEM?" A storm was brewing inside me and I wasn't sure how much longer I could hold off before I exploded. Adam had some nerve asking that question. He had some nerve talking to me at all. I faced him as I stormed outside of the swanky lobby of the swanky palace he'd brought me to. The concern on his face was the only thing keeping me from making a scene. It was the concern that made me take one deep breath and then another in an effort to calm down. I'd managed to smile and thank his parents for being hospitable, which they were. It wasn't their fault their son was a complete and total asshole. Or maybe it was partially their fault. They did raise him, after all.

"My problem?" I pressed a hand to my chest. "You think I'm an idiot. That's my problem."

"What? Why would you say that?"

"You brought me here so that your mother could ask me questions. You wanted her to get into my head since you can't. You want her to get to know me since you refuse to because you're too caught up in your own head to realize that your shit stinks like the rest of us."

"Jesus." He exhaled heavily, raking his hair with his fingers. "I . . . yeah, I fucked up. I'm sorry, but for the record, I only did it because you lied to me."

"I lied to you?" My voice rose and I was fully aware that we were making a scene in the middle of a fancy neighborhood but I didn't care. "Please explain how I lied."

"Your name isn't Stella Thompson. It's Eva Guerra."

"You knew." I took a step back, then another. "You bastard. How long have you known?"

"I just found out. My brother's friend did a search on both of you and it turns out he's a friend of Stella Thompson's. You should have told me."

"I . . . " I looked away, taking a breath as I processed this. He just found out. "Does that mean your parents know? Do they think I'm crazy?" I shook my head. "I guess it doesn't matter. It's not like I'm going to see them again."

Adam opened his mouth and closed it, shaking his own head. "Why didn't you tell me?"

"Because I wasn't sure you'd believe me."

"Well, you should have let me decide that."

"That's rich coming from the guy who brought me to meet his mother so she could tell him whether or not I'm crazy."

"That's not . . . " He cocked his head. "Fine, yeah, that's exactly what I was doing."

"Why would you do that?"

"I needed to know that I wasn't wasting my time with you."

"Because I may or may not be crazy and that's not good enough for your prestigious lifestyle?"

He didn't answer. He didn't have to. I shook my head, disappointment winning out. More than anything, I was sad that he felt that way, especially since I liked him. I reminded myself that I'd kept my actual identity from him. It didn't matter. He'd brought me here so that his mother could psychoanalyze me and it was embarrassing.

"You're an asshole."

"I am and I'm sorry. I shouldn't have done that. I should have just asked you directly."

"Do you know what it's like to grow up thinking something is wrong with you? For every single outburst to be overanalyzed and probed as if I were some kind of experiment?" I pointed at the building. "Shit like that makes all of those memories come flooding back. My mother, my adoptive mother, pays good money for me to see Dr. Maslow. Money we don't have. I've been surrounded by head doctors all my life, so that little stunt was not very covert."

"In her defense, she didn't know I was bringing you for any of that."

"Oh, so she just asks every single girl you bring around about their childhood five seconds into meeting her?"

"Honestly? Yes. She really does." Adam let out a short laugh and dammit, I felt myself laugh a little.

"That's ridiculous."

"Hey, you saw the amount of hugs you got in ten minutes. We're pretty fucking ridiculous."

I laughed again and followed him back to his car. After we got in, I took a breath and exhaled, realizing I felt lighter. Even though I hadn't told him, I was glad he knew and that he seemed to be on my side in all of this. I was clicking on my seatbelt when I felt him looking at me and glanced up to meet his eyes.

"What?"

"I really am sorry." He brought a hand up and caressed the

side of my face with his thumb. I nodded my acceptance for his apology because I couldn't quite seem to get the words out of my mouth.

"Where are we going?" I asked after a moment, after he'd dropped his hand from my face, turned the car on, and started to drive.

"To excavate."

"Excavate what? Dinosaur bones?"

He didn't respond, but as he pulled into a cemetery and drove down the street, passing the endless plots, I started to feel like I was going to hyperventilate. I looked over at him.

"Please tell me we're not going to dig up a person."

Adam's smile was wolfish as he glanced back over.

My shoulders hurt from shoveling dirt and we had barely made a dent on the plot. I exhaled, wiping my forehead with the back of my arm.

"Don't they have machines that do this?"

"They do."

"So why are we doing this?"

"Because it's part of the initiation."

"To dig a hole in the ground?" I set the shovel into the ground and looked at him. He was just standing there, all cool as a cucumber as he watched me do the hard work. "Please don't tell me I'm digging my own hole."

"You're not. Yours is back at The Manor."

"So whose is this one?"

"Who knows?"

"What do you mean who knows? Adam, you're not making any sense."

"Keep digging, Eva. I'll let you know when you're done."

"This is ridiculous."

"You know what's not ridiculous? Fifty grand in your bank account in a few days if you pass these little tests."

I kept digging. A little faster now. I exhaled and set the shovel down again, about to reach for my water bottle, when I felt the shovel tap something. I glanced up at Adam.

"I thought you said there was nothing in these plots."

"I didn't say that."

"I think I just . . . I think I just hit something."

"You should keep digging."

"Adam, I think this is a casket." I stepped away, taking my shovel with me.

"You should open it."

"What?"

"You should open the casket."

My heart roared as I stared at him. He was completely serious. I took a step toward the hole. I definitely hadn't dug six feet. Not even two. How was there a casket buried so close to the top?

"I can't see," I said. "I need a flashlight."

He walked over with his cell phone flashlight on and aimed it at the ground. Sure enough, there was a glossy brown casket there.

"I don't know if I'll be able to open it," I said.

"Try."

"Are you going to help me?"

"Nope."

"Why not?"

"Well, what you're doing is a crime and while you could go to court and argue that I helped you commit this ridiculous crime, I think we both know I'll have a better lawyer."

"You're framing me?" My jaw dropped as I stood up. Taking my gloves off one by one, I threw them at him, then continued walking as he walked backward. I pushed his chest. "After you took me to your mother's house so she could diagnose me because you thought I was crazy, now you're framing me?"

"Relax." Adam laughed loudly, putting his phone away to dodge my slaps. "I'm kidding dammit."

I stopped hitting him. "What?"

"I'm kidding. You do need to open the casket though." He took a deep breath and let it out, still chuckling.

"It's not funny."

"It's actually pretty funny." He looked at his phone and played the video.

"I will murder you if you show that to anyone."

"I'll keep it in my private collection." He grinned and it caught me off guard. "Open the casket."

"Right." I blinked, grabbing the gloves from the ground and the shovel.

Adam decided to help me after all. After the door to the casket popped up, he stepped back again. I grabbed onto his arm as I looked inside. There didn't seem to be a body in there, just a garment bag. On top of it was a white envelope with the name Stella Thompson. I reached for the envelope first and hesitated on the bag. What if it had human remains in it? The Swords did seem sick enough to do something like that, after all. Fifty grand, I reminded myself. Fifty grand. I stepped forward, reached down, and grabbed the garment bag. It definitely didn't have anything heavy in it.

"It's a cloak," Adam said. "Read the note."

I ripped open the envelope and took out the card, reading it as he illuminated his flashlight on it.

You have been hand-selected to join The Swords.

Should you pass our test, you will be welcomed into our organization.

Doors will open.

Money will flow.

Opportunities will arise.

Unbreakable bonds will form.

The Swords is a historically male-driven society.

You are one of the few women chosen.

This gift is not to be taken lightly.

When it comes time to make your choice tomorrow tonight, keep that in mind.

Choose wisely.

Wear this tomorrow.

9 p.m.

P.S. Don't take your meds.

Don't take my meds? How did they even know about my meds? I put it away and unzipped the bag. It was a white and gold cloak.

"When do I get a red one?" I zipped it back up.

"When you're an official member."

He helped me close the casket and put the dirt back on it. When we were done, he grabbed a spray can sitting nearby and sprayed a big red S on it. We walked back to the car, me drinking water and holding the bag. Him, carrying the shovels and gloves. Inside the car, I felt myself melt onto the seat as he drove.

"Hey, how'd you figure out my name was Eva?"

"I saw it at The Institute the other day."

"How?"

"I met your sister."

His words slammed into me. I sat up straight. "What?"

"I met your sister. She's in there, but her file has your name on it."

"How can that be?" I whispered. "So she's not missing."

"Missing?"

"That's how . . ." I shook my head and started from the top. I told Adam everything, from Karen to Stella to Dr. Thompson and Dr. Maslow. I tried to condense my whole life story into short paragraphs. I spoke fast and went in circles, but ended up coming back to the same point: I needed to meet my sister.

CHAPTER SIXTEEN

THE BURIAL WAS TONIGHT, BUT I NEEDED TO FIND AISHA ASAP. Adam said he would see what he could find in The Institute and begged me not to show up there. We decided last night that if Stella was in there and I was out here, the Maslows may have something to do with it. My hands itched with the urge to call Dr. Thompson, but I waited. I needed to be sure he wasn't in on this too.

I was standing outside of Aisha's one o'clock class, my gaze fixed on the door. I'd skipped Stella's Psychology of Motherhood class. In my defense, I'd gone to the class, and when I arrived and found a man teaching it, I opted out. I wasn't in the mood for lectures today and I certainly wasn't in the mood to take a class on motherhood given by a man who didn't know the first thing about womanhood to begin with. At three-fifteen, the doors to Aisha's class opened and people started spilling out. I caught a glimpse of her rummaging through her messenger bag as she walked, and started to walk in her direction. She was pulling out her phone when I reached her, and stumbled back a step when she glanced up and saw me standing there.

"I told you I didn't want to speak to you."

"I know. I know and I'm sorry that I'm here, but I need to

talk to you. I need you to tell me if you saw me last week and if so, what happened."

"You're not serious." She searched my eyes.

"I am."

She stared at me a moment longer before sighing and shaking her head. "Fine, but you have to drive me to my next class."

"Fine."

We started walking toward the parking lot. When we picked our schedules, we made it so that our classes were near each other's. It would make it easier to get around campus. We would take turns driving, because even though they were short five-minute trips, they added up. Aisha had a job on campus. My job was thirty-five minutes away. My chest squeezed as I thought of the children I'd left behind and Ms. Paxton. Even though the parish school was small, with only a handful of kids in each class, when four six-year-olds were together in a space it was like having sixteen of them. Besides, Ms. Paxton was old. She needed the help.

When I'd called to inform the school I wouldn't be able to go back to work for a few weeks, they sounded just fine, but Ms. Paxton sounded tired. I glanced over at Aisha, her kinky curls looked damp, as if she'd washed her hair this morning and it was still in the process of drying. Karen had spent a lifetime straightening my hair and buying products that would ease the curl to the point that she'd finally achieved her goal. My hair no longer knew what it wanted to be, so it chose waves. I guess it figured that having no other choice left, it would compromise.

"So," Aisha said, pulling me out of my thoughts. "Talk."

"I need you to tell me when the last time you saw me was and what happened."

"Okay." She eyed me suspiciously for a second. "Last Friday at The Institute's cocktail hour." At the sight of my frown, she continued, "They held an open bar event for psych and med majors and I asked you to go with me."

"So I went with you? In your car?"

"In your car."

"And then what happened?"

"We were all drinking and talking. You kept looking at some guy you wanted to talk to but said he was way out of your league. I kept telling you that you were crazy because no one is remotely close to your league and the guy was hot but seemed like an asshole." She shrugged. "We laughed about it and everything was cool until that man showed up."

"What man?"

"You seriously don't remember?" Aisha stopped walking suddenly and turned to me. "You went to the bathroom, but you were taking really long, so I went to check and you weren't there. I don't know what bathroom you went to, but whatever." She shook her head and waved a hand. "When you finally came back, you were talking to a man. Arguing with him. It was weird. I'd never seen him before and I mean, we've been friends since high school, I thought I knew most of the people you knew. The argument seemed serious, so I went over there to intervene; you know, I was always in your corner."

"And?" I swallowed, the "was" in her sentence forming a knot in my throat.

"And you snapped at me. You went off and I mean off. And you know what, Eva, I'm used to your mood swings, but you went off in front of all of my peers and it was not cool. My professors were there, people I have to see every day." She shook her head. "It was not cool."

"What did I say? Why did I snap?"

"You told me I needed to mind my own business and back down. To be honest, I don't know what else you said because I was in such shock, but you started going off about how I wanted to fuck that man you were talking to. It was embarrassing."

"What?" My frown deepened. "I can't believe I said any of that."

"Well, you did. I'm not going to make that up, Eva. Besides, one of my friends, or so-called friends, got it on video and played it back for me at a party the following day. As if I needed to relive that."

"Aisha." My heart roared in my ears. I swallowed, trying to clear my clogged-up senses. "I know you hate me right now and I know you don't trust me, but I need you to get me that video."

"What the hell is going on with you?" She was looking at me like I was a stranger. "Are you off your meds?"

"I am not off my meds." My jaw ticked. I hated when people threw my meds in my face as if drugs that diminished my senses and drowned out my emotions were some sort of messiah. Aisha knew this too, but because I hurt her deeply, I tried not to let that statement cloud the conversation at hand. "What happened next?"

"Next." She blew out a breath. "Everyone started to leave. I told you that I never wanted to talk to you again and left with a friend from one of my classes because I refused to get in the car with you, and that was that."

"Jesus." I hit the clicker to unlock my car.

"What is this?"

"What is what?"

"What is this car, Eva?" Aisha pointed at the car.

"It's a long story. That's one of the reasons I need to talk to you."

"I don't understand." She looked at the car like it was some sort of death trap and not a brand new, black BMW with all the bells and whistles. "How'd you get this? How can you afford this?"

"I can't."

"So how do you—"

"Look, do you want me to drive you to your next class or not?"

"Yeah."

"So get in and I'll answer your questions."

"You seem like you have more questions than answers."

"You're not wrong." I pushed down the driver's seat and slung my backpack into the backseat. Aisha pushed down the passenger's seat and did the same. Only then did she look back and see the backpack I was using, and look at me with concern.

"How'd you get a designer backpack?"

"It's not mine. None of this is mine." I started the car. Aisha finally closed her door and put her seatbelt on. I glanced over at her and said the words aloud that I hadn't been able to say to anyone else. "It's my sister's."

"You don't have a sister."

"I do now."

She searched my face for a long moment. I started to drive. At least it gave me something to focus on while she was psycho-analyzing me. We didn't say a word during our drive and when I parked in front of the building to her next class, she just sat there, looking out the window quietly.

"I don't understand," she said after a long moment.

"I don't either. I really don't. Friday and Saturday are totally blank in my memory. I don't remember those days at all."

"Were you that drunk?"

"On Friday? I must have been."

"How did you end up with this car? With this backpack?" She eyed me closer now. "With those clothes."

I explained to her what happened, beginning at the mental institution and ending at The Manor, though I was careful not to go into detail about that. I only said that it was where they'd dropped me off and where I'd been staying. When I finished the recount, I looked over at her, expecting to find a look of disbelief, and sure enough, it was exactly what I was rewarded with.

"I don't want you to take this the wrong way." She said the words slowly, as if preparing for my impending blow. I practiced patience, focusing on my breathing and reminding myself that sometimes reacting to negativity wasn't the smart move. I needed her in my corner.

"I love you, Eva. You know I do. I always will. You were the only one there for me when my mom left us. You put our names on the prayer list at church and dragged me there every Sunday until I couldn't help but go willingly. I will forever be grateful to you for a lot of things. But you need help. I don't want to blame all of this on Karen. She was never a fit mother. She wanted to whitewash you and change you into something you could never be. I get that. I do. Some parents suck, but at some point, you have to take accountability for your own actions. You need serious psychological help. You've always wanted a sister, so you've created one." She paused to look around the car. "You created a rich, perfect sister. The daughter Karen always wanted."

"I didn't." I shook my head. "She's real. Dr. Thompson gave me all of these things so that I'd help find her."

"Dr. Thompson." Aisha sighed, taking her phone out and tapping. I watched as she googled Dr. Thompson. When his face appeared on the screen, she glanced up quickly, eyes wide. "That's the guy."

"What guy?"

"The one you were arguing with at The Institute." She

looked at her phone again and clicked on the first profile. "He works closely with the Maslows."

"I know. He's a neurologist there."

"Do you think there's any chance they slipped something in your drink while you were there?"

"The Maslows? No way. Why would they do that?"

"I don't know." She shook her head and looked at the screen again, then back at me. "Maybe they're trying to help you control your disorder by allowing you to live two different realities."

"I'm not schizophrenic."

Aisha pursed her lips. I knew that look. It was her judgmental no comment. I hadn't been on the receiving end of it often, but when I was, I always felt myself shrink. She had a way of making people feel inferior and according to Dr. Maslow, I had a bit of an inferiority complex thanks to events in my past.

"Are you saying you don't believe what I just told you?" I asked after a few seconds of maddening silence.

"I'm not saying I don't believe the events that took place, but you said it yourself, you don't even remember what really happened those days. For all you know, you never left The Institute on Friday and by the time you woke up on Sunday, they were able to feed you whatever they wanted your reality to be." She looked at her phone again, then at me. "Shit. I have to go. Listen, I think it's best if we take some time apart. You sound like you have a lot of issues to work through."

She grabbed her bag and left the car. I didn't move.

On my way to The Institute, I thought about what Aisha said. What if this was one of their innovative experiments? What if all of this was a lie? What if I had been kept in The Institute all of those days? If that was really the case though, how had I been at Karen's on Friday?

CHAPTER SEVENTEEN

A T NINE O'CLOCK ON THE DOT, I MADE MY WAY DOWNSTAIRS. The Manor seemed darker than usual, the light coming from the flicker of every other candle as I walked down the long corridor. I wasn't sure how I knew where I was going, but I headed to the left, towards the dungeon doors that led to actual dungeons. A memory of a naked woman on a rock and monks surrounding her flashed in my mind and I froze, midway.

"You were doing so good," a voice said.

"Keep going," said another.

"Where are you?" I looked around, panicked. I wasn't drunk, so I knew I wasn't imagining things, but everything lately seemed to lead to second-guessing myself.

"Where are we? Where are you? Where is anyone?"

I pressed my back to the wall behind me, the edges of the portrait hanging there digging into my back as I looked around. There was no one in the hall. They must have been talking to me through a speaker. I turned my attention to the ceiling and saw a small black dome camera I hadn't noticed before. There must have been a speaker somewhere as well.

"I wouldn't push up against the walls if I were you," one of the voices said that I was sure was Will's. "They move."

At that, I shook my head, nearly smiling. This wasn't a haunted house. The house was creepy, I'd give them that. It was old and mysterious with even stranger things happening inside of it, but moving walls wasn't something I was going to fall for. That was, until the frame behind me clicked, and the floor beneath me shifted so quickly, the only thing I could do was press my palms to the wall behind me to keep from falling. The spot where I was standing was a half-circle that spun around, and as I continued to press my palms onto the wall beneath the frame, I realized I had just been taken to another room, one I had no idea was behind the long, dark corridor. In front of me stood three red cloaks.

"I told you the walls moved." That was Will, though I couldn't see his face, but having them in front of me, I knew the one in the center was Adam, the one on the right was Will, and the other was unknown to me at the moment.

"What the hell is this place?" I asked, once my words found their way to my mouth from underneath the knot in my throat. I let go of the wall tentatively and stepped forward, away from the frame.

"The Manor." The third guy cocked his head. "I assume you're sober."

"You know what they say about those who make assumptions."

"Let's start." That was Adam, all authoritative, as he passed me my cloak.

He turned around and Will and the other guy picked up a candelabra that was beside the door. At first, I thought it was for show, but he continued holding it as Adam walked over to the wall behind them and turned a doorknob, pushing the door that blended into the wall open. I wondered how many secret passages and doors this place had. Were there any that led to my bedroom? God, I hoped not. With the door closed behind us, we walked further onto the lawn. It was freshly cut. If I stopped walking, shut my eyes, and just inhaled, I could transport myself back to Karen's lawn on a day that the neighbor had just mowed it.

"Freshly cut grass is my favorite smell," I said.

"Interesting," Adam responded, though he didn't turn around. "You realize it's a distress signal the grass is releasing because it's just been wounded by the blade, right?"

"It has a name," Will mused.

"Green leaf volatiles," Adam responded.

"Are you a botanist?" I blinked. "How do you even know this?"

Neither of them answered. I stopped talking and focused on the distress signal the grass was sending out. The walk seemed to go on forever and I was dying to ask how much longer we had till we got there, but didn't. I looked over my shoulder and was surprised at how far from the house we'd gotten. As I looked up, I saw the house next door. It looked similar to The Manor. Eerily so. There was only one light on and with it came the outline of a woman standing by the window. I wondered if she could see us, and if so, if she would tell someone that a group of men led a woman into the woods and left her there. From what I gathered, that was what they were here to do. As we reached the entrance of the woods, where the long pine trees started, I felt myself shiver. I looked over my shoulder one last time, in search of the woman at the window, but she was gone, as was the light.

"How much longer are we going to walk?" I crossed my arms to fight the breeze now circulating.

"We're almost there."

I'd been dodging so many people calling me crazy and

now that I was walking deep into the woods I realized maybe they were right. What sane person would let three guys lead her into the woods in the dead of night? What sane person would let them lead her there knowing they meant to bury her alive. I reminded myself that the task came with dollar signs and potential answers and that was what I was here for. A few more steps and the trees seemed to open up and clear around a large circle. From here, I could see three buildings, much smaller than The Manor, but buildings nonetheless. *The forbidden ones*, I thought, as we stopped in the midst of them. They seemed to be surrounding the circle perfectly. Will walked over to a spot in the clearing and reached down, pulling up a rope with him. I brought up a hand to cover my gasp. I looked down and realized there were black ropes everywhere. If you were just taking a walk in the woods, you might miss it, or think it was just material left behind from a campsite. As I walked closer to where they stood and saw the outline in the grass of a rectangle, I knew it was the box in which I would be buried. My head was woozy from the shots I'd taken and I was grateful for that.

"How deep is it?" I stepped closer and looked inside. It was too dark to see, even with the candelabra Will carried. The thought of going in there at all wasn't a welcome one, but I'd signed up for this and I'd see it through. "Am I supposed to . . . jump in there? What now?"

"No. Now we wait." Adam turned toward one of the buildings.

Not knowing what else to do, I faced it with him. The two buildings on that side were plain and windowless, at least I thought they were until a light switched on. The guys didn't move, didn't make a sound, but the energy in the air changed. My skin prickled as I spotted someone walking toward us from that direction. They were cloaked, and from their height, I couldn't tell if it was a man or a woman.

"Is this the Chancellor?" I whispered.

"No. A messenger."

The person stopped walking a few feet away from us, right beside one of the black ropes that lay over a rectangle.

"You have been chosen," the figure said. It was a man. A monk, I realized, to my horror, considering what I saw the other night. "Hand-selected by the Chancellor for an opportunity of a lifetime. The Swords is the oldest prestigious society. Before The Eight, before Skull and Bones, before The Family, before the Freemasons, before Quill and Dagger, and before The Swords themselves came to existence, a creed was formed between Jesus and his apostles. Twelve men would lead alongside Him. Twelve men would tell the stories of His miracles."

The monk paused. "Later, in Rome, another great man by the name of Giovanni de' Medici would bring another group of men together. Six men would form what you now know as The Swords." He signaled at the ground beside me. "Every Sword is tested, as you will be tested tonight. Since the dawn of time, our society has been male-driven, only allowing women to join every thirty years. You may be wondering why. You may be wondering why you wear a white cloak and not a red. The red cloak signifies blood. The blood that has been sacrificed in the past to allow you to be here tonight. Tonight is the most grueling of our tests. Spending the night underground, in a coffin, is not an easy task. Despite the measures we've taken to ensure safety, you will find it difficult to breathe at times. We provide you with oxygen and water. Inside you will also find a latch that connects to this black rope."

He paused again and lifted an arm. "Tonight, your partner

has chosen to join you in this task, to show you that he too knows about sacrifice."

My head whipped toward Adam. He'd be in the coffin with me? I'd die. I'd become claustrophobic and . . . I couldn't do it.

"If you cannot bear to stay inside, use the rope," the monk said. "If you do before daybreak, you will no longer be a contender to join The Swords. I'm sure you have questions we can answer afterward. Good luck."

With that, the monk turned and walked back to the building he'd come from. My head whipped toward Adam again.

"You're going in there with me?"

"Relax. It's a two-person casket."

"There are two-person caskets?" I was breathing heavily.

"We're about to get in one." Adam looked at me. He turned to me and grabbed my shoulders, making me face him and meet his eyes, though I could barely see his eyes in this lighting. "You're going to be okay."

I nodded, focusing on breathing, on relaxing. I stepped away from him, reached down, grabbed the rope, and grunted as I tried to pull it up. As I let it go, I exhaled. "This is too heavy."

Adam reached down and pulled it open with ease. I wasn't a weakling. I did fifty push-ups daily. I could carry my own weight and then some. Somehow, I couldn't open that lid.

"If we need to get out . . . " I looked at Will.

"We'll get you out."

"So you'll stay here all night?"

"Yup." That was the third guy. "All night."

"What if you fall asleep and you don't hear us shout? Has that happened before?"

The three of them looked amongst each other. Finally, Adam nodded as he looked at me.

"It won't happen tonight." Adam squeezed my hand. "Trust me, I scream pretty loud."

"Okay." I took a deep breath. "Let's do this." I looked at the ground. "How deep is this?"

"Not classic burial deep," Adam said. "Three feet? Maybe four?"

"Deep enough that I can't climb out on my own." A chill ran through me.

"Why would you need to climb out on your own?" Adam asked.

"I don't know what you're going to try to do to me in there."

"Jesus Christ." He ran a hand through his hair. "Are you serious? You'd rather be buried alone?"

"No. I don't know." I crossed my arms. "Let's just do this."

They helped me get into the casket. Adam came next, slowly lowering himself beside me. Once we were settled, both of us lying on our backs facing up, Will and the third guy stood over us, only their cloaks visible in the dim moonlight. They looked around as if making sure we had what we needed and shut the lid over us. I shrieked. Adam laughed.

"It is not funny." I bit my lip. "This is crazy. Why do you do this?"

"To achieve your full potential."

"How the hell is being buried alive achieving your full potential?"

"It's mind over matter," he said. "Mind over matter."

"This is crazy," I whispered. "You did this by yourself?"

"Yeah."

"And did you *achieve your full potential?*" I asked, mocking him.

"I'm not sure I'll ever achieve my full potential, but I keep trying." The smile in his voice made me smile.

"I spoke to my friend Aisha."

"What'd she say?"

"She told me what happened on Friday and confirmed that I have no memory of it." I turned on my side, surprised by how much space was actually in this casket. I couldn't see Adam, but I knew the moment he turned his face toward mine.

"At all?"

"At all. She did say something interesting though about them doing an experiment on me during those days. Is that legal? Could they take my memory? Is there even something that does that?"

"Fuck, I hope not." He looked away. "Some people say electric shock therapy does that sometimes."

I nodded. I'd heard that. I turned on my back again and scooted a little closer to Adam. He brought an arm around me and I closed my eyes. It was strange, to feel safe inside of a box while being buried underground.

"Tell me about your upbringing," he said after a moment. "Did your parents attend Ellis?"

"No. Well, I don't know. I was adopted. My adoptive parents didn't."

"How old were you when were you adopted?"

"I was a baby, five months? I can't remember. I'd have to ask Karen."

"So you don't remember anything before the adoption happened."

"Or much after. Don't they say we truly don't remember anything until age three?"

"Depends on the person. The human mind was built to withstand trauma. We box things up and filter out things that can deter us from moving forward."

"Tell me about Karen."

"Karen." I sighed. "She's nice. We're not the best of friends, but we look out for each other."

"Was she who you were talking to the other night?"

"Yeah. She's in Florida. She says I visited her on Friday night, but I don't remember. I went over there and her neighbor said the cops were called, Karen was taken to the hospital. It was a big mess."

"Is she okay? Why was she in the hospital?"

"She allegedly pulled a gun on me and shot into the air and I guess even she went into shock over it."

"What the fuck? She tried to shoot you?"

"It seems that way."

"Seems that way? What the hell kind of mother tries to shoot her daughter?"

"Well, yeah, that's the thing, I know I'm a huge pain in the ass but I don't think she'd pull a gun on me for no reason."

He stayed quiet.

"What? You're not going to say it's no wonder you ended up at The Institute or it's no wonder you need meds to calm your crazy or whatever other generalization comes to mind?"

"I wouldn't say those things." He pulled me closer.

"You took me to your mother so she could tell you I was crazy."

"Are you ever going to let me live that down?"

"No, probably not."

"I guess I'll have to live with it," he said. "But just so you know, my mom already invited you to Thanksgiving, so you'll have to get over it by then."

"What?" I laughed.

"I'm not kidding."

"Does she think we're dating?"

"I mean, I didn't say otherwise."

"You're joking."

"Not joking." He shrugged. "I chose to be buried in a casket with you. I'm pretty sure we're past the dating question."

"We haven't even had sex." I frowned. "Don't people have sex and then decide whether or not they want to date?"

"Is that what you do normally?"

"I don't normally date."

"What do you mean?"

"I mean I don't normally date. I usually have sex and that's it. One-night stand, no strings attached."

"You're that afraid of commitment?"

I bit my lip and thought about it. "I'm not afraid of commitment. I'm afraid of disappointment."

"Got it."

"You're a dater though. I can tell. You like having girlfriends."

"I haven't had an actual girlfriend in a while, but I'm not opposed to having a girlfriend. Why haven't you had a boyfriend? You're drop-dead gorgeous. I can't imagine you went through high school without a million guys trying to date you."

"I was gone for a lot of it. The Institute. When you're there too often people start creating this narrative about you. I think they thought if they got too close to me and hurt me that I'd do something drastic."

"That's not fair."

"Neither is taking me to see your psychologist mom."

"I already apologized for that."

"I know. That time, I was kidding."

"So, one-night stands, no strings attached," he said as if mulling it over. "Sounds lonely."

"I like lonely."

"Hm."

"Hey, Adam," I said after a long bout of silence.

"Yeah?"

"Did it occur to you that they could kill us by throwing dirt on us and leaving us here?"

"It hadn't occurred to me, but thanks for putting that in my head."

"I'm just saying. What if that happens?"

"What if my best friends try to kill me?"

"Yeah."

"Well, fuck, Eva, I don't know. I guess I'll be dead and won't have a chance to give it much thought."

"You seriously trust them?"

"With my life. Obviously."

"Okay." I nodded against his shoulder.

"You're going to trust us with your life?"

"I'm going to think about it. Who knows, maybe I'll unlock my full potential and become the queen of this weird castle."

"Achieve, not unlock." Adam chuckled. "This isn't a video game."

"You sure about that?" I raised an eyebrow even though he couldn't see me. "So, what'd you do with your money?"

"From The Swords?"

"Yeah."

"Deposited it into a Roth IRA account."

"Damn."

"What?"

"That's why the rich keep getting richer. Here I was thinking about spending it on a car."

Adam chuckled. "You're funny, Eva."

"I must be. I don't think I've even seen you smile this much, let alone laugh."

"Where do you see yourself in five years?"

"I guess I should have expected achieving my full potential to come with a side of questions like these."

"I'm curious and we have all night."

"I want to teach first grade."

"That's cute." I could hear the smile in his voice. "You know you're going to get attached to the kids, right?"

"I know."

"I'm surprised you're okay with that being that you're such a commitment-phobe."

"I'm not a commitment-phobe. I just prefer to be alone."

"Hm." He stayed quiet for a moment. "Hey, Eva."

"Yeah?"

"Do you realize I've had my arm around you this entire time, in this hot, box of death, and you haven't even pulled away once?"

"Interesting." I smiled. I hadn't noticed. "I guess I feel comfortable with you."

"I like that."

"Of course you do. You're trying to have sex with me."

"I'm trying to date you." He chuckled. "And have sex with you."

"Hey, Adam." I looked up, even though I couldn't see his face. "I really like you, despite reason."

"The feeling is mutual." He kissed the top of my head. "I would kiss you, but we need to save oxygen."

"We should have taken our cloaks off." I gasped. "What if we overheat?"

"Just stay calm and we'll be fine. We have water. Try to get some rest. The ceremony will be ten times more exhausting than this."

"This isn't the end?" I groaned, banging my head against his shoulder.

"You want to be the queen of the creepy castle, don't you?"

"Ugh. Stop talking."

At some point, I fell asleep. When I woke up, it was noises above us followed by a bright light and two guys standing over us, looking down into the casket we were inside of.

"Congratulations. You survived the night," Will said, grinning.

"Good job," the third guy said. "Damn. No crying or pounding on the door. I'm jealous. And impressed."

"Jealous and impressed because Wolf pissed himself the night of his burial," Adam said.

"Fuck you. Burying people alive is a form of torture." Wolf scowled.

Will and Wolf pulled us out slowly. I felt sore everywhere, and after a few steps toward the main house, my knees began to weaken. I stopped walking and held my knees as I breathed.

"Go ahead. I'll catch up." I put a hand up.

"We don't leave people behind." Adam walked back over to me and lifted me into his arms.

He carried me to the house, gave me Gatorade and food, and then carried me up the stairs to my bedroom. I couldn't stop thinking about our conversation or the possibilities between us.

CHAPTER EIGHTEEN

IT WAS FIVE TWENTY-THREE WHEN I GOT TO THE INSTITUTE, AND because of that, the valet guys were packing up and not taking any more cars. I left mine up front and walked inside without a second glance their way, wondering if this was how Stella did it. I was wondering a lot about Stella after my conversation with Aisha. Did she really have such a bad attitude? I knew I had one, but even I had my limits and would never scream at Karen in front of people, and I definitely would never scream at a stranger for no reason like she did to Aisha.

I bypassed my usual steps of checking in and waiting for Dr. Debbie Maslow. Instead, I barged straight into her office, but found it empty. I'd wait. Debbie didn't leave this building until well after six and I knew she'd be back in no time. I shut the doors behind me and walked in. Her office was massive and unlike Neil's, hers looked like something that belonged in a museum. A larger than life portrait of her grandfather hung over a fireplace behind her desk. He was wearing a white doctor's coat and smiling in the painting. It was one of those things that always made me stop and stare. His blue eyes seemed compassionate and his expression was soft.

According to Debbie, who normally shifted attention away

from her personal life but was always willing to talk about her grandfather, he was one of the best human beings to have ever lived. He was smart too. Both Debbie and Neil were direct descendants from two of the greatest minds in psychology, and therefore, were basically royalty in the psychology world. Not that either one of them would ever boast about it. The only reason I knew was because I'd done my own research on them when I got old enough to have questions that went unanswered by Karen. The door opened behind me and I turned to find a surprised-looking Debbie walking in.

"Did we have an appointment today?"

"No. I hope you don't mind my being here at this time, but I didn't know where else to go."

"Of course not, Sweet Pea." She signaled for me to take a seat. I walked around her desk and sat in my usual chair, and she took her own seat beneath the portrait. "What's going on?"

"You look tired."

"I am tired." She let out a laugh. "Belinda had a five a.m. meet this morning and I had to drive them. Then I got a flat tire on the way back so I had to move all of my appointments down an hour. Let's just say I've had better days."

"Ouch." My eyebrows rose. "Is she still doing well with that crew stuff?"

"Well enough to be offered a scholarship." Debbie grinned. "She's attending Ellis in the fall."

"That's amazing." I smiled. I'd met Belinda a few times and liked her so much.

"So, what brings you here?"

"I'm having trouble remembering what happened to me last weekend." I blurted out the words and watched her reaction. She had none.

"Okay?"

"I was here on Friday for a cocktail event."

"Yes, I know. We spoke."

"We did?"

"For a long time. We talked about *Schitt's Creek* and how Belinda and I love it and you said you'd binged it with Aisha."

"Was I drunk?"

"You seemed fine." Her brows pulled in slightly. "You don't remember any of that?"

"No. At all." I gnawed on my lower lip for a beat. "And Aisha said I embarrassed her and yelled at her in front of everyone."

"When was this?"

"Right before the event was over."

"I must have stepped out before that happened."

"When was the last time you saw me?"

She tilted her head slightly and looked at a spot on the bookcase beside us. "You said you needed to use the restroom and I said I was leaving, so we walked together."

"The restroom in the lobby?"

"I'm not sure. You took the elevator up with me, I had to get my purse and keys, and then, well, I'm not sure where you went."

"I'm not sure either."

"There was a storm that night. The drive home was a pain." She blinked at me. "What was the last thing you remember?"

"Nothing. I remember waking up here on Sunday morning."

"Here?" Her eyes widened. She leaned forward and powered up her computer. "Who discharged you?"

"No one. I just got my stuff and walked out."

"What room were you in?"

"366."

She glanced over at me, her gaze uneasy, and looked back at the computer, typing something. "Why are you coming to me now? Why didn't you come before?"

"I don't know. I guess it didn't bother me before, but then I went to see Karen and she wasn't home." I bit my tongue, unsure of whether or not I should say what was on my mind. Finally, I decided to come out with it. I met her gaze again. "Her neighbor said we got into an argument. Karen went inside to get a gun and had passed out. I don't know. I don't remember any of this."

"Where is Karen? Is she in the hospital?"

"No." I shook my head. I didn't want to tell her anything about Karen right now.

"Is she not home? Is she in Florida? She goes there when she needs to get away. You know Karen doesn't like to hang around when things get rough." She shot me a pointed look. "If you two got into an argument, I wouldn't be surprised that she went over there."

"Maybe."

"What was your fight about?"

"I don't know."

"I'm having a difficult time helping you here, Eva." Debbie rubbed her temple with the tips of her fingers.

"I just . . . what if it wasn't me who went to Karen's house?" I licked my lips. "What if it was someone else?"

"Someone else like who?"

"I don't know. Someone else."

"But your neighbor said she saw you."

"I know."

"So who would it be?"

"Someone who looks a lot like me." I shrugged. "Someone like my sister."

"Eva." Debbie sighed heavily, dropping her hands. "I know how badly you've always wanted a sister, but come on."

"I'm just saying, it's possible."

"Is it though?" She shot me a look as she opened the first drawer of her desk and took out a file. She opened it and started reading. "Age five, Eva Guerra suggests she saw a girl who looks just like her playing in the park. Age ten, Eva Guerra chased after a family in the mall, losing her mother in the process, because she saw a girl who looked just like her and believed it was her sister. Age fourteen, Eva Guerra claims she saw a girl at a Halloween party who looked just like her, but she couldn't be sure since they were both in costume." Debbie shut the folder and looked at me sympathetically. "I'm sorry, but you have an ongoing history of believing this."

"So you're saying I'm crazy." I batted away the tears that pricked my eyes. "You're saying I'm making all of this up." I stood up. I couldn't believe after everything, she was still lying to me. "I shouldn't have come."

"Eva, wait. I don't want you to leave like this. I know how upsetting this is to you, but you need to hear it."

"I don't want to. I get it. I'm crazy. I'm bipolar, maybe more. Maybe I'm imagining all of these alternate realities of my life. Maybe I'm doing it for attention. Maybe I'm doing it so Karen can take pity and listen to me. Maybe I'm doing it because I wish I had you as a mom and not Karen. Maybe I'm looking for ways to make my life better, the way we all are." I wiped my face. "You know who believes me? Dr. Thompson. He believes me and he'll vouch for me."

"Oh, honey." Debbie lowered her gaze.

"What?"

"Dr. Thompson is missing."

"What?" My heart jumped to my throat. "What do you mean missing?"

"He and his son went on an adventure to climb Mont Blanc and there was an avalanche. They haven't reported any survivors."

I stumbled back with the news and ran out of her office, taking my phone out and dialing his cellphone in the process. Straight to voicemail. Fuck. It was just my luck that the only impartial person in the entire world who could vouch for me had now gone missing, or worse.

CHAPTER NINETEEN

ADAM

SHE WAS DRUNK WHEN I FINALLY SAW HER IN THE MANOR. Drunk and alone. I wondered how often she did this. It was clear that the bottle in her hand was her own. We didn't keep Jameson in stock in The Manor. It wasn't that I didn't enjoy it from time to time, but on the rare occasion I allowed himself a drink, I chose Glenfiddich. I crossed my arms and pressed my side against the doorframe, just watching her.

"Fuck all of them," she said, taking a shot. "Fuck all of them."

"You may want to slow down." My voice made her jump. "You're going to pass out, or worse, throw up all over our kitchen."

"I don't throw up." She turned to face me.

Even with a scowl on her face, she was incredibly beautiful.

"You might throw up." I pushed off the doorframe and walked over to her. "And then you'd have to clean it up because I sure as hell am not cleaning up your vomit."

"You won't clean up my vomit but you'll spend the night

with me in a coffin?" She raised an eyebrow. "I'm glad to see you have limits."

I shook my head, trying to keep from laughing. "I have a thing about vomit."

"I went to see Dr. Maslow today," she said.

"What?" My heart stopped. "We said you'd stay away for now."

"I know, but I just had to see her."

"And?"

"She lied to my face again. She even went as far as pulling out my file from the drawer where she keeps it and started reading all the times I imagined seeing my sister."

I hated that Dr. Maslow did that to her, but above anything else I hated that it affected her the way it did. Eva was all tough exterior, but I saw her, really saw her, and knew she felt things deeply.

"She also said Dr. Thompson is missing. He went on a trip with his son and there was an avalanche."

"Dr. Thompson?"

"Yep."

"Did you check the news?"

"There's nothing on the news about him yet, only the avalanche."

"Hm." I didn't even know what to think anymore. Was this another ploy to get Eva to drop all of this or was it real? Why would Debbie Maslow make that up though? It made no sense. None of this did.

"Do you believe in God?" she asked suddenly, catching me completely off guard.

"Why are you asking?"

"Answer the question." Her words were slurred as she closed the distance between us, bottle dangling in her left hand. "Do you believe in God?"

"I believe in facts."

"So you don't believe in God?"

"I don't know."

"Some people take the bible to be facts."

"And I don't judge those people." My eyes stayed on hers. "Isn't that one of the things in the bible? Do unto others as you would have them do unto you. I live by that."

"So you are familiar with the bible."

"I think everyone is familiar with that phrase." I felt myself smile. She looked cute and completely wild like this. "Do you believe in God?"

"Of course." She blinked. "Even in my darkest days, in my darkest moments, I've always felt Him by my side."

"That's good."

"I don't anymore." As she blinked, tears trickled down her face. "I don't feel Him anywhere anymore."

"Maybe you should stop drinking. Stop numbing yourself."

"You're probably right." She frowned, stumbling as she took a step toward me. I reached out and caught her.

"You okay?"

"Yeah." She didn't move though, just stayed against my chest and looked up at me. "You're so handsome, Adam Astor."

"You're so beautiful, Eva Guerra."

"Sometimes I find that the only thing that makes me smile these days is when I think about that kiss we shared."

"Yeah?" My heart pounded.

"What if I kiss you right now?" Her lips brushed against mine.

"What if I let you?"

"You shouldn't. You shouldn't want to date me or to come to Thanksgiving. You shouldn't want me as a girlfriend at all."

"Why not?"

"I'll ruin you," she whispered. "I ruin everyone."

"I'm already ruined, Eva."

I pressed my nose against hers. She closed her eyes and leaned forward just a touch, and when her whiskey-fueled lips touched mine, and her tongue coated my own, I felt my chest rattle. How many women had I kissed? Thirty? Forty? How many times had I kissed her? Twice? Three times? Somehow, this felt different. She tasted like wildflowers, untamed and unexpected. Our tongues danced the length of a song, two, twelve. Our hands explored over our clothing and I knew I needed to stop this, pull away. She was drunk and I wasn't going to let this escalate, but every time I tried to stop, she leaned in and deepened the kiss. When I felt like I would explode if I let her keep going, I pulled away, panting.

"Let's go to bed." I took the bottle from her hand and set it on the counter, walking her up to her room.

When she was fast asleep, I left her room and locked the door. I didn't know if she'd wake up in the middle of the night, find me there, and try something, and I didn't trust myself not to let her.

CHAPTER TWENTY

EVA

MORNING ARRIVED TOO SOON. I FLINCHED AS I OPENED MY EYES, confused as to why I'd woken up until I realized someone was calling my phone repeatedly. I reached for it and picked it up as soon as I saw Karen's name.

"I'm home."

"Okay. I'll be there soon."

I got up, brushed my teeth, showered, and got dressed in ripped carpenter jeans, black Converse, and a black T-shirt. I wasn't in the mood to sift through Stella's designer shit, and now that the cat was out of the bag, I wasn't sure I had to. I was halfway down the stairs when I saw two people walking up. Two women. One of them was wearing a nun outfit—a black and white dress to the knee and black veil on her head, while the other was dressed in blue jeans and a white frilly blouse. I'd never seen either one of them here before and it took me a moment to convince myself that I wasn't hallucinating. They were talking to each other quietly and smiling. When they saw me freeze in the middle of the stairs, they stopped and looked at me. They were definitely old enough to be my mothers.

"Good morning," the nun said. "Are you feeling okay?"

"I . . . yes. Thank you." I looked at the two of them and saw no distinction in their faces, a realization that made me feel instantly woozy. "Are you sisters?"

"Yes." The one in plain clothes smiled.

"Twins. Are you twins?"

"Yes." She frowned. "Are you okay?"

"I'm not sure." I grabbed onto the rail beside me and sat down slowly. "I'm sorry. I just haven't had anything to eat."

"It's okay." The nun looked at her sister. "Get her some water. And bread."

The one in plain clothes ran down the stairs and disappeared to the right. The nun sat down beside me.

"You should be in bed thinking about the sacrifice you'll be making."

"What sacrifice?" My eyes searched hers.

"It is your duty to fulfill whatever the Chancellor asks of you."

"I don't understand. I was already buried. I was already initiated."

"More may be asked of you. You have a sister, don't you?" She stood suddenly. "It's the thirtieth year, Child, and sacrifices come in threes."

The other woman gave me a slice of bread in a napkin and a bottle of water before they walked up the stairs. I continued my walk down, my sneakers squeaking with each step I took. Why had she asked me if I had a sister? Did she mean I'd have to sacrifice Stella? Or maybe Stella already sacrificed me. I followed the sound of the piano, which was playing a very familiar and very unexpected song. Outside the closed door, I closed my eyes and just listened, the notes transporting me to another time, another place, before Karen started drinking heavily and I was constantly in and out of The Institute. It was so long ago, I had to squint my eyes to get a glimpse of what my life looked like under this lens. I turned the knob, pushed the door open, and Adam stopped playing and looked up. I cleared my throat. I decided not to tell Adam about this yet. It was too much crazy to lay on one person at once.

"I thought you weren't Catholic."

"I'm surprised you remember anything about last night at all." Adam smiled. "Would you like me to play S'vivon?"

"I don't know what that is."

"I didn't think you would. Normally people who are married to one religion don't think about the others."

"But you do." I walked to the couch across from him and sat down.

He gave a small shrug. "Let's just say my mother went through a crisis when I was a teenager and my entire family had to learn about multiple religions as she tried to figure out what she believed in."

"Oh." I tried to picture what that would be like, but couldn't. Between Karen, *Full House*, and *Family Matters*, my idea of a family unit was entirely warped, tittering between what I knew and what I'd never achieve. "Which did she decide on?"

"She thought she could be Buddhist for a while, but went back to Catholicism. Apparently, it's a bitch to give that one up. The guilt eats away at you slowly every second you turn your back on it, and by the time you realize it and go back to confession, you're so guilt-ridden, you're almost having another existential crisis."

At that, I chortled. It was so relatable. Every time I met a guy on Bumble I had to give myself a pep talk about how it wasn't wrong, truly.

"I definitely didn't expect you to be playing 'Ave Maria,'" I said finally. "It was beautiful."

"Don't tell me it's your favorite."

"It's everyone's favorite. I think that song transcends religious belief. You have no choice but to appreciate it when you hear it."

Adam didn't say anything, but his eyes were smiling, and I felt myself smile with them. There was a knock on the door and we both faced it as it opened and a priest walked inside. My frown deepened, heart leaped so high it lifted me to my feet. Adam stood as well.

"Please. . ." The Priest waved his hands. "You don't have to stand. I'll only take a second of your time." He smiled at me as we continued to stand, and walked over to us. It was a kind smile, but after everything I'd seen here, I wasn't sure I believed the sincerity behind it. When he reached us, he turned to Adam. "Four more called to RSVP this morning. I told them in jest that it was too late, but they didn't seem to accept that. I just wanted to let you know before you saw my email."

"That's fine. Four won't make a huge difference. Sometimes, people don't show up."

"My child." The Priest reached up and set a hand on top of Adam's shoulder. "Everyone will show up tonight. I don't know who you're expecting, but our people don't RSVP unless they're going to show. They've waited years for this."

"Years?" I asked. "Don't these happen every year?"

"Not like this." The priest took his hand off Adam's shoulder and faced me with the same smile.

Adam and I waited until he walked out and shut the door behind him before we both sat down again.

"Priests, monks, what's next, nuns?" I whispered. "This is like elementary school all over again." I shook my head. "And you've never had women before this?"

"We invited some a couple of years ago but it didn't work out. They couldn't handle the burial."

"Which makes the fact that I'm here now even weirder."

"You or Stella?" He raised an eyebrow.

"Both of us," I said. "I had a key to The Manor as well."

"What do you mean?"

"The key to the front door was in my backpack."

"How'd you get it?"

"I don't know."

"You don't know."

"I don't remember. It must have happened Friday."

"Shit. That makes sense. That was when we dropped off the letters." Adam looked at me. "Well, the ceremony is tonight. Are you ready?"

"Am I ever?" I shrugged. "I have to go see Karen."

"I'm coming with you."

I stared at him for a moment. "If you come, you're either on my side or against me. I don't want you acting like we're okay and then go behind my back to figure out whether or not you believe me."

"Hey, I'm with you. One hundred percent with you."

"Noted." He nodded.

In the car, he was fine until he got on the highway. Then, he had no idea where to go. I directed him on where to go, where to turn, what roads to take.

"You really don't know your way around here."

"I grew up in the city," he said. "My parents went to Ellis though, met there. It wasn't ever really a question of whether or not my brother and I would attend, it was a matter of when." He glanced over at me. "How'd you end up at Ellis?"

"The Maslows."

"The Maslows?" He frowned. "I don't understand."

"It's difficult to explain."

"Try me."

"Karen says I was always a difficult baby—"

"Sorry to cut you off, but have you always called her Karen?"

"You have to make a left here." I pointed at the upcoming block. "Yes, for as long as I can remember she's been Karen."

"You refer to her as your mother."

"Well, she is my mother."

"You two don't seem close."

"Not all mother-daughters are, but it doesn't change the fact that she raised me."

"Where do I go now?"

"Right here." I pointed at the streetlight.

"So Karen said you were always a difficult child."

"Yeah, and somehow at church it came up in conversation." I paused, frowning. That wasn't right. "Apparently, during my baptism, which was late, I was baptized when I was ten months."

"That's late?"

"For a Catholic, yes," I said. "You weren't baptized?"

"I was, but I was a baby."

"Anyway, during my baptism, I was throwing a tantrum. Karen thought it was because I hadn't napped. Luisa, our friend from church, one of the Dominican ones, said I needed food. Father Murray said the devil was inside me."

"What?" Adam's face whipped toward me. "Don't tell me they bought into that."

"Well, I was shrieking when the water was poured on me. Then when I was around three years old, I started saying something like 'burns, burns' and you know holy water only burns the wicked."

"What?" He laughed. "That's crazy."

"If you really want to know my story you need to keep an

open mind." I scowled. "It's not easy for me to say all of these things to someone like you."

"Someone like me?"

"A spoiled, smart, hot guy who doesn't believe in God."

"I never said I didn't believe in God. I would just rather stick to facts. And science." He slowed at the end of the block. "You're going to have to tell me where to go."

"Oh crap. Sorry. Turn around. I'm two houses back, to the right."

Adam made a U-turn and parked in the driveway, behind Karen's old, white Buick. I took a deep breath as I opened the door. Adam followed closely behind me. I rang the doorbell, but before I'd even let my hand fall to my side, Karen had opened the door, leaving the screen door closed between us.

"Eva?" She switched the porch light on. "Where's your key?"

"I don't have it with me."

"Are you sure you're Eva?" She frowned. "Where was your sixth birthday?"

"McDonald's."

"How 'bout your seventh?"

"Also McDonald's." I looked at Adam who probably hadn't been to McDonald's in his life. "I had a thing for the Hamburgler."

"Who's this?"

"Adam. He's a . . . friend."

"A friend?" Karen eyed him closely. "A rich friend."

"Are you going to let us in or not?"

"Definitely Eva." Karen smiled as she opened the door for us and closed it quickly behind us, turning three locks.

"Why do you have so many locks?" I frowned. "Even if I had a key I wouldn't have been able to get inside."

"One can never be too careful these days." She walked over to the kitchen. "I'm making tea."

Unlike Adam's parents' large granite island and sleek appliances, ours was plain. Karen had done very little remodeling since moving into the house in 1991. She had replaced the countertops because they'd chipped and the appliances from white to stainless steel when she found out my Aunt Carmen in Florida had replaced hers, but the floors were still the same little white tiles and the cabinets were still the same washed wood. I sat in my usual spot at the table. Adam sat beside me, adjusting in the wooden seat as he tried to get comfortable. It would be an impossible task. Our furniture wasn't made for giants.

"How was Florida?"

Karen turned around and crossed her arms. "Humid. Loud."

"How's Carmen?"

"Missing you."

"I miss her too." I felt myself smile a little. Carmen was Karen's deceased husband's sister. Karen was an only child, but his siblings had welcomed her into their family and treated her and me like their own. Karen was still staring at me when the kettle began to whistle. She turned around and busied herself.

"You drink tea, handsome?"

"Sure. Thank you."

"Where'd you meet Eva? That swanky Ivy League school?"

"Yes, ma'am."

"I'm surprised she brought you here." She turned around and set a mug in front of Adam and one in front of me. "Eva's big on one-night stands staying one-night stands."

Adam's head whipped in my direction. I felt my face burn as she turned around and poured her tea.

"We haven't had a one-night stand."

"Yet." Karen raised an eyebrow and sat across from us, setting her mug down. "Eva is a very difficult person. She's moody, she's outright mean sometimes, but she's going to make someone very happy someday."

"Oh my God." I brought my tea to my lips and drank. *What was she doing?*

"She's a good person," Adam said.

I closed my eyes and shook my head, setting the mug down.

"She is," Karen agreed, "but like I said, she has an attitude problem, which was why I thought it was weird when a couple of weeks ago she showed up here acting like the doting daughter."

I sat up straighter. "This was the night you went to the hospital?"

"Yes. Which, I guess I owe you an apology. I thought you'd abandoned me and didn't go visit until it dawned on me that it wasn't you at all."

"How'd you figure it out?" That was Adam.

"At the hospital, I had a policeman come visit. He told me you'd been in a car accident. When I asked if you were okay, he said you were fine, minor injuries, but that you were in another hospital recovering." Karen pursed her lips. "I called every hospital. You weren't registered in any."

"What did she say when she came?"

"She started out by being nice to me, for starters. She called me mom, not Karen." Karen raised an eyebrow. "I should've known then."

"What did she say though?"

"It was mostly small talk, but when I told you . . . her . . . that she needed to leave and take her meds, she started panicking. That was when she told me she was your sister."

"What did you say?" I inched forward, feeling my heart in my throat.

"I told her to get out of my house. I'd had enough of you. Enough of the lies and exaggerations. Enough of the back and forth." She shook her head. "It was too much. She came on the eve of Esteban's death. I'd just gotten back from an emotional Mass."

"Oh, God. I forgot." I shut my eyes briefly.

"You didn't come last year so I figured you wouldn't show this year either."

"I was in Florida last year and went to Mass there with Aunt Carmen."

"Well, shortly after I got home, you got here." Karen paused. "She got here."

"Why'd you get a gun?" I asked, remembering that detail. "Why do you even have a gun?"

"I had a break-in a few weeks ago. Something you'd know if you answered your phone." She raised an eyebrow.

"Were you home? Did they take anything?"

"I wasn't. They rummaged through my office, but I don't think anything is missing."

"You don't think anything is missing?"

"Our passports are still there. Our social security cards. Esteban's watch collection is untouched."

"So you got a gun."

"So I got a gun."

"And were you going to shoot me with it?"

"Well, at that point I figured it wasn't you after all and she wouldn't leave."

"So you were going to kill her?"

"No. I was going to scare her off, which I did," Karen said. At the sight of the shock on my face, she continued, "She came in here pretending to be you. Why would she pretend to be you for a full ten minutes before telling me the truth?"

"I don't know."

"Where were you on Friday anyway?"

"At a party."

"A party." Karen scoffed. "Of course you were."

"A school function," I said. "Not a fun, college party. Either way, I don't have any recollection of it, or Saturday. I woke up on Sunday at The Institute, in a bed, and got picked up by the cops. That was where I learned of Stella's existence." I paused for Karen. "My sister. The one who came here."

"So it's true."

"Either that or I was cloned, but I don't think anyone has the resources to do that yet." I looked at Adam, who shrugged.

"You woke up at The Institute. How perfect. What did your perfect little doctor say about that?"

"Nothing." I bit my lip and chanced another glance at Adam, who was looking at me.

"Eva thinks Deborah is the most perfect person on the planet and Deborah eats it all up." Karen scowled. "For years she's tried to pit her against me and for years she's won."

"That's not true."

"It is true. You were just too caught up in her web to see it clearly. Do you think you could really get into Ellis without her backing?" Karen scoffed. "Please."

"I've had a 4.0 GPA since the ninth grade, Karen. Yes, she wrote a letter of recommendation, but I made it there on my own."

"At what cost?"

I shook my head and bit my lip harder, refusing to answer, refusing to look at Adam or Karen. Instead, I stared into my tea.

"At what cost, Eva? You don't want to say it in front of your boyfriend? Does it embarrass you? It should."

"At no cost," I whispered.

"No cost? You left your job at the parish school. A damn good job that you were damn good at. You isolated yourself from your friends. You don't answer the phone when I call. This girl, your sister, was talking about some cult you joined."

"She told you about that?" I met her eyes then. "What did she say?"

"Something about you needing to get out of there and her not being able to help you. I was waving a gun around at who I thought was my own daughter. I wasn't really paying attention to details at that point."

"Oh, God." I put a hand on my stomach and looked at Adam. "Is there any way she copied the key? Copied the card? Is there any way she sent it to me so I could go in her place?"

"Didn't you say her father made you go in her place?"

"To look for her because she was missing."

"Eva, that makes no sense," Adam said. "A man at a police station tells you to go to The Manor, in front of the police officer, to look for his missing daughter?"

"What are our taxpayer dollars going to?" Karen's fist slammed on the table, rattling the cups. "This is what I don't understand."

"The nun said there was a sacrifice to be made." I swallowed. "What if Stella is sacrificing me?"

"What sacrifice?" Adam frowned. "For The Swords?"

"I saw a nun today and she said, 'It's the thirtieth year and sacrifices come in threes,'" I said. "What does that mean?"

"Well, we've always said all bad things come in threes," Karen said. "All good things too. It's the trinity."

"You used to know a nun," I said. "The one who helped you adopt me. What was her name?"

"Sister Marie." Karen smiled. "Very nice nun."

"Marie?" My heart pounded in my ears. "Do you have a picture of her?"

"A picture?" She stood, frowning. "I don't think so. She worked at the front office in your elementary school, remember? She may be in the background of an old album."

As Karen walked out of the kitchen and into the living room, where the photo albums were, Adam leaned over.

"Was the nun's name Marie?"

"I'm not sure, but that woman, the one who serves the food and cleans The Manor. She said she's been working there over forty years. Her name is Marie."

Adam sat back, stunned. Karen walked back into the room with three albums in her arms. She set them on the table between us. I grabbed the first one, she grabbed the second, and Adam looked between the two of us.

"I don't know what I'm looking for."

"Nuns," Karen and I said at the same time, both in the same short-fused tone.

The three of us leafed through the albums and stopped every so often to show pictures of nuns, but saw nothing.

"Here she is!" Karen held her book up as she stood and laid it on top of ours, pointing at the picture. Adam and I both stood and hovered over the album. It was Karen carrying a baby, her husband Esteban, and a nun. Karen and Esteban were all smiles. The nun had a small smile of her own. She was young, younger, but it was definitely, without a doubt Marie. Adam and I looked up at each other at the same time, our foreheads nearly touching, our eyes wide, horrified.

"That's her," Adam said. "That's Marie."

Karen brought a hand up to her mouth, her eyes brimming with tears.

I took a step back.

Adam looked as shell-shocked as I felt. When he looked back up, he looked at Karen.

"She spoke to you?" Karen asked finally. I nodded. "Did she ask your name?"

"Do you think she'd remember me? I was so small then."

"Of course she would. She was so proud to have helped us. She sent a card for you every Christmas, every birthday." Karen exhaled. "I don't understand any of this. She definitely knew you had a sister. She must have. She never said a word."

"This is all so fucked up," I whispered.

"Fucked up doesn't even begin to scratch the surface," Adam said. "I have to go to work tomorrow and I don't even know how I'm going to act when I see Stella again."

"What room is she in?"

"366."

Karen and I looked at each other. A chill ran down my spine. It couldn't have been a coincidence that I always stayed in room 663, could it? I thought hard to that Sunday when I'd woken up there. I was all out of sorts, but it wasn't like it had been my first time running to The Institute and staying there. I was what they'd call a regular. All of the halls looked the same. All of the rooms looked the same. The staff all wore the same uniform. But something was off that morning. Something I couldn't pinpoint until this moment.

"I was in room 366 that Sunday," I said finally.

"Are you sure?" Karen asked.

"Positive."

She did the sign of the cross and muttered a prayer under her breath.

"She had a tattoo on her right arm," Karen said suddenly.

"A cross?" Adam's namesake apple bobbed.

"Yes." Karen's brows pulled together. "So you did see her."

"I did." He nodded slowly and looked over at me. "And she denied having a sister."

Those words hit me like a brick. She knew about me, obviously. She showed up at my house and tried to pretend she was me, yet she denied I existed? My head felt like it was spinning and I was beginning to think everyone was setting me up.

CHAPTER TWENTY-ONE

W E WERE WALKING TOWARD THE CHURCH IN THE WOODS FOR MY ceremony and I still hadn't met the Chancellor, but I would tonight. It was odd, wearing a white and gold cloak in the midst of all of the red cloaks in front of us and behind. All of the men walked in pairs. One of them holding a lantern, illuminating the way for their partners.

"Is the Chancellor the highest up in the society?" I asked.

"No. There's one higher than him."

"Is there a chance that you'll become Chancellor one day?"

"Impossible. I'm not a man of God."

"You mean like a monk?"

"Even monks don't become chancellor."

"So you have to be a priest?" I whispered.

"Basically." He glanced over. "And beyond that to be his boss."

My mouth fell open. "So like a Cardinal? Bishop? Archbishop?"

Adam nodded gravely as we reached the front of the church. It had double wooden doors and as the right one opened before us, I smelled the familiar incense. Adam placed the lantern in his hand down beside the rest of them outside of the door and led the way inside, walking to the front of the room. What I thought was a chapel was more like a small cathedral, with a dome ceiling and paneled windows. Despite the lack of light, it seemed like everywhere I looked I found something beautiful to look at and I was sure it would take me days, maybe even weeks to see all of the artwork. There was a panel of saints on the other side of the altar. When we reached the front, Adam bowed and did the sign of the cross. I did the same and slid into the second row, right beside him, before focusing my attention on the cross with Jesus on it that sat atop of the altar. A priest walked onto the altar, wearing white and gold like I was, taking in the room as he smiled.

"Welcome, brothers and sisters." He opened his arms as if he was hugging the entire room. "I see new faces and old, but that doesn't mean you're getting wrinkles." He chuckled as the crowd laughed. "Where are our sisters? I saved the first row especially for you."

At the sight of twelve red cloaks walking toward the front and taking a seat in the row in front of me, I wondered if I should stand and join them. Adam nudged me, answering my question. I stood and sat directly in front of where I'd been sitting, hating that I was the only one wearing white and gold while they were all wearing red.

"Welcome," the priest said, smiling at me. I smiled back and bowed my head. There were whispers in the room that he quieted when he began speaking again. "Don't worry, I won't be holding Mass today. There are too many sinners in this room and I'm afraid none will be able to take the bread."

The room laughed again. I felt myself smile. I liked this priest. He reminded me of Father Murray from my church.

"The Swords, has, from the beginning of time, been the most prestigious secret society. Forget the Skulls, forget The

Family, forget the Masons. No secret society has been able to wield power in both the church and the state. Together, we are powerful. Together, we are worthy. Together, we have the power to change the world. These were the words spoken by our founder. They are words I say to you today. They are words your presidents and chancellors and leaders will recite for years to come."

"What makes us different? What makes The Swords important? Worthy?" He walked forward and stood right at the edge of the altar. "We combine science and religion. We delve into the psyche, explore the mind, and go past barriers that were put there. Sometimes these barriers are put there by others, and sometimes we put them there ourselves. Barriers are a form of protection. They're important. But you're a Sword now and barriers are meant to be broken. So, let's begin, shall we?"

Two young monks dressed in brown cloaks brought out a bench and set it at the center of the altar, behind the priest. The priest raised his hands in the air and everyone in the room stood, including me.

"If the ladies of The Swords would please step forward and circle around the altar," he instructed, then looked at me. "Not you. Not yet."

The women on either side of me stepped forward and stood facing the altar. I hadn't taken a good look at their faces, but I knew some of them were much older than others by the way their shoulders slumped a bit, as if they'd been carrying the weight of the world on them far too long. The priest walked up to the first one to his left and did the sign of the cross over her head as she bowed her head. He continued on, going down the row of women as we all stood and watched. When he reached the last one, he glanced over at me and signaled me to walk over. I fought the urge to look at Adam behind me, to seek his counsel.

When I made it to the front, two of the women parted without even looking at me, and I took a step up to where the priest stood. He did the sign of the cross in front of me and I bowed my head slightly. When I looked up again, he put his palm over my forehead and left it there as he spoke.

"Can you see?"

"No," I whispered, not with his hand on my forehead and the sleeve of his robe blocking the view.

"Yet we see for you."

"You have allowed yourself to become trapped by the outside world, your family, your past, your origin, and have blinded yourself to what is real, what is important. Tonight, this changes. Tonight, we will reach the root of your anger, your pain, and we will set you free." He pressed his hand a little harder. "Leave us, Swords."

I couldn't see, but I heard the whoosh of robes moving, the patter of footsteps as they departed, the door as it closed, and the sound of silence as they followed his directions. Only then, did the priest take his hand off my forehead and let me see for myself. The women were there, their heads bowed to us. I looked at the priest, who was watching me closely.

"You're a child of God."

I swallowed, nodding.

"Do you attend Mass on Sundays?"

"I try."

"Your parents are Catholic?"

"Yes." The word came out a whisper.

"Are they alive?"

"My mother."

"You were adopted." He glanced at the women beside me. I nodded. Instinctively, my gaze followed his and I saw a few of their heads raise before quickly lowering into a bow. "How old were you when you were adopted?"

"Months old."

"Too young to have any memory of your birth mother."

I nodded again.

"Would you like to remember?"

"I . . . how?"

"Don't question me. Answer the question. Would you like to remember?"

"Yes."

"Lie down."

I did as I was told, lying down on the bench that felt like it was made of rock, my back already complaining with discomfort. I turned my head to look at the women, who were still standing, heads still bowed even as the priest busied himself at the altar. I grabbed the fabric of my robe to keep the dress I wore underneath covered.

"Many think that because The Swords haven't allowed women to stay in recent years it must mean we're becoming an all-male society," he said as his hands moved the chalice on the table he stood in front of. "But The Swords would be nothing without women. After all, there would be no men without women. There would be no Christ without Mary."

"Without women, we would cease to exist and that is true for the entire world, not just The Swords." He walked back over to me holding a gold chalice between two fingers. "Because we are cognizant of that, we handpick the women we invite to join. Every thirty years, one of those women must make a choice, a sacrifice, for the greater good of the society. For us to grow, flourish."

My heart quickened as he spoke, but I didn't dare speak. Even if I wanted to, I couldn't find my voice, my words, my questions.

"Women have been making sacrifices since the beginning

of time. It is why the world continues to spin on its axis. It is why life does not stop. The day women stop making these sacrifices, the sun will stop shining and Earth will stop spinning. We will no longer have anything to hold us together."

"Now, I will ask you to drink from this chalice, one that all of your sisters have drunk from before you. You will free your mind tonight. You will let us see through your barriers and into your depths. Tonight, you become a Sword."

He walked over to me and kneeled beside my face, holding the chalice to my mouth. "Drink."

I hesitated. All his talk about sacrifice making me think of death, making me question whether or not that would be my fate tonight, but I looked at the women with their heads bowed, and thought of Stella, and Dr. Thompson, and the woman the monks had been having sex with. I thought of all of the men standing outside of these walls. Would they let me get very far if I ran? Did I even want to run? He promised me memories. He promised me freedom. Wasn't that what I was here for? And so, I tilted my head slightly and drank from the golden chalice, swallowing slowly as the liquid spilled from either side of my mouth. The priest wiped my face gently as I drank. It tasted bitter. When he was finished pouring the wine in my mouth, he stood and stepped back. My vision got hazy quickly, the room spinning as my heart sped up. He spread his arms open once more and said, "Sisters."

I could barely make them out, only flashes of red as they walked onto the altar and surrounded me. Their chants filled my ears. Their movements blurred with my vision. I tried to place the chants, what they were saying. It sounded familiar, too familiar, and then just before my eyes shut the world out completely, I realized where I knew it from: it was what the monks had been chanting around the naked woman.

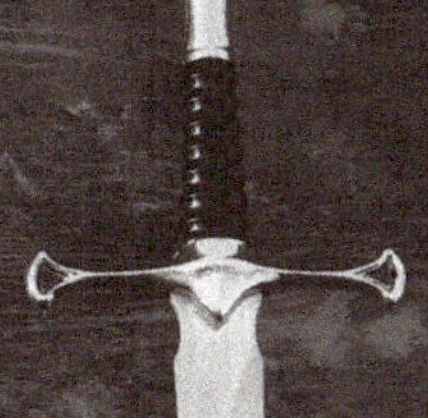

CHAPTER TWENTY-TWO

ADAM

THEY WERE TAKING LONG INSIDE AND I WASN'T SURE IF I WOULD BE allowed back in. I hadn't been there for a woman's initiation before. Truth be told, part of me didn't actually believe in the whole women's history in The Swords until I saw the row of women standing in front of me. There was something eerie about all of it. If they'd been so important to The Swords, why hadn't they recruited more of them? Why hadn't they been included in the narrative they spun every time a new member joined?

I hadn't gotten a good look at any of them, just the back of their heads as they stood there. When the priest said they initiated women every third year, I became even more confused. The last time we had women here was two years ago, not three. The Swords didn't count failed initiations though, so those women were written off anyway, no mention of them spoken outside of the core members who were there when they were. Every third year. The words seeped back into my head. Had they stayed, this would have been their third year. *Shit.* I tried to think of any commonalities they had with Eva, with Stella, but none came up. As far as I knew, they didn't even have siblings, so Eva's theory of multiples wasn't valid. One thing I knew for sure is that I hated being kept in the dark. I was the president of the goddamn secret society and I had no idea what was happening right under my nose. Why have a president at all? For pretenses?

When the heavy church door opened again, my heart stopped. One woman peeked her head out, her head was not only cloaked, but her face was veiled now, a red sheer over it as if to block her identity.

"Mr. Astor. Please come in."

I was aware that she'd said my name, but seemed to be frozen, rooted to the spot. The hum of the conversation happening around me ceased as they watched me finally gather my thoughts and lift my feet to walk over. The woman held the door open just enough for me to walk inside. The church was dark with the exception of the candles lit in the front, circling the altar. My gaze became transfixed on the front of the room. I wasn't sure what I expected to find inside, but it wasn't this. The women's heads were bowed as they stood, covering something in the middle. A bench maybe? Was that where Eva was? My heart was in my throat as I walked over and sat in the center of the pew the woman led me to. I tried to go through the motions of what I'd do if this was a repeat of what we'd seen that night of the party. My pulse quickened at the thought. Even though I wasn't a believer, I'd always respected the sanctity of the church, but if anyone tried to rape Eva, I'd kill them all. With what? I didn't know. I had no weapon, but I'd make do with whatever was on the altar if need be. It was sick. The whole thing was sick. The fact that I could even sit in a church and think about using their crosses as defense tools.

I thought back to the night I'd been initiated and how weird it had been for me. I thought being buried alive had been enough of a test and figured the initiation ceremony would be a welcome party. I hadn't expected to be drugged or questioned. They'd used psychedelics as a form of therapy, a way to let go of the past and past guilt. Before that night, my anxiety, which I hadn't dealt with since I was a teenager, had found its way back into my life, making it difficult to focus on simple tasks. By the time The Swords sent their calling card, I was desperate. It was something no one would have guessed and how could they? After all, I was smart, good looking, worked out, was charming, privileged. I was also exceptional at hiding my emotions.

For me, initiation had been a transcendence. From the burial to the altar. The psychedelics they used were unlike anything I had ever taken, but they served their purpose. When they worked. I was a believer that all drugs, even the ones with a bad reputation, could be used to serve a helpful purpose. After all, there was science to back them up. I wasn't an idiot, though. I'd seen the experiment go wrong. It only happened once, but it had been enough for me to know that not everyone could handle it. As I sat there, knee bouncing, I hoped like hell Eva was one of the ones who could. The priest was speaking in Latin now, facing the cross and Jesus, his back turned to the spectacle behind him. The women's heads were all bowed as if in prayer. I couldn't see Eva, but I knew she was in there. She was quiet. I hadn't seen many quiet ones. I'd seen a lot of guys try to do a lot of crazy things while under the influence.

I scooted forward, my knee hitting the back of the pew in front of me as I tried to get a glimpse of her. I could see the white and gold robe. Finally, the women shifted and I saw her lying on a bench in the middle. She looked like a version of Sleeping Beauty, with her hair cascading to one side and her hands neatly placed over her midriff. A peaceful smile replacing her usual scowl. The priest turned back to her, this time waving that thing filled with incense as he chanted. The women began to walk around her, chanting along with the priest. Then suddenly, they all stopped. The priest turned and faced them and I knew he was waiting for something. Normally, the person on that bench stood, or spoke, or sat up and swayed as if they were drunk out of their mind. In the church, you could hear a pin drop, until Eva gasped loudly, her chest coming off of the bench as if being pulled by a string. I wished suddenly I hadn't chosen last night, of all nights, to watch *The Exorcist*, because it was the only thing that came to mind as I sat there.

She sat up, her hands on either side of the bench, and began to speak in perfect Spanish. At least it sounded perfect to me. It wasn't like I knew enough to understand it or know whether she was pronouncing things correctly. Unlike my brother, who could have a perfect conversation in Spanish if he wanted to, I'd taken Mandarin and German instead. What good was it doing me now? The priest asked her a question, which she answered, then another, and another, until they were having a full conversation right before his eyes. The only thing I could make out clearly was the name Karen spilling from her lips before she began to cry. I fought the urge to stand up and demand they stop.

CHAPTER TWENTY-THREE

EVA

MY EYES OPENED SLOWLY, FIGHTING AGAINST THE BEAMING SUN to open fully. As my vision adjusted, I realized I was in my bedroom. Inside The Manor. I didn't remember anything about last night, but I definitely expected to wake up in the woods. I heard myself groan.

"You feeling okay?"

"Jesus." My head whipped toward Adam.

"You were in bad form last night. I stayed just in case." He swung his legs off the bed and sat at the edge, his back facing me.

"Just in case I died?"

"I know how to perform CPR." He shot me a smirk over his shoulder that I knew I would've felt down to my core had it not been for the fact that I felt like absolute shit.

"Well, I can officially say I've slept with a guy twice without seeing his penis." I tried to sit up and fell right back down.

"Third time's a charm, right?" Adam chuckled. He stood up with a stretch, his shirt riding up high enough for me to see the definition in his abs.

"I'll hold you to that." I brought my eyes back to his and lifted a hand to my forehead. I felt clammy. "What did that priest give me?"

"LSD."

"What?" My eyes widened.

"I wasn't sure if you'd done it before."

"I've never cared to experiment in that department." I sat up and stretched as well. "Is that legal?"

"For them to give you drugs?"

I nodded.

"For fifty grand?" He shrugged a shoulder. "I'm going to make us breakfast, unless you need me to bathe you."

"I don't." My cheeks warmed.

"So I'll meet you in our usual spot."

"Our usual spot?"

"The piano room."

"Right." I smiled. "I'm feeling very slow today, sorry."

"Take your time."

I watched him walk out and shut the door behind him. As soon as he was gone, I sighed into my pillow. I still felt high. LSD was definitely something I wouldn't be doing again. I didn't remember anything about last night, but I could have sworn I saw Karen. It couldn't be right. I mean, unless somehow she was there last night, but that was impossible.

We spent the majority of the day hanging out with Will and Wolf. I'd made it a point to wear a dress today, it was lavender with small white flowers, just above my knees and cinched at the waist. I loved the way it fit me because it was sexy without being too revealing. When Adam saw me walk downstairs in it, his heated gaze told me it was the perfect thing to wear. We'd spent the majority of the day touching, holding hands, brushing fingers, hugging as we laughed at Will and Wolf's jokes. I felt like I was completely in. Maybe that was the point of all of the tests, not to prove to them that we were worthy, but for them to give us time to let it all sink in and make us realize that we belonged to this family. There were still people around who had attended the ceremony, but even though we'd spoken to some, most of them were mingling amongst themselves and with women I'd never seen before.

"Why are there so many women here?" I looked at Will, who was beside me.

"Members are allowed to invite people to spend the night on the night of the ceremony. It's basically the only night we have an open-door policy like this. Even when we throw parties, guests can't stay over."

"So these are, what, their wives?" I looked at the crowd again.

"I don't think Professor Wagner is married to his TA," Wolf said with a laugh as he pointed at the man in question. The man wasn't very old, maybe early forties, but the woman was definitely much, much younger than him.

"She can't be much older than me," I said.

"She's not. Rae's a junior," Wolf said. "She'd be my pick if they let women join The Swords. She's got it all, brains, looks, her family has power. Too bad she's into older men."

"Married older men," Will added.

"Ew." I wasn't a saint, but I prided myself in having somewhat of a moral code.

Later, when everyone left, Adam and I finished up dinner and headed to the piano room. I was feeling a billion times better than I was when I woke up this morning, but so many things were still running through my mind and I'd spent the majority of the day trying and failing to sort it all out.

"What are you thinking about?"

"The Chancellor said something last night that made me think."

"What?"

"He said the world depends on women to make sacrifices. He said without their sacrifices the world would be a disaster."

"Makes sense. Women are often seen as selfless beings." He pushed the door to the piano room open and let me walk in before following and closing it behind us.

"He made it seem like I'd have to make a sacrifice."

"Last night?"

"In general."

"What's your concern? That they'll ask more of you even though you've had your official ceremony?"

"No. I mean yes, obviously, but no. Between what he said and what the nun said about my sister. I just . . . " I paced a few steps. "What if . . . " I shook my head, trying to gather my thoughts. "Would you be able to tell if one of the keys or cards is fake?"

"You mean the one you got?"

"Yes. I just . . . isn't it weird? Why would I be invited?"

"You said you had a 4.0 GPA. That would be a good reason for an invite."

"The same year they invite Stella? My parents didn't even go to college."

"Did their parents?"

I shook my head. "I'm the first person in my family to attend."

"Ever? Even community college?"

"Karen and Esteban both grew up in poverty. Education was a luxury."

"Education should never be a luxury."

"Well, unfortunately, not all of us are born into wealthy families. Or even middle-class families. To some people, education is the ultimate luxury."

"That's a sad reality," he said. "You want a drink?"

I nodded. He walked over to the small bar, his arm brushing past me and leaving a trace of fire as he went. I walked over to my usual seat, tucking a leg underneath me as I sat on the edge of the couch closest to the piano. He walked over, handed me a glass, clinked his against it in a toast as he held my eyes, and took a sip. I did the same. He sat on the piano bench, close enough that if I stretched out my leg, it would touch his. Even though we'd kissed and talked about dating, I still wasn't entirely sure where to go from here. So many things were happening at once that it felt dumb to even try to figure this thing between us out. Yet there I was, thinking about it every time he was near and trying not to think about it when he wasn't.

"Are you going to play?" I took another sip of the whiskey.

"What would you like me to play?"

"Anything."

"Anything like what?" He leafed through the book in front of him.

"I don't know piano music. Just anything."

"You know regular music. What's your favorite song?"

"I don't think I have one."

"You make things incredibly complicated." He sighed and picked up his drink.

"I said play anything. That's as simple as a request gets. I just like hearing it and seeing your hands move on the keys."

"You can see my hands from all the way over there?"

"Are you inviting me to sit next to you?"

"If that's what you want to do." His gaze burned into mine as he set his glass down.

A challenge.

I set down my own glass and walked over to him. My legs lifting when they touched the cold bench, and setting right back down when Adam moved closer, the warmth of his body so close to mine was as comforting as it was maddening. I didn't dare look at him. I knew if I did, I would find that we were too close and I didn't want to make the first move again. I refused. I focused on his hands, hovering over the keys, his long, thin fingers. Aunt Carmen used to say you could tell a lot about a man by his hands and even though I never fully understood that, I loved looking at Adam's. He kept his nails trimmed short and had callouses on the inside of his knuckles, from working out, I presumed. Other than that, his hands were perfectly unmarred. When his fingers finally began to move over the keys, a beautiful melody filled the air and I couldn't not stare at his hands.

"I've always wanted to play like that," I whispered.

"Why not take classes?"

"Another luxury."

"I could teach you."

"You don't think it's too late for me to learn?"

"Knowledge is timeless." He met my gaze, his fingers still moving on the keys as he spoke.

I felt my breath quicken as he inched closer. He continued playing even as he closed his eyes, even as our lips touched lightly, even as I brought a hand up to caress his face, to feel the prickle of the shadow of hair growing on it that reminded me that he was real, that this wasn't made up or in my mind. He stopped playing suddenly, the melody getting sucked into the kiss we shared, and brought his hands up to cup my face as he deepened the kiss, those long fingers sliding into my hair as his tongue moved against mine. He pulled back, both of us breathing heavily as he placed his forehead against mine.

"You've had a long day," he said.

"I've had a long life."

He chuckled against my lips, then pulled back, grabbed my hand, and stood. I followed him upstairs quietly, my heart galloping too quickly for me to even form words. He led me to my room and waited for me to unlock it. It was dark in there without the lamps on the nightstands on, but it didn't matter. The moment we shut the door behind us, our mouths found each other again. Our movements were frantic, our mouths starving, our hands ripping at each other's clothes.

I managed to pull his shirt over his head. He broke the kiss to allow it, tossing it to the other side of the room as his lips crashed against mine once more. He toyed with my dress, his hands sneaking underneath, setting my skin ablaze as his callused fingers moved against my thighs, my hips, my torso, and found my naked breasts. I grappled with the moan building in the back of my throat, trying not to expose just how much I wanted him, but when his other hand snuck under and set my panties aside, it was futile. The moan ripped from my mouth and was silenced by his lips against mine, his tongue licking along the seam of my lips to make way into my mouth. I broke the kiss to lift my dress over my head, tossing it to meet the same fate as his shirt, as he lowered my panties slowly down my legs with one hand, while continuing to explore me with the other. He dragged his mouth down my jaw, my chest, my abdomen, until it met the same fate as his fingers, moving against me, inside me, with the same fluidity and sensuality he used to play the keys. His fingers filled me, his tongue devouring me until I felt out of breath, shaking, and only gasping out incognizant words of approval.

He bit the insides of my thighs as he let me come down from the climax, his mouth working its way up my body again, his five o'clock shadow brushing against my sensitive skin as he did so. His hands slinked away momentarily, as I panted, staring up at him, my limbs relaxed. Adam looked at me as he removed his pants and boxers, then reached for a condom, his gaze meeting mine and holding it steady as he ripped it open and began rolling it on. I bit my lip as I watched, anticipation rolling through me. There were no words between us. I wasn't sure my heart could handle hearing whatever he was thinking. He normally didn't wear his heart on his sleeve, but he did tonight.

Sometime between the time he finished tearing away the rest of our clothes and finished applying the condom, I realized this was the first time I was having sex with someone I liked. Really liked. Someone I'd see every day afterward. Someone who knew me, truly knew me, and was willing to help me, despite his reservations. As he climbed over me and set his arms on either side of my head, my hands moved up to run over his chiseled abs. His eyes never left mine. He was so open, so bare to me, that my own chest began to cave with emotions. I brought a hand up to his face and brushed his cheek with my thumb, hoping he could see me the way I was seeing him. As he entered me slowly, fully, my hips billowing for more, which he gave, I realized that I didn't want him to be a stranger. With each thrust he gave, my back arched in acceptance, and with our eyes still connected, I knew that above anything else, I didn't want him to be one of the countless faceless men in my wake. I wanted him to be mine. It was a scary thought, one I fixated on as he started moving, really moving inside of me, but it was one that stuck.

CHAPTER TWENTY-FOUR

THERE SEEMED TO BE AN UNSPOKEN UNDERSTANDING BETWEEN US after last night. The feelings were definitely there. The potential was there. The promise of something bigger than anything I'd ever allowed in the past. It scared the hell out of me, but I wasn't going to shy away from it. Not this time. I'd always thought about love as something foreign that could never happen to me. Even the word *love* was one I hadn't spoken aloud. Ever. I'd never even told Karen, my own mother, that I loved her, not with words.

In the kitchen, we found Will and Wolf. They both looked at us, at our joined hands, back at us, and went right back to their breakfast as if it was the most obvious thing in the world that we were together. Adam stayed behind talking about his brother's hockey game and I excused myself to go outside with my oatmeal and coffee. I wanted to see if I caught a glimpse of Marie. I had so many questions I hadn't been able to ask. By the time Adam joined me outside, I was almost done with my breakfast and hadn't spotted anyone out there in the woods or near the house.

"I want to go to The Institute on Monday to see Stella." I looked at Adam.

"Are you sure that's a good idea? You were just talking about how you thought she potentially framed you."

"I know. I just need to see her. She's my sister."

He nodded a couple of times. "Okay."

"You're going to help me?"

"Yeah, why not?" He shrugged a shoulder. "My feet are already wet. I might as well jump in."

I felt myself smile. I couldn't remember the last time I felt that I had a male ally, if ever. It was that thought, and that thought alone, that made me swing both arms around Adam's neck. He breathed into my neck as he brought an arm around my body, pulling me closer.

"A hug from someone who hates hugs? That's pretty special."

"You're pretty special."

The following day, I dressed for Mass and snuck out of my bedroom quietly, careful not to wake Adam who was snoring lightly in bed. I rushed down the stairs and froze when I reached the backdoor and saw Will sitting there having breakfast.

"Another early riser," he said. "Want some eggs? I made too many."

"No, thanks. I'm kind of in a hurry."

"Hurry?" His brows furrowed. "Where are you going?"

"Church."

"Out here?"

"Out there." I pointed toward the woods.

"You're kidding, right?" He wiped his mouth and set down his napkin. "Does Adam know about this?"

"Nope."

"What kind of Mass do you think you're going to out there?" Will sat back in his chair. "You think it's just a regular ol' Catholic Mass?"

"A Mass is a Mass." I shrugged a shoulder.

"There's a reason we can't go."

"Because they don't let you, but Marie invited me to Mass. She said it's a special service. And she even said I could take a job there cleaning."

"A job?" Will scoffed. "Have you checked your bank account lately?"

I pulled out my phone and checked my account. I'd checked it last week and had one thousand and twenty-seven dollars in there, but that was before I paid my rent two days ago. I hadn't bothered checking since, knowing I was uncomfortably close to the red. I'd adopted an out of sight, out of mind motto when it came to debt. Looking at my account now, I gasped. $50,382.72.

"Told you. You don't need a job. The Swords is your job."

"I'll be back soon." I put my phone away and turned to the endless yard, my eyes set on the woods beyond it. As I started walking, I heard Will stand and curse. He was beside me quickly. "What are you doing?"

"Going with you. Obviously."

"You weren't kidding when you said your mother raised you right."

"She sure did, though in situations like these I feel like even she'd question my sanity."

"We're going to Sunday Mass, in the woods, in broad daylight. How bad can it be?" I glanced over. "What? What's that face?"

"I'm trying not to point out any statistics."

"God, you're morbid." I felt my chest tighten. He wasn't wrong though. How many people had died while they were simply praying? I looked ahead. We still had a couple of minutes to go before we arrived. "Where did you grow up?"

"San Diego."

"Long way from home."

"I'll be back there soon enough."

"You're pre-med?"

"Following my father's footsteps." He grinned. "He's a podiatrist."

"Ah." I smiled. "Is that your go-to podiatrist joke?"

"Pretty bad, huh?" He chuckled.

"Was your father a Sword?"

"Nah. He was here at the same time your . . . well, not your dad, but Dr. Thompson was. They were friends and neither one of them could get in even though all their white friends were invited. I'm sure you've heard about the racial inequalities happening then."

"Then?" I raised an eyebrow. "I didn't realize they ever stopped happening."

"Ain't that the truth." Will sighed.

"Is it the same for your sister you think?"

"Not really. It pains her to see it though. I mean, imagine being a black man's white twin."

"I honestly can't imagine." I smiled. "But you've made it this far."

"And I'll make it further." He smiled. "I have to say, as far as academia goes, things have gotten better than when my dad attended. I'm not the only black guy in my classes."

"And here?" I pointed back to The Manor.

"There will be more of us. And now we have you."

"You mean a woman?"

"A Hispanic woman who doesn't come from a rich, privileged family. That's gotta count for something."

"Except I'm the only woman here."

"You know you were the one I was supposed to hunt?"

"Hunting?"

"Try to recruit."

"Oh. How'd you figure it out?"

"There was an email I was included in. I wasn't supposed to be, but it was between the Chancellor and someone else. They never signed their name and the email didn't have one either." Will shook his head. "The email had your name, Eva Guerra, and a picture."

"Can you show me the picture?"

"Let me check." His brows pulled in as he reached for his phone in his pocket and scrolled through it. We stopped walking just on the other side of the black ropes on the grass, where the caskets were buried. Finally, Will handed me his phone. "Grainy."

I looked at the photograph in question and felt the color drain from my face. It was a picture of me, with my long hair, before I'd cut it to my shoulders to look more like Stella Thompson. I was wearing a white Stones T-shirt and ripped shorts. Both things which I no longer had and hadn't since two summers ago when I donated them to the church, which meant the photograph must have been taken before I was even attending Ellis.

"You're shaking," Will said.

"Can I screenshot this and text it to myself?"

"Sure."

I did, sending it to myself and Adam with the message, "wtf?"

"What's wrong?" Will took his phone back.

"This confirms that I didn't get a fluke invitation."

"Even if you did, they deposited the money into your account, right? Not Stella's?"

"Good point." I nodded.

The church bells rang out making us both jump a little. The bells rang again. We looked at each other and walked faster. Will hurried as well. We slowed down as we reached the doors. There was a woman there, a nun who seemed to be watching the monks and nuns as they walked in. At the sight of us, she frowned.

"May I help you?"

"Marie invited me to Mass."

The nun looked at me, looked at Will and back at me. "You're not dressed for Mass."

"I'm wearing a dress." I looked down at the floral maxi dress I wore. "And a jean jacket."

"Your face isn't veiled. I can't let you in."

"What?"

"Ma'am, we'll sit in the back," Will said in his good-behavior voice.

"I'm sorry. I can't let you in either." She looked at him. "We're holding a special Mass today."

"A special Mass?" Will frowned. "It's not even a holiday."

"It's an initiation."

"My initiation was the other night." I looked at Will, who looked just as confused as I felt, then back at the nun.

"Yours was. Ours is now." She made to move. I moved in front of her. She took a step back and arched an eyebrow. "Excuse me."

"I'm sorry, but I just really need to see Marie."

"I'll tell her you were looking." She stepped forward again and brushed past me.

I watched as she walked up the steps and ushered a few more nuns inside. Will stood beside me without saying a word. We both continued staring at the nuns, with their heads bowed and eyes to the ground. The very last one looked up briefly, so briefly I almost missed her, but when our eyes met I felt the earth shake beneath me. Will's hand on my shoulder, squeezing his own confirmation, was the only thing I had to let me know this was real. Once the doors shut, I managed to look at Will, who was still looking like he'd seen a ghost and in a sense he had because it was my face on the nun who was walking inside.

"Was that Stella?" he whispered.

"I don't know."

"Let's find out." He grabbed my arm and pulled me to the other side of the church. "There's a back door here somewhere that they used to get in and out."

My phone vibrated in my back pocket, but I ignored it.

Will's phone vibrated in his pocket and we both looked at each other.

"It must be Adam."

"I'll text him back," I whisper-shouted, pulling my phone out and seeing his name next to a missed call on my screen. I shot him a quick text: *at the church in woods. We'll be over there soon.*

Adam: wtf? We're not allowed there

Me: Emergency

The phone rang immediately. I ended the call and shot him another text.

Me: can't talk. Will is with me.

There were no little dots after that, so I put my phone away and looked at Will, nodding that I was ready to keep going. We continued walking. The windows were just slightly higher than we were; the church was built on a concrete platform. Basement maybe. We seemed to be walking into the ground as we continued on. This side of the church was definitely steeper than the other. Will stopped walking. I stopped behind him, then looked over his shoulder to see a wooden staircase and a door. He pointed to it and we both walked faster in that direction. Just as Will set his hand on the doorknob, a person appeared in the woods, moving toward us and we both froze.

CHAPTER TWENTY-FIVE

"WHAT THE HELL ARE YOU DOING HERE?" WILL WHISPER-SHOUTED.

"What are you doing here?" Adam asked, his eyes wild on Will and me. "Are you insane?"

"Stella's in there dressed like a nun." I pointed at the church. Adam's eyes widened as he looked at Will.

"We *think* Stella's in there dressed like a nun," Will said.

"They specifically told us to stay away this weekend."

"Marie invited me to come."

"What?" Adam's voice broke out of the whisper and the three of us cringed.

"And the nun by the door said they're having their own initiation. What does that even mean?"

"I don't know." Adam wasn't whispering, but at least his voice was lower.

"Why is it so quiet?" I looked up, trying to gauge whether or not Mass had started.

"The walls are soundproof."

"What?" Will and I said simultaneously.

"Why would they soundproof their walls?" Will asked.

"Do you really want to find out?" Adam shot the two of us a pointed look.

"Yes," Will and I said simultaneously.

"Shit," Adam swore under his breath. He looked at the building beside us, then at the door above the stairs. "It's probably locked. It has to be locked."

"Let's find out." I rushed up the stairs, Adam and Will at my heels. I turned the knob slowly. "Unlocked."

"I'll go in first." Adam stepped forward. "Stay behind me."

I nodded and looked over my shoulder to see Will nodding. We walked inside, quiet as mice, and took a right. We could hear voices coming from below us. Adam stopped walking suddenly, bringing a finger to his lips as he pointed down. I covered my mouth with both hands, realizing we were standing right above the altar. Normally, they'd have an organ in this spot, storage, something, but it was completely empty. We crouched down to look at the church. The nuns were all veiled, like the one at the door had said.

It looked like a regular Mass, with the priest up front and the nuns all standing as they listened to him speak.

"You will give us your silence," he said. "That will be your sacrifice. Silence."

"Silence," some chanted.

"The ceremony will take place in two days. Until then, silence."

"Silence," they said in unison.

Adam, Will, and I looked at each other. The Mass continued. We signaled each other to leave, and we did just as quietly as we'd arrived. Back at The Manor, we followed Adam to the library, where he pulled out book after book from the shelves and dumped them on the large desk.

"I've never looked at these," Will said.

"I've only looked through a couple."

I walked over and opened the one closest to me. They were

photo albums and judging by the fashion and discoloration on the prints I could tell they were old.

"The dates are on the spines."

I closed it and looked at the date. 1935. Damn. I opened it again and looked through. There were only men, not surprising, in each of the photographs. Posing with hunting rifles, dead deer. I paused at that and looked up at the stuffed deer head displayed over the fireplace. I'd never understood the reason for those until this moment. It was a remnant of what survived from their time here. Maybe a way to not be forgotten. I pictured a bunch of old white men drinking scotch surrounding this very fireplace, talking about how their great-grandfather hunted the animal.

"What are we looking for?" I set the book down with a thump.

"Help me get the black books down." Adam reached for the rolling ladder and set it in front of where the black books were, high up on the last shelf.

Will shut the book in his hand and walked over. I followed, heart in my throat as I watched Adam climb.

"How old is this ladder?"

"Old," Will said, and the ladder, as if it could speak, creaked in agreement.

"Be careful." I grabbed the edge of the ladder as if it would make a difference if it dismantled.

"Worried about me?" Adam looked down, the edge of his mouth tugging into a smile.

"Shut up." I gripped the edge harder. He chuckled as he reached for the first book, then another.

"You're not going to be able to hand those to us." Will stepped back and reached for me to follow suit. "Just let them fall."

"I don't think these will survive a fall." Adam inspected the dusty books.

When both of his feet were on the ground, Will and I moved forward as Adam turned around and set the books down on the desk, a cloud of dust rising as they thumped. The three of us stood over the books. Adam picked one up and tilted it so we could see the year on the spine. 1915. The pages were intact but looked brown; unlike the deer on the wall, these pages were barely withstanding the test of time. The photographs of the monks were black and white. All posed. The next book, 1920, was more of the same. Adam brought down four more books. It wasn't until we got to 1930 that we saw a difference. There were nuns in these photographs. Nuns laughing, playing soccer, posing with rifles. As the photos went on and the monks joined the pictures, their smiles diminished.

"This is so weird," I whispered, reaching to turn the page. I gasped at the next photograph and looked up at Adam. "This is what we saw."

"What? When?" The question came from Will.

"The night of the party. I saw this." I pointed. "Monks surrounding a naked woman."

"What were they doing?" Will turned the book toward him. "Chanting?"

"At first." I flipped the page and braced myself. There was a naked man standing on the rock the naked woman lay on. The photograph was grainy at best, but that much was easy to make out, his penis was erect as he stood there.

"Dude, is that the priest?" Will leaned closer to the picture. Adam and I did as well. My eyes swung to the next image, which showed the naked woman a little better.

"Doesn't that look like Marie?" I said, my voice a whisper.

"Must be her mom or something," Will said distractedly.

Adam and I looked at each other. "I think we need to get the album for 1960."

Adam walked back up the ladder and brought down the 1960 album, placing it on the table.

"Why this one?" Will asked.

"One of the nuns said every thirty years there's a sacrifice."

"And you think this is it?"

I looked through the album quickly. Unlike the first album where the nuns made an appearance and looked happy, they seemed despondent in all of these. When I finally reached the picture we were looking for, it was like a carbon copy of the first, but the naked woman wasn't Marie. I'd never seen her before, yet something about her was eerily familiar. Feeling the blood drain from my head, I grabbed onto the side of the desk.

"Watch out. I think she's going to faint," Will said as my knees buckled.

Adam caught me before I hit the ground and carried me over to the couches on the other side of the desk.

"I'm fine," I managed once I was on the couch.

"What happened?" Adam asked.

"It happens sometimes." I waved a hand. "I'm fine."

"Vasovagal syncope," Adam said.

"What?" I blinked, focused on my breathing.

"It's a condition that would explain your fainting spells. It's caused by intense heat, intense fear, intense emotions."

"I don't experience intense emotions." I buried my face in my hands.

"Okay." Adam pulled away and walked over to the mini-fridge, bringing a can of soda with him. "Here. This may help."

"I think that might be my birth mom." The words left my mouth as slowly as I sat up.

"The lady in the picture?" Will's voice went so high he nearly squeaked. "The one being raped by the priest?"

"Yes." I flinched.

"You've never seen your birth mother," Adam said.

"You can't tell me she doesn't look exactly like me."

He stood up and walked back over to the desk, examining the lady in the picture. "Damn."

"If that woman is my mother it would explain some things."

"She's not wrong," Will agreed.

"What would it explain? That they invited you here to rape you?" Adam's jaw ticked. "That Dr. Thompson maybe set this up so his own daughter wouldn't be the one on the receiving end, so he fed you to the wolves instead?"

"I don't know." I set the soda down and walked over to the desk to flip through the rest of the pictures. I took my phone out and snapped pictures and sent out a text. "I have to show these to Karen."

"I thought Karen didn't know your adoptive mother?"

"She didn't. Marie facilitated the whole thing." I raised an eyebrow. "What a coincidence."

"I'll tell you what, this is a lot more than I bargained for. I'm here for the connections." Will sat on the couch, his wide eyes bouncing between Adam and me.

"So am I, but what will that matter if our legacy is tarnished by priests who rape?" Adam asked.

My phone vibrated in my hand and I glanced down to see Karen was calling. I answered quickly.

"Did you get my text?"

"Where did you find that?"

"At . . . it doesn't matter. Doesn't she look like someone?"

I bit my lip, glancing back up and meeting Adam's gaze as I

waited for Karen to say she agreed with me. Or not. You never knew with Karen.

"Of course she does. She was your daycare teacher."

"What?"

"At the parish church. That's Ms. Penelope." Karen paused and I could hear someone speaking in the loudspeaker. She was probably calling me from work. "People always used to say you looked more like her daughter than mine, which was obvious with your complexion and features, but I didn't think much of it." Karen paused. "Oh my God, do you think that's her? Your mother? It can't be, can it?"

"I don't know. How old would I have been in daycare? Do you have pictures?"

"I'm sure I do. I put you in there at Deborah's insistence. You must have been four? It was the year Esteban's health took a turn for the worst."

I took a seat in the leather chair behind me. "Can you look for pictures when you get home?"

"Sure. Where did you find this? That secret society place?"

"Yes."

"I think you need to get out of there," she said.

In the past, I'd taken comfort in Karen's discomfort. This time, I was crawling with it and I didn't like it one bit.

CHAPTER TWENTY-SIX

ADAM

When I received an ominous white envelope with my name on it, I was immediately skeptical. It only deepened when I actually showed up at The Manor and was told I'd be given fifty grand for joining The Swords, but then I heard the stories about how they came to be. How a group of men who met in a lab came together because of their joint interests. Their interests being cadavers, the human body, and how it functioned. They were grave robbers at first, borrowing the freshly buried for the purpose of science. They were making a real difference with their findings. Later, a man bought The Manor and his wife bought the house next door and it became the home of The Eight, our brother society. The secret societies on campus learned early on that if they didn't stick together, they'd go down. The Skulls went down. There was no anonymity there. The Eight have nearly gone down countless times, including last year, when they were nearly exposed. Somehow, they'd stayed afloat. The Swords were the most secretive of all and I never fully comprehended why until now.

They were cloaked by the monks and priests and possibly the

archdioceses. They were swimming in their blood, rotting in their lies and I knew that no amount of handwashing would ever make me feel as though I didn't have blood on my own hands. Not the kind of blood I'd gotten on my hands when I'd been allowed to cut open a cadaver last year—something only medical students were allowed unless you were a Sword—no, this was the kind of blood I'd never rid myself of. I'd accepted their money, I'd bought into all of their lies, recruited people for them, and sold them the same twisted dreams. It wasn't the money that attracted people to these societies, though it helped. It was the prestige. It was rubbing shoulders with world leaders and having certain people on speed dial. They weren't in these societies for what they could get out of them right now. This wasn't a movie. They weren't driving around Lambos and partying with rappers. They were in it for the favors they could and would cash in later, for the connections, for the honor. I knew about the monks. I was told by the person who recruited me, just as I'd told Will. The monks were there. The nuns were there. Why they were there or what they were doing was a mystery to me, but I didn't meddle.

I was never normally at The Manor. I had my own apartment, after all. An apartment I had barely visited after Eva showed up on our doorstep. Now there I was, worried about Eva and what she may be in for. After a long shower, I dressed and sat at the edge of my bed, thinking. I needed to think. I needed to remember everything that was said the day they named me president of this chapter. Everything that was asked of me. Everything that I swore I'd do for them. And I would. I knew deep down that I'd signed myself over to The Swords when I accepted everything they'd given me, but if that included giving them Eva, I'd have to draw a line. Thirty years, they'd said. A sacrifice, the nun told Eva. They were obviously functioning on some sort of code. I only hoped I could crack it before it was too late.

CHAPTER TWENTY-SEVEN

EVA

WHAT WAS THE CORRECT THING TO SAY TO THE TWIN SISTER you'd never met? *A sister who may or may not have fed you to the wolves.* I wiped my clammy hands over my jeans and stood up, pacing the parking lot for what seemed like the millionth time. Adam told me to stay in the car. He told me not to go inside under any circumstance. He also stuck Will with me and there was no way I could outrun him, so I was staying put.

"What's taking him so long?" Will huffed, crossing his arms as he looked toward the building.

"The daytime staff leaves at six," I said. "He's probably waiting for the main doctors to clear out."

"How often do you come here?"

"These days? Twice a month."

"And before?"

"A lot more than twice a month."

"What were you in for?" He eyed me sideways.

"Everything under the sun." I faced him. "From anger issues to hallucinations."

"Hallucinations?"

"When I was little, I saw a little girl who looked like me. I chased her halfway through the mall and got separated from my mom. I lost sight of the little girl and security found me, but I swear it was my twin."

"And they said you hallucinated it?"

"They said I wanted to have a sister so badly, I made one up." I shrugged, looking away.

"Well, joke's on them."

"I think the joke is still on me." I shook my head. "I've spent my entire life seeing things through fogged-up lenses and they're starting to clear up."

"You think they knew about your sister and were purposely lying to you about her?"

"I think they lied to us both."

"Do you think they lied about your anger and all of your other issues too?"

"It's hard to say." I looked over at him again. "When someone tells you who they are, do you believe them?"

"Do you?"

"I guess so." I looked away and blinked the unexpected tears that burned my eyes. I'd spent so much of my life putting up barriers to avoid getting hurt. I'd turned my back on Karen when she tried to help, and lashed out when she acted protective toward me. As much as it pained me, I saw that now. Will's phone started vibrating in his hand and I wiped my face as he answered.

"We're on our way." He glanced up at me as he hung up the phone. "You know where the entrance to the B-Wing is?"

"That's where she is?" My chest tightened.

"Apparently." Will and I started walking. I picked up my pace and he followed. "What's in the B-Wing?"

"Trouble."

It was the only word I could use to properly describe it. Of course, to the staff and doctors, the B-Wing probably meant opportunities for new discoveries, but for those on the receiving end of the treatments, it meant endless days that looped together and confusion. I thought about the day I was picked up by the cops, the day this all started, and came to the same conclusion I did that evening. I must have been in the B-Wing. Before the initiation with The Swords, I'd never done drugs willingly, but the only time I'd ever felt close to that euphoria followed by a murky aftermath was when I'd been in the B-Wing. As we approached the side door of the building, I took a deep breath and shook my nerves away. The door opened before us and Adam appeared, wearing his slacks, dress shirt, and tie. He looked like he belonged here. Not the way I did, inside one of those rooms being watched and studied twenty-four hours a day. He belonged like he could one day be running the place that housed people like me. I tried and failed not to picture it—us on either side of the glass.

"Hey." Adam took my hand suddenly, and the picture dissipated. I glanced up at him. "You sure you want to do this?"

"I need answers." I took a deep breath. "I'm nervous."

"Hey, we're here." Will placed a hand on my arm briefly.

"The cameras are covered," Adam said, looking at Will.

"How'd you manage that?"

"I called Nolan. He brought Marcus."

"Who's Marcus?" I asked.

"An Eight." Will looked at me and back at Adam. "They know about this?"

"I wasn't not going to tell my brother."

"And of course he had to tell Marcus." Will shook his head. "We haven't even told The Swords about this, Adam. If they find out—"

"They can't find out." Adam let go of my hand. "We don't even know what we're dealing with here. Once we do, we'll let some of the others in, if we can."

"What do you mean if we can?" I frowned at Adam. "I thought The Swords were a family."

"All families have secrets."

"This one isn't supposed to," Will said.

"Yet it does. You know that better than anyone. Look at all of the crap we found yesterday. You think everyone knows about that?"

"Probably not." Will scowled. "Definitely not the black members. Otherwise, they wouldn't have joined."

"Times have changed," Adam said, his voice hopeful.

"Not enough," I said so that Will wouldn't have to.

"I know, and I hate that." Adam's expression softened as he brought his hand back to mine. "But if we want things to change, we need to do it together and that means getting to the bottom of this."

The three of us started walking up the stairs toward the fifth floor. By the fourth, my thighs were feeling the burn. Adam and Will were walking ahead of me as if they were in a race to the top floor. I held on to the rail between floors four and five and paused to take a breather. They walked back down to me.

"You okay?"

"Fine. Just out of shape, obviously," I huffed, looking up at them. "What the hell do you two do? Run marathons for fun?"

"Actually, we do." Will chuckled. "Maybe you should train with us."

"Maybe you should fuck off." I put both hands on the rail, still breathing heavily. "Okay, let's go."

"We're almost there," Adam said, grabbing my arm when I reached him on the landing between the stairs.

"We don't have walkie-talkies or something to make sure the cameras are turned off for sure?" I asked when we reached the door.

"No, we have cell phones." Adam took his out and pressed Marcus' name on his phone. "We're on five. Are we good? Okay." He hung up and put the phone away. "The nurses are on the third floor, which means we have exactly fifteen minutes before one of them comes back up to do her rounds. We stick together, you got it?"

I gave a nod. Will gave a nod. Adam opened the door and we followed him down the hall.

"Damn, this is fancy." Will looked on either side of us.

We were surrounded by windows. The entire building was built like that, with Plexiglas instead of concrete. Debbie said it was built that way so it wouldn't feel like a prison. The glass was supposed to make the patients feel calm and not trapped. It always had the opposite effect on me. I couldn't even count the number of times I envisioned myself barreling through it and falling to my death, but that was then. I hadn't been to the B-Wing in years and was seeing it in a different light now. Instead of drinking the Kool-Aid and accepting everything they told me, I was questioning it. The way I'd once questioned Karen. I'd spent so much of my life being angry at her and using her as a scapegoat for my flaws that I rarely ever paid attention when she bad-mouthed the Maslows. Back then, it felt like jealousy. Now it felt like . . . truth. Adam stopped walking suddenly and knocked on the door beside us, taking my hand in his when he dropped it from the door.

"Can she just open the door?" Will whispered. "Why wouldn't she just leave?"

"The only reason we're walking freely right now is because Marcus handled the cameras and alarms. Otherwise, we wouldn't have been able to open the door to this floor," Adam whispered back.

"Her door won't open," I said. "Not without us unlocking it."

"What?" Adam frowned. "Are you sure?"

"Positive." I took the badge he had clipped on the pocket of his dress shirt.

"Wait." He reached out for my hand just before I slid it. "They'll have it on record that I was the one who opened the door."

"Fuck." That was Will. "Why didn't you think of this before?"

Adam shook his head, looking annoyed at himself, and took out his phone. "Hey. Can you open the door for me from there? What do you mean he's on his way over?" He hung up the phone and slid it in his pocket as he looked over at us. "He says Nolan is on his way with the key."

Not even four seconds later, we heard footsteps coming from the direction of the elevator. The three of us froze. A carbon copy of Adam walked toward us, wearing the same pants, dress shirt, and tie. I did a double take. Nolan kept his hair long, but he had it tied up today, so from the front he looked identical to the man standing beside me. He walked up to us, card in hand, and slid it into the reader. The door clicked.

"What do you want now?" The voice sounded so much like mine, that I had to take a step back to remind myself that there was a real person outside of my head who sounded like that.

Nolan stepped back and signaled for me to move forward. "You should do this."

With my heart in my throat and shaky hands, I reached up and turned the doorknob.

CHAPTER TWENTY-EIGHT

"**A**RE YOU ALL COMING IN WITH ME?" I GLANCED OVER MY SHOULDER. "Only if you want us to," Adam said. "We could leave the door open in case you need us and wait for you here."

"I'd like that." I took one last deep breath and let it out as I stepped inside.

She was reading a book, perched up on a bench beside a window when she looked up and spotted me. She shut the book and stood quickly, blinking as if unsure what she was seeing was true. She took a step forward. I took one toward her. It was like looking in the mirror and being seen for the first time in my life. Her hair was much shorter than mine, her curls looping around the frame of her face perfectly. She reached up and it took everything in me not to flinch as she set her hand on my face and caressed it softly.

"You're . . . me," she whispered, her hand moving from my face to my hair. "Your hair is straight."

"I straighten it."

"You even sound like me." Her eyes jumped to mine. "Are you in my imagination?"

"I'm not." I reached out and pinched her lightly, smiling at the way her eyes widened.

"You're really here."

Her voice was so soft, so kind, that I had to fight to remind myself that this was the same person who showed up at Karen's house pretending to be me. This was the same person I was taking the fall for at The Manor. The one who'd set me up for . . . I wasn't sure what exactly, but whatever sacrifice they had in mind for me. Rape. Pregnancy. Death. I wasn't sure.

"We need to talk."

She nodded, dropping her hand and stepping back toward the bench. She didn't turn around and give me her back though; I wasn't sure if it was out of fear that I might disappear or because she thought I'd attack. With the way my heart was beating, I wasn't sure which I wanted to do more. She sat down on one side. I walked forward and sat down on the other, my knee bent all the way to the glass beside us. I glanced outside.

"You have the nice room."

"Are you stuck in here too?"

"No. I snuck in."

"Oh." She stared at me. "To get me out?"

"Can't you leave on your own will?" I frowned, looking at the door, remembering she was locked in. I'd never been locked in. Not that I could remember, but then, I hadn't been in the B-Wing for a long time.

"I can't leave on my own anymore." She glanced down at her wrung hands. "Not for a while."

"Why?"

A shrug. "They think I'm having an episode. Imagining things."

"Because you told them about me?"

"Probably."

"How did you know about me?"

"I found your file." Her head snapped up.

"Why did you go to my house and pretend to be me?"

"Because . . ." she glanced outside briefly. When she looked at me again, her eyes were filled with tears. "I needed to make sure you were being treated okay. I had such a good life and you . . . that neighborhood, that house, that . . . woman." She wiped her face. "She was mean. I'm sorry."

"Well, I was pretty awful to her." I smiled sadly. "And we both ended up here, so your life wasn't so perfect after all."

"My father did everything he could to protect me."

"So why are you here now?"

"Because I need to be."

"According to who?"

"I was hallucinating." She brought her feet up and hugged her knees. "I keep seeing you everywhere."

"I'm not a hallucination. I'm real."

"That's what you say every time."

"When?"

"When you come here."

My heart pounded harder. "What are you talking about? When do I come here?"

"On nights like these."

"Stella, I've never seen you before. This is our first time meeting face to face."

"Sure." She pursed her lips. "Next you're going to tell me you didn't cut my hair this short."

"What?" I frowned. "I don't know what you're talking about." I put my hands up. "Let's start over. Why did you go to Karen's house and pretend to be me?"

"I already told you why."

"How did you find out about me?"

"I told you that as well. And they say I'm the crazy one." She huffed out a laugh. "Last time you were here, you cut my hair against my will. I told you I didn't like my hair this short."

"You're sure it was me?" I inched closer. "Stella, look at me."

She did, her eyes scanning my face before nodding. "It . . . well, she looked like you. Like me. But no. I guess it wasn't you. She had longer hair and her skin was lighter. Her mouth wasn't full like ours."

Stella nodded.

"How did you get my address?"

"I told you. I found your file."

"How did you know I existed?"

"I saw you. I've seen you before, but the night of the party here I really saw you. I confronted my father about it."

"You were the one Aisha saw arguing with him," I whispered.

"After, I went to Dr. Maslow's office."

"She must have countless patients. How'd you find mine?"

"It's the only file they keep in their top right corner, in the locked drawer. Neil does the same with mine."

"How'd you get the key?"

"I took it from Debbie's keyring."

"And then you went to Karen's?"

"I tried to explain it to her since my own father didn't believe me, but she didn't believe me either, and the minute she realized I wasn't you, she flipped out, got a gun, aimed it at me. I hightailed out of there."

"Did you get into a car accident?"

"I don't remember." She frowned. "I think I went straight home."

"And then?"

"Then I told my dad everything again. He called Neil. They brought me here. I've been here since."

"So you didn't go to The Manor?"

"I did, to escape this." She waved around the room, "But Neil greeted me outside."

"Outside The Manor?"

"I guess he had someone following me."

"Was he inside or outside of the gates?"

"Inside. Why?"

"I think they're all in on it." I swallowed. "Where's your dad now?"

"Home, I assume."

"Has he visited you?"

"No." She shook her head sadly. "Why?"

"Have you heard from him at all?"

"He sent me flowers the other day." She smiled. "Pink lilies."

"And you're sure they were from him?"

"It had his name on it and was written to Baby Girl. Why?"

"Debbie told me your father had gone missing during a hiking trip with your brother."

"My brother?" she laughed. "Now that's bullshit. My brother barely goes outside. He'd never agree to hiking."

"Then Debbie lied." I felt my heart sink as I spoke those words. Was that possible? I'd seen the news article. *One* news article. "Your dad made me go to The Manor. He told me to pretend I was you. He gave me your car, your schedule, everything."

"And you did it?"

"He told me you were missing. He said you'd gone to The Manor and then poof, disappeared."

"Why would he want you to pretend to be me?"

"Because obviously someone is after you. After both of us."

"Who?"

"I don't know, but there's more though."

There was a knock on the door, followed by it opening slightly and Adam peeking inside. "We have to go. Marcus can't keep the cameras down much longer without it looking weird."

"I'll be right there."

He looked between Stella and me and nodded as he stepped outside again.

"Nolan Astor?" Stella looked at me, brow arched.

"His brother."

"Adam."

"Yeah."

"I'm in a class with them." She sighed heavily. "I miss my classes."

"I went. As you." I took a deep breath. "I think you should leave with us."

"Now?"

"Yes, now."

"They'll know." Her eyes widened. "If I leave, Neil will know. They'll know we're on to them. As it is, I had to bribe one of the nurses to make copies of your file for me." She stood quickly and lifted one side of her mattress, taking a folder out and handing it to me. "You need to take this with you."

"Just come with us."

"I can't."

"I know you're scared. I get it, but we can call a news station and tell them our story. If it's out there in public, they won't be able to lock us up, will they? Or we can hide. We can—"

"This is Neil and Debbie Maslow we're up against. For all I know, they fired my father over this. I need to find more information on why they did this to us. Why would they keep us away from each other? Why not introduce us? Me staying in here is the only way."

"We can find information together."

"So, stay."

"You know I can't do that." I clutched the folder and looked away. "If I stay, neither of us will have a way out." I reached out and set my hand on hers. "Please come with me."

"I can't." She blinked unshed tears. "I've been here too long. I'm scared of what awaits me outside of these walls."

"You don't think I'm scared? I'm terrified, but we can stand together. We can figure this out together." I squeezed her hand and swallowed. "I also think I found our birth mother."

"What?" Her mouth dropped. "Where? How?"

"In The Manor. They have photos. There's a woman who looks just like us. There's more, but I'm running out of time."

"You need to get out of there, Eva. You need to get out of The Manor. You're safer in here than out there."

"I'm done with playing it safe." I stood up, holding the folder to my chest. "I need truth."

"Truth always comes with a price."

"I'm ready to pay whatever it costs."

CHAPTER TWENTY-NINE

"How was it?" That was Nolan.

"As weird as it would be if you just met Adam for the first time tonight."

"I can't imagine." Nolan stopped walking in front of the building, and we all stopped with him. A male figure walked out of the building and started walking toward us. I froze. "That's Marcus," Nolan said.

Marcus was a brown-skinned, green-eyed guy with curly hair. He was as cute as he was tall, and he was incredibly tall.

"He's Dominican too," Nolan said. "But he's legit Dominican."

"At your service." Marcus grinned. "You're Eva?"

"Yes. It's good to meet you." I felt myself smile because of his infectious smile.

"I'm glad we got that out of the way." Adam took my hand in his as he stood beside me. "Did you get the cameras back up?"

"Do cows moo?" Marcus cocked his head. "I also made it so there's less of a time lapse between the time they went down and back up. You guys took longer than the fifteen minutes you promised."

"She was meeting her sister for the first time. She couldn't exactly rush that." Adam squeezed my hand tighter.

"I'm just saying, you have a five-minute window of nothing on the system, so it's not as seamless as it would have been if you'd only taken fifteen minutes," Marcus said. "My cousin said they don't check the cameras anyway unless something is really wrong."

"Your cousin works there?" I asked.

"Rolando Fernandez. He's worked there for years. Started out as a janitor and worked his way up to head of security. You know him?"

"No." I shook my head. "Maybe if I see him."

"Maybe." Marcus shrugged a shoulder. "Anyway, he wasn't exactly thrilled about our little rendezvous."

"I can't imagine why. Adam paid him a lot of money for this," Nolan said.

"You paid him?" I glanced up at Adam.

"Silence isn't free." Adam shrugged a shoulder.

I tuned them out as we walked toward the parking lot. I'd been so focused on getting in there, meeting Stella, and getting out, that I hadn't stopped to think about all of the effort it took to do it without being discovered. I guess if it had been up to me, I would have gone in there without shutting the cameras down, looked for her, and probably gotten caught along the way.

"What's that in your hand?" Adam nodded at the file Stella had given to me.

"My file."

"She took it?" His brows rose. "How long will that go unnoticed?"

"She said she paid someone to make copies."

"Damn." He glanced over his shoulder. "Do you think she'll tell anyone about tonight?"

"I don't know." I chewed on my bottom lip. "I don't know if I trust her not to."

"If one of us goes down, we all go down." Will set his hand on my shoulder. "We're here for you, Eva."

"We all are." Nolan and Marcus came forward and set a hand over Will's.

It was odd, but feeling the weight of their promise on my shoulder made me feel invincible. Maybe that was the beauty of the secret society. It wasn't about the network and connections. It wasn't about the money. It was about the camaraderie, because having one another's backs and taking the fall for and with someone was the ultimate sacrifice.

"We'll see you tomorrow night," Nolan said, stepping back. "I have to get up early for practice."

Nolan, Marcus, and Will all said their goodbyes and headed to their cars, while I got into Adam's with him. He switched on the ignition and sat there for a moment, looking over at me.

"You sure you're okay?"

"I don't know." I rested my head on the headrest and looked over at him. "I should be happy, right? I'm not alone in the world like I thought I was all this time, but I just . . . " I sighed heavily and glanced back at the building. "I just wish it would be that simple. I have a sister, the end. Not this."

Adam reached over and put his hand on mine. "What do you need me to do?"

"I don't know."

"Do you want me to look at that folder before you dive into it?"

I shook my head and looked at him again. "I need to do it."

"Let's go home and do it together then."

As he started driving away, I looked back at the building and thought about the sister I was leaving behind. I couldn't force her hand though. I needed to give her time. I just hoped she'd do it before it was too late.

CHAPTER THIRTY

"WHEN YOU SAID HOME I THOUGHT YOU WERE TALKING ABOUT The Manor." Eva sat in the car, eyeing the small cottage I'd parked in front of warily.

"Is this okay?" I brought her to my house without a second thought. "I just figured we should stay away from The Manor right now. Just in case."

"We could've gone to my place," she said, chewing on her bottom lip.

I set the gear to drive. "That's fine."

"No." She glanced at me quickly and smiled. "This is fine. I want to see your place."

Once we got inside, I let her explore the place while I ordered Chinese food for us.

"This place is cute. Not where I'd expect you to live." She sank down on the couch, still clutching the folder. "I thought you'd live in Billionaire's Row."

"My parents aren't billionaires."

"Their vacation condo or whatever they call it is there."

"True."

"Nolan lives there, I bet."

"He does, actually." I brought two glasses of water and set them on the coffee table.

"You bring me to your house and you give me water?" She arched an eyebrow. "Where's the whiskey?"

"You want whiskey?" I chuckled, setting the glass of water down.

"You have whiskey?" she sounded surprised.

"What kind of German do you think I am? Of course I have whiskey."

"Isn't whiskey an Irish thing?"

"Scottish, technically, but yeah. These days, Germany produces more whiskey than Scotland though."

"Damn. I didn't know I was going to be getting a history lesson with my nightcap."

I couldn't help but to laugh. She was entirely too amused by me and I liked it. I liked that she let herself go around me, that she let herself just *be*. I poured us some of the Macallan 18 my father gifted me for my birthday last year. I'd only had a few glasses of it with him, Nolan, and Will. I wasn't much of a drinker, but my father told me it was a good bottle, and I knew Eva would appreciate it.

When I walked back to the living room, she was looking through the photo album on my table. My mother had set it there last month when she visited and I hadn't bothered to move it. It was the only thing that was of sentimental value in the house. Everything else belonged to the landlord. Between school, my internship, and The Manor, I was rarely home and didn't care to decorate much. Of course, I'd signed the lease before the Chancellor asked me to move to The Manor, otherwise, I would have saved my money.

"Scottish whiskey," I said, handing her a glass.

"Not German?" she gasped. "I'm offended for you."

"I just stated facts. I didn't say I actually drank it."

She shook her head, smiling as she took a sip of the drink. "This is good. Really good."

"I thought you'd like it."

"Where's your mom from? She's not German."

"Greece."

"Greece. That's my dream vacation." Her brows rose. "Have you been?"

"Every year. Mom moved here for college and stayed for my dad, but she can't stay away from her family for too long. Dad says if they lived here, they'd probably have to move to a compound that fit all of them."

"They must be close."

"Very." Adam smiled, thinking about his *yiayia*.

"Do they really have huge weddings?"

"Ridiculous weddings. My last cousin who got married probably had three hundred people, and half were family."

"Damn. I've always wanted to go to one to see how it compares to the movie."

"I'll take you." I grinned as I took a sip of the whiskey. "You know, after you come to Thanksgiving and all that."

Eva laughed.

I picked up the folder between us and waved it at her, asking for permission. She nodded and picked up her glass again as I moved closer to her and opened it. Inside, there was a page with numerous pictures of Eva. The nurse who made copies of the original folder for Stella must have gotten all of the photos and placed them together on a page so that they'd all be on one sheet. Eva when she was a baby, a toddler, a little older, a tween, a teen, and now. I looked at her.

"How long did you say you've known the Maslows?"

"My whole life." Her voice was a whisper as she reached over and touched the photograph where she was around six or seven months old.

"They don't even see babies." I frowned. Eva took the folder from my hand and started looking through the rest of the file.

"Apparently they did." She handed me the paper she'd just scanned through. "What do you think this means?"

The paper had no names, but the birthdates were the same and there were three, not two of them on the page. I didn't look up until I finished scanning the page. Eva had already moved on to another one when I looked at her.

"Do you think there's a chance you have a third sister?"

"Why do you say that?" Her eyes widened when she looked over.

I held the page up. "There are three people on this page and they all have the same birthday."

"Right. Wouldn't that mean three different babies born the same day?"

"Three adopted babies, all girls, with the same birthdate, and the same agency?"

"Where do you see the agency?" Eva took the paper from my hand and looked at it again. "Oh shit. St. Nicolas' Orphanage."

"We need to go there and ask questions."

"Karen tried that when I was hell-bent on finding my birth mother. They said she didn't want to be found."

"It's not about your birth mother, Eva." I turned to her so that our knees were touching. I needed her to understand the gravity of what I was trying to come to terms with. "If you have another sister, that means there are three of you. Three women who have been in contact with The Maslows since they were babies. You and Stella were both invited to The Swords and Will did some digging, the third girl? She also has your birthday. Is that a coincidence? I don't think so."

"But she didn't make it there either. Only I did. Not only that, Stella said Neil Maslow was the one who stopped her from going inside The Manor that night. He made her go to The Institute, while Dr. Thompson made me go in her place."

"I'm not saying this makes any sense. I'm just saying we need to consider that you have another sister involved in all of this."

"The girl," she whispered, her eyes flicking back to his. "The visitor."

"What visitor?"

"Someone keeps visiting Stella at The Institute. She said she thought it was me, but then decided it wasn't. I guess she looks like us but not identical? Is that possible? Is it possible for triplets to not be identical? Or for two to be identical and the third not to be?"

"It's possible for multiple fetuses to have different fathers, so yes, I'm sure it's possible for one of you not to have shared the same sac as the other two."

"Oh my God." Eva brought her hand to cover her gasp as she stared at me. "I think it's a nun. I think our sister is that nun Will and I saw."

CHAPTER THIRTY-ONE

I'D HUNG UP THE PHONE WITH KAREN A FEW MINUTES AGO AND couldn't stop pacing. She'd been drunk when I called, which meant I had to repeat myself more than a few times.

"What are you doing?" I walked back to the couch and plopped down beside Adam, who was furiously typing into his phone.

"I contacted our family lawyer so he could look into the orphanage and I sent these to my mother, but she's still on her flight, so she won't be able to answer until she lands." Adam sighed heavily, looking at the papers again. "They must have separated you when you were just days old."

"But Karen didn't adopt me until I was five months old," I said. "So where was I during those five months?"

"I don't know."

"Is it normal to separate multiples like that?"

"When I first started at The Institute, I was in Neil's internship program. I'd wanted to go into psychology like my mother, but I wasn't sure whether I wanted to see patients or do research work." He set his phone and papers down and looked at me. "This was my first semester here, before I was recruited by The Swords and decided to go into neuroscience instead. That was when I learned about the Twin Study."

"The one where they got people who looked almost identical but weren't actually twins," I said.

"Yes, that's one of them, but prior to that there had been a longitudinal study about multiples. Originally it was about actual twins, triplets, etcetera. Part of the deal for twins to qualify for their scholarship is that they answer a series of questions from The Institute. It's really no big deal. Nolan and I were done in a day. That was where we first met Nora and Will," Adam explained. "I keep thinking back to that day. Dr. Maslow was riveted by the fact that Nora and Will were twins, one black, one white, and such different experiences growing up."

"Did they do that longitudinal study on them?"

"No. They didn't go back."

"How does the longitudinal study work? Weekly basis? Monthly?"

"It takes place over a long period of time. They're conducting some, unrelated to multiples, that they've been doing for over sixty years."

"How is that even possible? Wouldn't most of the subjects die?"

"Yes, and then the research falls on the next generation. They have one on socio-economic backgrounds in which they take a single parent and follow them through the course of the child's life, then when the child is old enough, they follow them, and so on."

"So basically they're studying them in order to see if and when they break the chain people fall into when they're born into a certain situation," I said.

"Exactly."

"But why us?" My voice grew louder as my thoughts poured in quickly. "Why not tell us about each other? That wouldn't have been against the code of the orphanage. And to add insult to injury, we were all at The Institute at one point or another and they chose to keep us apart."

My words seemed to silence Adam. For a while, we just looked at each other, possibilities running through each of our minds. Impossible possibilities. Finally, Adam swallowed and reached for my hand as if I was a patient he was going to deliver a deadly prognostic to.

"If they were using you for a study your guardian had to sign off on it."

"You mean Karen?"

"Who else?"

I shook my head. Karen had been just as outraged as I had. More so, maybe. I couldn't imagine she'd sign me over to them, not after all the awful things she had to say about Debbie and Neil. Unless she did sign me over to them and lived with the guilt all these years? It would explain a lot—the drinking, the blame she placed on me, the way she acted as if siding with the Maslows was a stab in the back.

"We need those papers," Adam said. "The contracts with The Institute and the ones from the orphanage."

"Dr. Thompson would have had to sign off as well. He doesn't seem like the type who would," I said.

"You're right." I sighed, stretching my arms over my head.

"You tired?"

"Of thinking about this, yes. I just want to go to a bar or a movie or somewhere and hang out in a regular place doing regular-people things."

"Let's go then. No one is stopping us." He stood, offering me his hand. "Besides, I haven't taken you on a proper date."

I smiled and took his hand.

The restaurant he took me to was in Billionaire's Row. It was one that was really popular and always had a line out the door and tonight was no exception.

"We're never going to get in," I said as he circled the block for a parking space.

"Good thing my friends own it." He dialed a number. "Hey, any chance you can get my girlfriend and me a table tonight? Yes. No. We're parking." He hung up and grinned at me. "Done."

"Your girlfriend?" I raised an eyebrow.

"Is that a problem?"

"I guess not." I smiled, linking my fingers with his. "Who's your friend anyway? The one who owns this place?"

"Logan and Amelia Fitzgerald." He eyed me. "You know them?"

"Is that the girl who went missing last year?"

"Yep. Will and I found her in one of the plots."

My mouth dropped. "Did she fall into one of the holes?"

"She'd been buried alive."

"But . . . like as part of initiation?"

"She's an Eight." Adam shook his head slightly. "She'd been left for dead there."

"What the actual . . . and you found her? How?"

"By chance."

"How long had she been there?"

"Days."

"Damn. I don't remember reading that in the paper."

"That part was never reported."

"The part where they found a missing girl buried alive was never reported?" I said slowly to make sure I wasn't making this up, even though it sounded far worse than anything I could make up, and I'd made a lot of shit up throughout the years.

"I know how it sounds, but a lot of factors went into it."

"Like the involvement of two secret societies." I raised an eyebrow, then it hit me. "Logan Fitzgerald? The hockey player?"

"Yup. They got married recently. Eloped, really. Just the two of them. They didn't even invite us." Adam scowled.

"You really like weddings, don't you?" I couldn't help but to smile.

Adam shrugged a shoulder. "Free booze."

"You barely drink."

"So I guess I just like weddings."

"I think it's cute."

"Thanks. I think." He parallel parked.

As we were walking into the restaurant, a couple was walking out. My eyes widened when I realized what couple. It was Logan and Amelia Fitzgerald, both dressed like they were fresh off a photo shoot, casual in ripped jeans and black T-shirts, but hot nonetheless.

"Speak of the devil," Adam said. "Or devils."

"Look who's talking." Logan chuckled. "We're not the ones digging up graves."

"Hilarious." Adam gave the woman a hug and kiss and gave Logan a quick hug. "How long are you in town for?"

"We're leaving right after tomorrow's game," the woman said. She smiled at me. "Hi. I'm Amelia."

"Eva." I set my hand out to shake hers, but she leaned in for a kiss instead. "Nice to meet you."

"Logan," Logan said next, as if he needed any form of introduction. I didn't even watch hockey and I knew who he was.

"Eva."

"Nice to meet you. So, you're Adam's girlfriend?"

"I guess so." I smiled.

Logan looked between us and at Adam a little longer, as if asking a question without words.

"She's a Sword," Adam said after a beat. I was surprised by his admission. I thought secret societies were supposed to be kept . . . secret.

"Oh shit." Logan arched an eyebrow at me. "An official Sword?"

"According to my bank account," I said.

Logan and Amelia laughed.

"You made it through the initiation then," Logan said.

"I did."

"I don't think I've ever met a girl Sword," Amelia said. "Have I?"

"Nope." Logan said the word slowly, the *p* popping loudly in it. The two of them were totally scrutinizing me and I wanted nothing more than to get out of there.

"Hopefully this initiation will be the first of many," Adam said, taking my hand in his.

"Well, we're going to be late if we don't leave now. Our table is available for you," Logan said. "Dinner's on us. Welcome to the family."

"Thank you so much," I said as we said our goodbyes, then turned to Adam. "That was so nice of them."

"They're Eights. They're family."

"Logan Fitzgerald is an Eight?" My brows rose. "Probably the only thing in life that can put him in that number."

"Meaning what?" Adam dropped my hand as we reached the table and sat across from each other.

"Meaning he's a ten in every other aspect of life. Even his wife is a freaking ten."

Adam let out a laugh, shaking his head.

"What? You don't use numbers to categorize people's looks and achievements?"

"Not particularly."

"Yeah, I don't either." I shrugged a shoulder when he shot me a look of disbelief. "Okay, fine, I didn't, but Aisha does and it kind of rubbed off on me."

"Hm. Do you miss her?"

"Yes." I picked up the menu. "But, apparently I've fucked up too many times for Aisha's liking and she feels her life is better without me in it."

"Fucked up how?"

"I guess she got tired of my mercurial attitude like everyone else in my life."

"There's nothing wrong with your attitude, Eva."

"Give it some time. I push away everyone I lo—" I stopped talking before I said the word and felt my face grow hot with embarrassment. Adam smiled, but didn't say anything.

"You said the police picked you on Sunday morning, right?" he asked after a while.

"Detective Barry did. Yeah."

"We should go see him."

"I think he's siding with The Maslows."

"Why?" He set his menu down.

"He was at Karen's house the day after Stella was there. He left his card with our new neighbor." I pursed my lips as I thought about it. "Why would a cop put me in that position to begin with? Why would he agree to letting me go to The Manor, by myself, to look for a missing girl?"

"Maybe Thompson paid him off."

"And you think he's going to be helpful in this situation because?" We both paused to put our order in. Since we'd already had Chinese food, we went with dessert. When the server left, I looked at Adam again. "Detective Barry probably wouldn't be there right now and if he was, he wouldn't talk."

"So our only hope is to go directly to The Maslows."

"Are you kidding?"

"This is why justice is never made. People go after the people lowest in the chain of command and that's not where change is made."

"I'd rather go back to The Manor and see what else we can find. If Debbie and Neil are involved, they must have a reason. Besides, The Manor is swarming with clergy. I'd bet they have more to do with all of this than The Maslows."

"Oh, the good Catholic girl is finally coming around?"

"I never said I was a good Catholic girl." My gaze swung toward his.

Adam picked up his phone, pushed a button, and pressed it to his ear. "Will, go to the library and see what you find on Neil Maslow. What? What do you mean? When?" Adam shot a glance in my direction and the horror in his eyes was enough to make an uneasy feeling settle in the pit of my stomach. "Yeah, we'll be there in an hour."

"What happened? What'd he say?"

"The Chancellor stopped by today. He said there would be an initiation tomorrow night. Everyone, including you, should wear their red cloaks."

"Another initiation?"

"A historic one."

"What does that mean?"

"He didn't say."

"A sacrifice," I said, thinking about that nun again.

Adam didn't say anything, but the color draining from his face was enough for me to know what he thought about that.

CHAPTER THIRTY-TWO

W E SAT AROUND THE PIANO SURROUNDED BY BOOKS AND laptops. It would have been a nice scene, two well-to-do boys and a rebel sharing a moment, if Will hadn't been googling *sacrifice* while I leafed through more picture books. Adam sat beside me and set his hand on mine.

"You okay?"

I shook my head.

"If it's too overwhelming, we'll stop."

"We can't stop. There's about to be a sacrifice and we don't know if it involves a shirt, a goat, or me."

"Don't say that. It won't involve you." He squeezed my hand.

"You know it has to, one way or another." I turned to face him. "You better get used to the idea of seeing me naked and tied down while a bunch of monks rape me."

"Don't put that picture in my head, Eva." He squeezed his eyes shut. "That's not going to happen."

"It happened before and we just stood there, watching, doing nothing."

"I wish we hadn't, but we didn't know what was happening."

"You don't have to know the full details to know the difference between right and wrong."

"We'll be ready next time."

One of our phones vibrated on the table and we all paused. Will stood and picked it up, sliding to unlock. His brows furrowed when he saw whatever was on it.

"Oh shit." He glanced up at Adam, turning his phone so we could see it. "My brother just sent me this. Look at the headline."

It read: **Nun Kidnapped.** It was accompanied by a front shot of The Manor.

"When did this happen?"

"Today." Will took his phone back and started texting. "A while back I'd told my brother I'd seen some creepy nuns and monks around here. He must have remembered our conversation."

"Yo, did you guys see the news?" Wolf appeared out of breath at the door of the room. "The nuns are freaking out."

"What?" Adam stood. I followed. "Where are they? What are they saying?"

"I don't know. They're congregated outside on the lawn but they look pissed."

I didn't stand around to keep talking. I let go of Adam's hand and marched out of the room, practically sprinting to the back door. When I opened it, I saw all of the nuns standing around the lawn, talking over each other, some pointing fingers at some of the monks. None of them seemed to notice my arrival, so I kept walking, looking for Marie. I needed to find Marie. She was the one I needed to direct all of these questions to, not Debbie, not Dr. Thompson, not Detective Barry. It all started with Marie. I weaved through the crowd of brown and black and white robes and tapped on one of the nun's shoulders. She looked confused when she saw me.

"Where's Marie?"

"I don't know." She frowned, grabbing my arm. "What are you doing? Everyone is worried sick about you."

"What are you talking about?" I yanked, trying to get free, but she gripped harder.

"She's right here," she said. "Wendy hasn't been kidnapped."

The nuns around us turned and looked at us. One of them, the woman who had spoken to me by the stairs, walked over and pulled us apart.

"This isn't Wendy." She looked at me. "Are you okay?"

"What do you mean that's not Wendy?" the other nun said.

"Mind your business, Sister," she said scowling at her. She turned to the other nuns. "This is not Wendy. It's a lookalike." She pulled me away from the crowd.

"What was that? Who's Wendy?" I asked once she let me go.

"Eva." That was Adam, rushing toward us. "What the hell?"

"I was looking for Marie," I said against his chest as he pulled me close. "We need to find her."

"Sister Marie?" the nun asked.

"Do you know where she is?"

"She should be at the chapel. Cleaning." She looked in the direction of the woods.

"Is . . . does Wendy really look like me?"

"You could pass as twins," she said, looking back at me.

"Do you know where I can find her?"

"Wendy?"

"Yes."

"She's been kidnapped."

"By whom?"

"They haven't said." The nun looked around and leaned in.

"I think it's one of the monks. I saw them arguing last night and it didn't look very good."

"Did you tell the police?" I lowered my voice to match hers.

"Of course not." Her eyes bounced to our surroundings. "If I tell them, I'll get sent away. That's how things work around here."

"Why stay?" The question came from Adam's lips. "We've seen some pretty messed-up things."

"My daughter is here." Her eyes filled with tears when she said it. "Not here, she's not one of us, but she and her family live nearby. It would break my heart to move far away from my grandchildren." She put a hand on my arm. "Listen, I have to go, but if I could give you one piece of advice, stay away from here."

She walked away and I felt something sit on my chest.

"You can stay at my place."

"What?" I blinked up at Adam.

"You can stay at my place for now."

"I have my own place, Adam. The only reason I'm not there is because I need to find out what happened to me and Stella and now possibly Wendy."

"I'm just trying to help."

"I know. I'm sorry." I sighed heavily, fighting the urge to take it out on him. I needed to stop blaming others for things they couldn't help just because I felt like I was spinning out of control. I turned toward him and wrapped an arm around his waist. With the way his eyes widened, I knew he wasn't expecting that. "Thank you for helping me. I mean, I know you have to get to the bottom of it as well, for The Swords and all, but thank you."

"I'm here for you." He pulled me closer and kissed the top of my head.

"I need to find Marie. That lady said she was back there cleaning."

"Let's go." Adam started walking me into the woods. When I glanced over my shoulder and got the full scope of how many monks and nuns were here, I held his hand tighter.

"Do you think maybe Wendy left of her own accord? Maybe she was the one who was supposed to be sacrificed?"

"Maybe."

"But if she's gone and Stella's not here, it would fall on me."

"Stop saying that. Can you stop saying that?" Adam ran a hand through his hair. "Jesus."

"It's not that far-fetched."

"It is, Eva. People don't sacrifice people. We're not the freaking Aztecs."

"Do you see the people standing in your backyard right now?" I nodded in the direction of the house we were walking away from.

"Clergymen and women, yes, not murderers or rapists."

"I was raised Catholic and even I'm willing to admit that a lot of them are disgusting." I shot him a look. "Adam, we saw them raping a woman. Various women if we take the photographs into account. My mother may have been one of them." A sudden wave of nausea overcame me and I stopped walking, letting go of his hand and setting it on my stomach. "Oh my God. Do you think my father is a priest?"

Maybe it was because I grew up without one, but I was so fixated on my birth mother, I hadn't thought about who my father could have been. Adam was looking at me like it was making him sick as well, but he didn't say no.

"I mean, wouldn't it be?" he asked finally. "Assuming that was your mother in the picture and they invited you and Stella here."

"Oh, God." I put my other hand over my mouth when my stomach rumbled. "I think I'm going to be sick."

"Who cares?" Adam said. "Honestly, what does it matter? Look at how you turned out, Eva. You're in Ellis freaking University. You did that on your own. You had Karen, and sure, you didn't see eye to eye but she obviously loves you despite that. You have Aisha—"

"Had." I blinked away unshed tears. "Had Aisha."

"You have us." He reached for my hand. "You have me."

As I stood there, I felt something shift inside my chest. Maybe it was the butterflies flapping all around inside of me. Maybe it was the circumstances and the fact that out of everyone I knew, everyone I'd met, Adam was the only one who stood next to me and meant it. Whatever the case was, I decided right then and there that this wasn't casual, this wasn't a blip in my story. He was exactly what I never knew I needed and I wouldn't push him away. Not purposely, anyway. With those thoughts in mind, I got on the balls of my feet and kissed him, his arms wrapping around me as my mouth moved against his. I pulled away quickly, not because I wanted to, but because I hadn't lost sight of what needed to be done. His hazel eyes searched mine and without saying a word, I knew he saw what I was trying to tell him.

We started walking again until we reached the church. The door was open, and unlike the other morning, it didn't look as daunting, maybe because I knew it would be empty. As we walked up the steps and walked inside, I braced myself to face Marie. Sister Marie. That was how I knew her. Finding her wasn't an issue. She was on her knees, scraping the floor with a tool, and looked up at us and back down as if she'd been expecting us.

"Darn monks with their gum." She set the tool down and stood. "I take it you're not here for the cleaning position."

"I need to know why I'm here."

"Why you're here?" She raised an eyebrow. "How would I answer that?"

"You helped my mother adopt me. You knew there were two of us." I paused because I still wasn't entirely sure about Wendy. She didn't look exactly like Stella and so I assumed she had a different father. When she didn't jump in, I continued. "Why did they separate us? Where is our mother?"

"Your mother is Karen Guerra."

"My birth mother."

"She doesn't want to be found. Your birth mother was a vessel, like I once was, like you'll be if it is determined you're the chosen one. I can't speak on why they separated the three of you, you'd have to take that up with the adoption agency, but I can say that because you arrived here on your own accord, you are more likely than Stella to be the one chosen."

"Wendy is . . . we're triplets?"

"Yes."

Adam set a hand on my shoulder and I glanced up at him, eyes wide. I'd spent twenty years of my life dealing with loneliness and feeling misunderstood and all along I had two other people I could have shared that with. Anger burned in my throat, unshed tears threatened. The moment seemed to be closing in on me, threatening to swallow me whole. I anticipated fainting. I waited for it to come. Waited for my knees to grow weak and my vision to fill with tiny black dots.

"Focus on breathing." Adam stood between Marie and me, setting both hands on my shoulders and holding my gaze. "Breathe."

I nodded and did as he instructed. When I knew I would be fine, I reached up and placed my hands on his forearms. "Thank you."

He didn't say anything, but he smiled with his eyes and that was more than enough. He stepped back beside me again and we both faced Marie, who had gone back to cleaning the pews.

"St. Nicolas' Orphanage." Sister Marie lowered her voice and looked around. "That's where you came from. Now, go on now, that's the only information I have and they're due to come back any minute."

"What happened to Wendy? Was she really kidnapped?" I asked as Adam grabbed my hand and tugged me in the direction of the door.

"That's what they say."

"What do you say happened?"

"I don't say anything at all, child." Sister Marie smiled. "It's better that way around here."

Adam ushered me out of the church just in time to see the mob of monks and nuns headed in our direction. I followed him around the building, deeper into the woods, until we reached a fence. I was about to tell him we had to turn around when he reached for it and pulled an opening.

"Get in."

I did and he followed. We walked in the direction of the house as the sun set behind us.

"We're really not allowed to be in the church?" I asked.

"It's banned."

"What would happen if they caught us there?"

"They'd probably kick us out of The Swords." He glanced over at me. "Take their money back and all that."

"Why though? It's a church."

"It's their church." He pulled out his phone and started typing.

When he finished, he showed me the screen. *St. Nicolas' Orphanage shut down in 2000.* I grabbed the phone and continued reading as we walked. *St. Nicolas' shuts down after controversies surrounded the adoption practices.* The article named people who had tried to get their adoption papers and were turned away, parents who tried to find out the truth for their children and were shut down.

"I think I'm still in shock about Wendy." I handed the phone back to Adam.

"It's a lot to take in. You just found out you had one twin, and now you find out you have two."

"And she's a nun, which would mean she was probably raised in the convent, raised by our mother." I looked up at him. "I spent so much of my time wishing for that and now that I know this I don't know what to do with it. Why did she keep her and not me? Or Stella?"

My heart sank as I asked the question. I wanted to find out the truth because I was tired of feeling unwanted, not because I wanted my feelings to be amplified. When we got back to the house, using a side door I'd never seen, and upstairs, I let Adam walk me to my room, but stopped as we reached the door.

"I'm sorry. I need space."

His expression gave nothing away, but his eyes were no longer smiling and I knew I'd hurt him. I set my hand on his.

"Just for a little while. I'll meet you in our spot later." I smiled.

"I'll be there playing some Chopin for you."

"I'm sure I'll love it." I licked my lips, unsure of what to do next.

We hadn't said goodbye to each other . . . ever. The few times we'd been apart, one of us had just left while the other was sleeping. This was uncharted territory and oddly enough, even though I needed space, I craved him more. He set his forearm on the door, over my head, leaning in.

"I can come in for a few minutes," he whispered against my lips.

"Only a few." I moved forward and kissed him.

CHAPTER THIRTY-THREE

I MUST HAVE FALLEN INTO A DEEP SLEEP, BECAUSE I DIDN'T EVEN HEAR when Adam left my room, but something woke me up. A scratching sound, like the legs of a chair moving against the hardwood. I opened my eyes and looked around in the darkness, but saw nothing, so I settled back into my pillow. In the distance, I could hear the piano. Closing my eyes, I pictured Adam's long fingers moving along the keys rapidly and smiled. With my left hand, I blindly reached for my phone on the nightstand, my eyes still closed. When I opened them, I googled *Kidnapped Nun*. The story hadn't been updated. In the corner of the room, I heard the sound again, *creak*. I positioned the face of my phone in that direction and screamed when I saw the outline of a person sitting there.

"No one will come," the voice said. A woman. A soft voice. I sat up rapidly, my feet kicking the sheets as my back met the headboard behind me.

"Who are you? What do you want?"

"I wanted to meet you. I've watched you from afar for so long."

"Wendy?" I swallowed.

"That's right."

"I want to see you."

I heard rather than saw her stand and walk toward the door, switching on the bright overhead light. She walked to sit back down. Her hair was curlier than mine and Stella's. Her skin was also darker. She was fresh-faced with tiny freckles on the bridge of her nose and light brown eyes. She was gorgeous. The kind of gorgeous that was unfiltered but could still land on a magazine cover. She reached down and brought a bottle of Blue Label up with her, setting it on the small table between the chairs.

"Come. Have a drink with me."

I stood slowly, grateful that I'd pulled on my pajamas before I fell asleep. As I walked over, I kept my eyes on her, examining, as she did me. She reached down again and brought up two glasses, setting them down in front of each other and pouring some whiskey into each of them.

"How'd you know I like whiskey?" I took my glass.

"Like I said, I've watched you from afar."

"You're the one who's been going to visit Stella at The Institute."

"Poor thing." Wendy lifted her glass. "No matter how many times I tell her, she thinks she's hallucinating me every time."

"So you're a nun. Who drinks." I swallowed some whiskey, loving the way it burned on its way down.

"Most of us do." She smiled and winked at me. "Don't tell anyone."

"So I take it you weren't kidnapped?"

"Nope. I did the kidnapping."

"What?" I choked on my whiskey and started hitting my chest as I coughed.

"I kidnapped a monk."

"Why?"

There was a loaded pause before she said, "Someone has to put an end to all of this."

"You mean the rapes?"

She nodded, her eyes welling with tears. "I'm tired of it."

"I'm sorry." I swallowed the lump in my throat. "You grew up with our mother?"

"Unfortunately." She glanced away briefly. "You and Stella got the best deal out of this. Stella especially, with her fancy car and doting father."

"Even Stella has issues."

"Bullshit issues." Wendy scowled. "You too. You were so hell-bent on defying Karen that you didn't even realize how good you have it."

"So she's bad? Our birth mother?"

"Not bad, but she kept me here. Don't get me wrong, I loved it before the monks got here." She started making circles with her pointer around the rim of her glass. "For a while anyway. Then I started seeing the parties The Swords get to throw. Sometimes I'd see them in the pool, drinking their beers, making out with girls, and I thought, why can't I have a life like that? I didn't choose this for myself. I haven't chosen anything for myself."

"Why didn't you come to me before? Why'd you wait until tonight?"

"Because. You've been so busy with Adam. Besides, the final sacrifice is tomorrow night."

"What does that mean?" I blinked, my eyes feeling a little heavy.

"It means it's my turn to kidnap you."

"What?" I tried to widen my eyes, tried to bat her away, but my limbs felt tired.

"Don't worry, sis. I'm not going to let anyone hurt you. It's just part of the game."

CHAPTER THIRTY-FOUR

I'D LET HER SLEEP LONG ENOUGH. I CONTINUED SAYING THAT AS I PACED back and forth in front of her door with the information I'd been given by the PI I hired. The key to her room burned in my palm, waiting to be used. I stopped pacing and sat down on the floor of the hall, my back against her door. According to my PI, St. Nicolas' was shut down for wrongdoings and giving out wrong information. Eva's mother had birthed her and her sisters here and according to the file, not in jail, but a regular hospital, and put two of them up for adoption. After doing more digging, the PI found that The Institute had been adopting multiples from St. Nicolas' Orphanage for years. From the time Debbie Maslow's grandfather and great-grandfather were alive. The study began as a way to examine Nature vs Nurture.

What better way than to rip siblings apart from birth and put them in different socio-economic households? I had to admit it was a brilliant study. It would have been if it weren't so inhumane. If it hadn't changed the fabric of these people so deeply. It wasn't just the way they grew up that changed them. Debbie and Neil Maslow found that by taking them away from each other from such a young age, they were altering their psyches. Compared to the children who stayed together, these babies showed signs of trauma early on. They were angered easily; their speech was delayed in some cases.

My PI sent videos he was able to get illegally. Videos that showed the kids, Eva, Stella, and Wendy, recorded separately as they spoke to their therapists, people they'd come to know as family rather than doctors. All these years, they'd been feeding them medication to numb the pain, maybe because of the guilt they felt for doing what they'd done, or maybe because it was the way of the doctor. If you can't fix something, medicate it. My stomach roiled. How would I give this information to Eva? It would break her heart. It broke mine and I hadn't been the subject of the experiment. I shut my eyes and saw one of the videos play in my head, of when Eva was just a child, maybe five years old, asking why no one wanted her. Debbie Maslow took on the role of doting caregiver in the video. She'd smiled softly and tried to hug Eva, who wouldn't let her. She told her that she was wanted, by Debbie, by Neil. She never mentioned Karen. Not once. It made me wonder a few things: Was Karen a bad person or had they vilified her in their narrative? Had they brainwashed Eva from an early age and molded her into a person who didn't trust her own mother? If you couldn't trust your own mother—the person who swore to protect you—then who can you trust?

I stood up and knocked on the door, bracing myself for the inevitable. There was no answer. I knocked again and leaned in, trying to hear if the water was running. It wasn't. Finally, I used the key to unlock the door and stepped into an empty room, with an empty, unmade bed, and the lights on.

"Eva?" I walked to the bathroom, then the closet. "Where are you?" When I exited the closet, I saw a bottle of Blue Label and two glasses set on the table.

One looked untouched while the other was drained of alcohol. I could guess which was whose, I just didn't know who the second glass was for. My frown deepened. Last night, after I left her room, I went to the piano. She'd come down and sat on the couch, watching me play for a few minutes before standing and walking out.

"Going to bed?" I'd asked.

"I'm tired," she whispered. "So tired."

She looked tired. She looked off. I berated myself for not standing from the bench and going after her, but I wanted to respect her wishes. I didn't want to push her away and just a couple of hours earlier she'd asked for space before she kissed me and pulled me into the room. The phone on the nightstand caught my eye. I walked over and picked it up. Eva didn't go anywhere without her phone hanging out from her back pocket. In my gut, I felt something was terribly wrong and my gut was never wrong. Well, rarely wrong. I'd been terribly wrong about her in the beginning. I took her phone and walked downstairs in search of her or anyone who may have seen her.

In the kitchen, I found Will and Wolf eating Pop-Tarts. They stopped talking and looked up at me when I stepped into the room.

"Have you guys seen Eva?"

"No." That was Wolf. His eyes were bloodshot and I knew he was high out of his mind.

"She was roaming the house this morning," Will said.

"Roaming the house?"

"She was in the library, then the piano room. She plays a hell of a Beethoven." Will's brows rose. "Symphony No. 5 she said. It sounded clean."

"Eva was playing piano?" I felt my heart pound faster, her cell phone in my back pocket feeling heavier as I stood there.

"Yeah. Why?"

"That wasn't Eva."

Wolf dropped his Pop-Tart. Will's face went from confused to horrified. The only person it could have been was Stella, but Stella was at The Institute. Wasn't she?

CHAPTER THIRTY-FIVE

EVA

S HE DIDN'T KNOCK ME OUT. I WAS GROGGY ENOUGH THAT I
needed help walking, but I chose to walk with her. I chose
to let her lead me into the woods and into the building
they slept in. I wanted to meet my mother. I wanted to know
my sister. I longed for family, despite what she'd said about our
mother. I wanted to know about her upbringing, really know,
but when I got to the building the only thing I could do was pass
out on a small, hard bed. When I awoke, there were four pairs
of eyes staring at me. Sister Marie was one of them. Wendy was
another. The other two were strangers to me, but they stood
and walked out of the room the second I sat up.

"This is for you." Wendy set a bag on the bed.

I looked inside and found some of Stella's clothes that I'd
been given by Dr. Thompson. A pair of underwear, grey Foo
Fighters T-shirt and washed-up, ripped-up jeans. Wendy placed
a toothbrush and toothpaste beside that. I looked up at her.

"Why did you bring me here?"

"We're trying to keep you out of harm's way," Sister Marie
responded.

"By drugging and kidnapping me?"

"It was a mashed up ZzzQuil, calm down. You act like you don't constantly mess up your liver." That was Wendy.

"The difference is I choose to mess up my liver, Wendy. No one else does it for me."

"Oh. Right. I forgot some of us actually have free will."

"What the . . . you can't hate me for not having grown up in this." I waved at the room, which was white and bare, with the exception of a cross holding Jesus.

"She's right," Sister Marie said. "When you turned eighteen you were given a choice. You chose to stay."

Wendy looked over at her and nodded. "For the greater good."

"For the greater good," Sister Marie responded.

"What's for the greater good?" I looked between the two of them.

"It's best you don't know," Sister Marie said, standing. She shot Wendy a look before leaving the room. "Make sure she's ready for tonight."

"How is it best I don't know?" I asked once she was gone.

"I don't agree with her. Shower, get dressed, and I'll grab us something to eat so we can talk."

I did as instructed. They had a small bathroom that was obviously shared by a lot, if not all, of the women living here. There were different kinds of soaps and shampoos, and a lot of colorful toothbrushes. I made sure not to mix mine with theirs and made sure I only used the things with Wendy's name on it. When I picked up the lavender scented shampoo, I froze. She used the same shampoo as Stella and me. As I washed my hair, I tried to think back to how I'd started buying it, but I'd been using it for so long I couldn't be sure.

When I was finished getting dressed, I sought out Wendy.

The house was small, unlike The Manor. It was also loud, unlike The Manor. Over there, the only noise came from the piano when Adam was playing or the guys when they were all having breakfast in the kitchen, which didn't happen often, since they didn't stay there every night. I followed the sounds of women laughing until I reached the kitchen, where some were having coffee and others were cooking. Wendy stood when she saw me.

"You can sit here. I made you a bagel and coffee. Is that fine?"

"Sure." I sat down in the chair she'd just evacuated and kept my eyes on the everything bagel. I wasn't sure where to look if I didn't. As I chewed, I looked back up and found the woman across from me staring at me.

"Oh, by the way, this is your mom," Wendy said, all nonchalant, as if that wasn't the biggest news of the century—of my life.

"What?" I coughed, slapping my chest as I looked at the woman across from me.

Her hair was covered, as was most of her body, in the black and white nun attire they all wore. She had a round face, was much darker than I was, and had eyes that were almost black. She didn't smile. Didn't say anything at all. Just watched me watch her. My heart launched into my throat. I set the bitten bagel in my hand down on the plate and wiped my fingers with the napkin next to it. How many times had I imagined meeting my mother? How many times had I rehearsed what I would say? Too many to count. Now that it was happening, I wasn't sure what to say or do. I wasn't sure if it was the same for her or if she just didn't care. She looked despondent. Distant.

"You're my mother?" I asked, my voice a whisper when I finally found it.

She nodded, but didn't speak.

"I have so many questions."

"She can't answer them," Wendy said. My attention whipped in her direction. "Sister Petra vowed silence."

"Silence?" My voice shook along with the rest of my body. "I'm seeing her for the first time in twenty years and she vowed silence?"

"We have prayer in five minutes," Sister Marie said, interrupting us.

I watched as my mother stood up, gave me a small bow that I guessed I was supposed to perceive as an apology, and walked away with the other women. My gaze stayed on her even as she walked out the door. My mother. The birth mother that Karen told me countless times didn't want to be contacted or found. The one we had arguments about day in and day out when I was a rebellious teenager. I finally saw her, finally met her, and she didn't even care.

"I told you." Wendy plopped down in the chair across from me, the one our mother had stood from. "You had a better life."

I blinked and realized tears were spilling down my cheeks. I wiped them quickly. "How could she not speak to me? Or react? She didn't even look happy."

"She's lived a difficult life."

"So have I."

"I'm not saying you haven't."

"That's not an excuse to not react to your own daughter." I wiped my face again and bit my lip to try to combat more from coming.

"Here are some truths, Eva." Wendy turned fully toward me and clasped her hands together on the table. She looked like she was about to work out a deal with me, which would have been humorous otherwise, since she was wearing a nun outfit.

"We were born in the Dominican Republic. We were brought here when we were barely three months old. We were taken directly to St. Nicolas' Orphanage, which used to be run by the Byzantine nuns. Our mother has always been a nun. She's never even had a boyfriend." She paused for a long time, waiting for me to acknowledge that I'd processed that. I hadn't. I couldn't.

"So if she got pregnant with us . . . " I frowned. "And that picture I saw . . . "

"The picture you saw was probably taken after we were born." Wendy licked her lips and took a breath. "You probably think the world is unfair. Maybe you don't like the president or your mayor or your mom, but you're allowed to scream and shout and protest. In here we have no voice. We're property. We're cattle. We're the women the suffrage movement didn't save."

"So why stay?"

"They stay because they truly love this path. They are genuinely good women who follow Jesus and do the Lord's work. They help those in need, really help them. They stay because they heard God's request." Wendy looked toward the door they all walked out through. When she looked at me again, her eyes were sad. "I stay because I'm the only one willing to fight the injustice."

"How are you doing that?" I pursed my lips. "Kidnapping monks?"

"Kidnapping that monk was just the beginning." Wendy's smile was slow and dark. "Tonight, one of them will die."

CHAPTER THIRTY-SIX

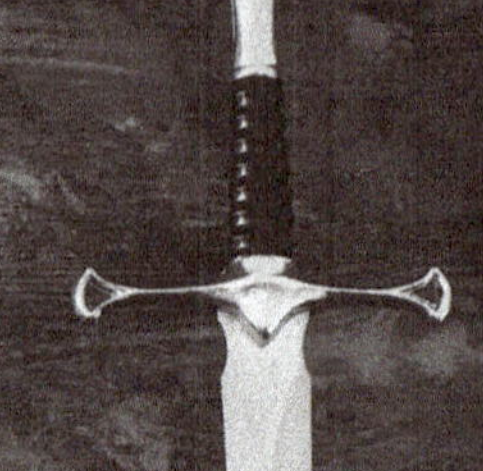

I WAS SITTING AT THE PRECINCT, ACROSS FROM DETECTIVE BARRY, and was doing everything in my power to not punch him.

"I'm sorry, Mr. Astor, but I really don't know what you're talking about," he said for a second time. "Maybe your girlfriend needs to get back to her treatments at The Institute."

I clenched my fists on my lap to keep from reacting. Normally, I had a good grip on my emotions. The art of processing and channeling them was something I'd learned from my mother, from my years in Tae Kwon Do, from my father who always taught me not to bottle things up. *"If you want to have a good cry, have a good cry, don't ever let anyone tell you men don't cry."* I wasn't sure how to control the anger I felt right now though. Not when the man sitting across from me was basically claiming my girlfriend was crazy. I'd always heard there were two types of cops: the good ones and the crooked ones. My privilege ensured that I only dealt with one type. To me, they'd always been good. They'd always been fair. I realized now, sitting across from Detective Barry, that Eva wasn't afforded the same fairness. Maybe because she was a woman, but more likely because she was a woman of color with no money and no power behind her last name. That enraged me even more.

I took a breath and stood, not even bothering to shake Barry's hand or say goodbye. Instead, I made my way to Officer Riley's desk. I trusted Riley. I knew Riley. My parents were friends with his parents and had been for a long time.

"Adam." Riley smiled as he looked at me, but quickly frowned when he saw whatever expression was displayed on my face. "What's up?"

"I need to speak to you outside of here."

"Sure thing." Riley glanced over in the direction of Detective Barry's office. "We can meet at the diner in thirty."

"See you there."

As I walked out, I felt Barry's eyes burning through me and hoped like hell Riley wouldn't tell him about our meeting.

Thirty minutes later, Will, Wolf, and I were sitting across from Riley. He'd looked surprised when he first got there and saw the three of us, who swallowed up the oversized booth at the diner. As he sat down, I introduced them to one another.

"He's the guy who came to The Manor," Wolf said disapprovingly. "Twice."

"Relax. He's on our side."

"You're going to have to tell me why I'm here," Riley said, looking at the three of us. "Is this about Barry?"

"I met with Barry to tell him that someone is in trouble. I asked him some questions and he lied, then he tried to turn it around and tell me the person in trouble needs mental attention, so I figured I can't trust him, not with this."

"And you decided to sidestep him and come directly to me," Riley said. "Why didn't you come to me to begin with?"

"Because you weren't involved, at least I don't think you were involved, but I guess we're about to find out. Did you arrest someone, a woman walking in a neighborhood, a few weeks ago?"

Riley leaned back in his booth and nodded.

"Do you know why?"

"They said she matched the description of a girl who had been reported missing."

"Do you have video of that?"

"Sure," Riley said. "I wouldn't exactly call it an arrest, more like we brought her in to keep her safe. Barry said she may not cooperate because she wasn't in good shape mentally."

"Do you have video?" That was Will's sharp question.

"I had my vest on that day from a prior call and I turned my camera on when I got off to get the girl." Riley's blue eyes bounced back to mine. "I'm sure you heard about Toby a few months ago. I didn't want that to happen again."

"Who's Toby?" Wolf asked.

"Another officer. His partner," I said.

"Hold up. Is she the one who forcefully arrested a pregnant woman?" Will asked.

"A pregnant woman on heroin who was trying to run in front of a car," Riley added. "Toby saved her life."

"Of course you'd say that. She's your partner," I said.

"Just like you say these guys are awesome even when we all know you do sick things like rob graves," Riley shot back.

"We don't do that anymore." Will smiled ruefully. "The school gives us access to the morgue so we can analyze the innocent people you guys kill all the time."

Riley's fists slammed on the table. "Our precinct has never committed a crime against those we try to help. It's not fair for you to pigeonhole me or us with what you see on the news. Some of us are genuinely trying to help and protect the community."

"He's right," I glared at Will. "And we need their help with this. I didn't call him here so we could hurl insults at him. He's one of the good guys."

Will sucked his teeth. Riley's face reddened.

"Look, I'm not defending everyone on the force. Lord knows there's work to be done. I'm not going to sit here and defend a flawed system that we need to fix, but turning against everyone in uniform isn't going to fix anything. I can show you Toby's video so you can see she saved that woman from death."

"The baby didn't make it though," I said.

"No, the baby didn't make it, and that eats away at Toby every single day. You think she's not traumatized? That she doesn't feel like a murderer? But she saved that woman's life and I hate to say it but with the amount of drugs in her system at the time, that baby may not have survived either way."

I looked over at Will. I'd brought him along because I didn't want my best friend to be uncomfortable having a swarm of police officers on our turf. Will had a run-in with a police officer last year and it had left a bad taste in his mouth, but Riley genuinely was trying to make a difference. I heard him go on and on about it every time our families had gotten together. He wasn't one of those cops who sat there not speaking about his job or dodging questions or making excuses for anyone who did bad things.

"I think this is a good idea," Will said, looking at me, "but we need The Eight in on this too."

"They're already in."

"In on what?" Riley asked. "Don't tell me you need us to go to one of your weird parties."

"That's exactly what we need." Wolf grinned. "Don't worry, you'll only be buried for twenty-four hours."

"You're joking, right?" The look on Riley's face was priceless.

"I need to see the video of the night you arrested Eva Guerra," I said, bringing purpose back to the meeting.

"Eva Guerra?" Riley frowned. "You mean Stella Thompson? That's who I took into the station, and please stop saying we arrested her."

"I need to see the video."

"Fuck." He took out his cell phone and scrolled through until he found the app, then scrolled some more. He set the phone on the table between us and faced it toward us, pressing play.

The video was dark. In the beginning the only sound was of Riley's breath.

"Are you going to get down?" It was a woman's voice, I assumed Toby. "You know I can't do it."

"Yeah, I will," Riley responded. "Shine the lights over there so it's visible on video."

A door opened and shut and then the video showed a woman walking, her back facing the camera. She was wearing jeans and a white blouse.

"Ma'am. May I see some identification?" Riley asked.

"What?" she turned around. Adam's heart stopped when he saw a bewildered-looking Eva.

"Your identification."

She nodded rapidly and reached for her backpack. Then, as if thinking better of it, she put both of her hands up and said, "I'm going to reach into my backpack and get it. Please don't shoot."

My heart cracked open.

"I'm not going to shoot you, ma'am," Riley's voice softened. "I want to help you."

Eva blinked and nodded as she unzipped her bag and rummaged through it, her brows pulling as she looked through the contents. She pulled out her wallet and then the ID from it. She looked at it before she handed it to him.

"Stella Thompson," Riley read. "Is that right?"

"Eva. My name is Eva Guerra." She shook her head, frowning.

"It says here your name is Stella Thompson. Is this a fake ID?"

"I don't have a fake ID."

"So this picture of you with a different name is in your wallet because . . . " Riley let the question hang between them.

"I don't know. I don't know. Look, I can't remember the last few days and I'm just tired and I need sleep and I—"

"I'm going to have to ask you to come with us."

"What?" Eva's eyes widened as she looked at the police vehicle. "Why? I've done nothing wrong."

"We just have a few questions for you."

"But I didn't do anything," she said.

"Please, Miss Guerra. It would be so much easier if you just came without me having to cuff you."

Eva buried her face into her hands. Then someone else came into the picture, a woman in a police uniform. Toby. She stood in front of Eva.

"Hey, I'm Toby. We just want to help you, Eva. Is it okay if we ride together down to the station? We promise you're not in trouble and you'll be free to go as soon as we're done with our questions."

Eva wiped her face and looked at Toby for a moment before nodding. As they walked back to the car she whispered, "I really don't remember what happened."

"That's it." Riley took the phone back. "That was the last time I saw her. Detective Barry took over as soon as we got back to the precinct. Did something happen to her?"

"She's missing."

"Missing," Riley repeated. "Missing like the time we picked her up?"

"It wasn't her who was missing that night, it was her twin."

"What?" Riley shook his head and signaled the waitress over. "Pot of coffee, please." He looked back at us. "I'm going to need at least that much in order to wrap my head around this."

"I agree," Will said.

"Buckle up," Wolf added with a chuckle.

Riley looked over at me again. "Maybe you should start explaining this to me and I need it to be detailed."

So, I did. I told Riley everything, from what happened after the night Eva was taken into the precinct to everything that followed. By the time I finished speaking, Riley had four cups of coffee in his stomach and a worried look on his face.

"You want me to get some of my people to go there tonight, behind Detective Barry's back, and basically work security in case anything goes wrong?"

"And we want you to record all of it."

"That's crazy, you know that, right?" Riley said. "Even if I can get a few to agree to do this, the whole thing is insane. Monks and nuns? Rape? What the hell are you involved in, Adam?"

It was my turn to lean back in my seat. What, indeed. I'd tried so hard to ignore the flaws in The Swords for so long. I'd convinced myself that just because back in the day they hadn't let black people join didn't mean they were racist. After all, Will was there. I'd walked away when I heard the members degrading women. Some vocalized their appreciation for the fact that there were no female members, while others said maybe The Eight was onto something by inviting them in. The Eight, who hadn't publicly been accused of a rape pyramid scheme only because of their powerful members. I'd physically looked the other way when I saw the monks having sex with that woman a few weeks ago. I was tired of it though. I was tired of sitting back. I was tired of not using my privilege for the greater good. I wanted to fix The Swords. I thought Will and Eva were a good start, but it wasn't enough. Fixing was a step in the right direction. Unfortunately, sometimes in order to fix a broken system, you had to dismantle the entire thing.

"Are you going to help us or not?" I looked at Riley.

"Fuck. Do I have a choice after everything you just told me? If I don't help you, I'm complicit in this and that is not what I signed up for."

The four of us shook hands. Riley took one more coffee and some croissants to go. As we watched him walk away, Will turned to me and said, "We need more like him."

I agreed and I knew that in order to do that, we all had to band together.

CHAPTER THIRTY-SEVEN

EVA

"I TRIED TO GET YOU OUT OF THIS, YOU KNOW."

I looked over at Wendy. We were sitting inside of Stella's apartment, waiting for her. I tried telling Wendy that our sister was at The Institute, but Wendy insisted that she'd gotten out and should be in her apartment any minute.

"How'd you try getting me out?"

"I called the cops."

"The night they showed up looking for Stella Thompson?"

"Yeah. Sister Marie said you were in trouble. I called for help."

"You called the cops." I laughed despite myself. "You think they wanna help me? They basically fed me to the wolves and wiped their hands with me. Even if they hadn't, you think they'd choose me over the rich guys in The Manor? That's like asking the Pope to choose between cardinals and monks."

"Pope Francis would choose a monk over a cardinal if the cardinal had done something wrong."

"Maybe." I shrugged.

"Not maybe," Wendy argued. "I know you weren't brought up in the church the way I was, but—"

"Are you kidding? Karen took me to church every Sunday, to CCD classes every Wednesday night, to bible study when I was finished with my communion and confirmation. I was heavily involved in the church. That twisted thing you're involved with has nothing to do with the church I know."

"You're not . . . you're not entirely wrong, but to be fair the nuns are truly followers," she said, and I finally got a glimpse of a woman who could be my sister, unable to admit when she was wrong, not aloud anyway. I felt myself smile as I shook my head.

"When you called the cops that day, why'd you tell them you were Stella?"

"Because you told everyone your name was Stella Thompson, and to be fair, I couldn't tell the two of you apart yet."

"Which is why you cut her hair."

Wendy shrugged and stood, walking over to Stella's bookshelf. She plucked out a thick hardcover and turned it over to me. It was Steve Berry's *The Malta Exchange*. "Have you read this one?"

"I can't tell you the last time I read a fiction book."

"Well, obviously Stella and I have better taste in books." Wendy smiled as she sat down and folded her legs beneath her.

"How are you so normal anyway?"

"Normal?" She glanced up from the book.

"You read thrillers, drink whiskey, talk normal, your name is Wendy, not Sister Mary or something."

"Contrary to popular belief, nuns don't always change their names. Not anymore anyway. Our mother did, Marie did, but that doesn't mean everyone has to." Wendy shrugged. "Besides, we're not nuns, we're sisters, and I'm technically a novitiate. I haven't taken vows yet. I'm not even supposed to be wearing the clothes, but it's not like the monks know one way or another. They barely understand English and they definitely don't understand us."

"The monks don't know English?"

"They're from the Ukraine," she said. "They were also put up for adoption through St. Nicolas'."

"The monks are all adopted?"

"Not like us. They went into the system when they were teenagers. Fourteen, fifteen, sixteen. Most of them are barely eighteen."

"Do you talk to them?"

"Sometimes. It's not like I know Ukrainian."

"But you kidnapped one of them."

"He needed to get out of there before tonight." She looked at the book in her hand. "I wish I could have taken more of them."

"Because they're nice?"

"Because they're kids, Eva." She closed the book with a thump and slid it into her purse. "They're children. They're doing what they're doing because they feel trapped."

"The way you've felt all this time." I met her gaze. She nodded slowly. "How do you communicate with each other? How do you hold Mass?"

"In Latin." She looked at the door. "Stella's taking too long."

"Maybe we should go to The Institute."

"Maybe you're crazy. It's the middle of the day. If we go there, we're screwed."

"Do you think you'll become a nun?" I asked, unable to drop the topic.

"Probably not."

"Did you go to high school?"

"I was homeschooled."

"Oh."

"Trust me, I got a better education than you did."

"I didn't say otherwise." I smiled after a moment. "But I was in honors my entire life, so . . . "

"I saw your grades."

"Did you know that there's a link between St. Nicolas' Orphanage and The Maslows?"

"Yes."

"Do you know why?"

"They were using us for their little experiments."

"What do you mean?" I swallowed. Of course, I'd already come to that conclusion, but hearing it as a fact was unnerving.

"Every single conversation and interaction you had with the fabulous Debbie Maslow was being recorded from the time you were . . . let's see . . . seven months old?"

I let that sink in. "Karen said I had anger issues as a baby. Maybe they were trying to understand it."

"Eva." She shook her head as if annoyed by my excuses. "They ripped us apart when we were just months old. They did the same thing to countless other twins and triplets. They did it on purpose. You think they didn't know we'd all develop anger issues? Depression? Anxiety? They knew."

I thought about it. I let myself believe that for a moment. Rewound the tape of memories in search of something to back up that claim. Time and time again, I found myself sitting across from Debbie, answering questions, accepting hugs, and listening to her tell me who I was. Had the study been about multiples living apart or about the way they could shape and mold human beings into being whoever they told them they were? After all, when someone tells you who you are constantly, it's only a matter of time before you start to believe them. I felt sick. A wave of nausea rolled through me. Without saying a word, I stood up and ran to the bathroom, crouching beside the toilet as I emptied whatever was in my stomach into the bowl. When I finished, I flushed and sat on the floor, my back against the wall. I wanted to see Adam. The thought seeped into my brain and sat there. I really, more than anything, wanted to see Adam. I looked underneath the sink, found an unopened toothbrush and used it before walking back to the living room.

"Do you have my phone?"

"No."

"I want to call Adam."

"Adam?" Wendy sat up. "Are you insane? He's one of them. If you call him our whole plan will go to shit."

"You haven't even told me what the plan is. You keep talking about how my life is so much better than yours and how you tried to save me and how you're going to end the injustice but you haven't told me how I fit into all of this."

The front door unlocked then, and opened. Wendy and I froze and looked in that direction. As Wendy predicted, Stella walked inside, shutting the door behind her, but she wasn't alone. Dr. Thompson was walking right behind her, and behind them, Debbie.

"What the hell?" I said loudly.

"Oh my God," Stella screamed, looking at Wendy. "You were the one sneaking into my room. You cut my hair, you bitch."

"What are you doing here?" I looked at Debbie, at Dr. Thompson. "And you, you've disappeared off the face of the Earth."

As I stood there, looking around the room, it occurred to me that maybe they were all in on this. Maybe I was the butt of the joke. Maybe the nuns had been right. Maybe I was the sacrifice they were all going to make tonight.

CHAPTER THIRTY-EIGHT

ADAM

NIGHTFALL CAME AND EVA WAS STILL NOWHERE TO BE FOUND. THE show had to go on despite that. I knew it better than anyone. They wouldn't let my absence pause whatever was going to happen. Not when they made it such a big deal, inviting all of the past members to partake in the big ceremony. They'd set up torches in a large circle around the clearing in the woods, surrounding the plots they'd dug. The ones closest to The Manor anyway. The woods were covered in buried caskets. There must have been three hundred of them wearing red cloaks. No one had checked IDs or faces; they just assumed if they were here, they were Swords or monks or nuns. The Chancellor himself said this was the most important ceremony of his lifetime when he called me this afternoon. He'd said it would be unforgettable and would unite us in an unbreakable bond. The most unbreakable bonds are the ones in which a crime is committed. The thought shook me to my core, but I knew it was true. If anyone spoke of the crime, we'd all go down. It was the way billion-dollar organizations dismantled time and time again.

"I was reading the history of this place recently," Wolf said. "They say it's built on a Native American burial ground. That has to mean it's haunted, right?"

"America is built on a Native American burial ground," Will said. "Where have you been?"

"Germany." Wolf raised an eyebrow.

"True." Will shrugged and nodded. "Your ignorance is semi-excused."

"Can you focus?"

They both looked at me and quieted.

"We don't know what's going to happen tonight, but we need to do everything we can to protect Eva."

"How do you know she's even here?" Wolf asked. "Maybe they took her away from here."

"She's here. We need to try to separate her from them before the ceremony starts."

"Okay, so we get her and take her somewhere else?" Will asked.

"Anywhere else. Away from here."

"Understood," Wolf said.

"Hoods up." I reached for mine and brought it over my head. With it on, it was difficult to see in this lighting, but not difficult enough. I'd know when I saw Eva. I just hoped I saw her before this started.

"Welcome, Swords." The Chancellor walked to the middle of the circle. He was the only one who didn't wear a hood, but a large pointy hat with a cross instead. "Welcome, Brothers. Welcome, Sisters." He opened his arms to everyone. "Tonight, we are all one, but we will ask our members to stand on the side of The Manor," he said. We were already on that side, so we didn't move. "Tonight is about unity. It's about sacrifice. It's about power. Long before we were a blip in history people have been using sacrifice as a sign of respect. As a way of asking for something. Tonight, we will be performing a ritual that has been performed alongside our Brothers for millenniums. This ceremony is one that is performed every thirty years. This year's, we've been looking forward to for a long time. We've been blessed with a trinity. Thirty years after the last sacrifice, we will make three sacrifices." He smiled then and stepped back. "Let us begin."

Three people stepped forward. I took a step forward. Was it Eva? I couldn't tell. The three people lit the wood they'd laid on the floor and it took me a second to realize what was happening. They were forging a fire between us, as if to make sure we knew our place.

It was the first time in my life that I stood still. Probably because it was the first time that I truly felt the weight of responsibility resting on my shoulders. My last name carried integrity, honor. It was one of the reasons I was the president of the secret society. When they asked me to do something, I did it. I wasn't compelled by a moral compass that others seemed to have. I only knew facts and calculations and those were the things I used to ensure I could do whatever was asked without getting caught.

It was what the men before me would have done. I followed a lineage of men who had led and fought in revolutions. Skilled workers who made money long before I was born. Plaques, busts, and photographs adorned my homes growing up. Reminders of what I should aspire to be like, of what others who came before me accomplished. Some would say that that in itself was a responsibility. The knowledge that not meeting certain requirements by a certain age meant failure. It was the sum of all of those things that drove me to try harder, to be better, to push myself to beat my twin in all things academia, since my brother had me beat in contact sports and other things.

But, as I stood there, my gaze on the licks of the flame, I realized I didn't know a thing about responsibility. And worse, I didn't want it. If being responsible for someone was going to make me feel this helpless, I'd rather not have it, because as she stepped toward the fire and stood still on the other side of it, my heart leaped into my throat. I knew that there were only two things I could do and both ensured the same outcome: we were all doomed. I would have loved to have thought the cops I'd thought to call would help, but we were outnumbered. No amount of hand guns would help, no amount of force. Worse, I realized, was that none of the people on this side of the fire held any power of authority over what was being done. It was church versus state and without a constitution or laws implemented, church would win. I lowered my hood and glanced at Will, who lowered his hood as well, and Wolf who lowered his, and Nolan who lowered his, and Logan who lowered his, and Mae and Nora and Marcus who lowered theirs. How wrong had we all been in the past to pin our societies against each other? Riley and Toby were standing a few feet away. They also lowered their hoods.

It was completely against the Creed for us to lend out hoods like this, but I had no choice. I needed backup and I wasn't sure who I could trust. An unspoken, unilateral, *what the fuck is happening* seemed to cross every single one of our minds. I closed my eyes for a moment, looking down at the ground as the priest who had stepped into the middle of the circle began to pray. The Chancellor had confirmed that there would be three sacrifices, but even as I stood there, I didn't know what to make of that. The crowd on the other side of the fire made way for six men to bring a bench to the center. Another person stepped forward, shoulders shaking. My heart dropped. *Was it Eva?* Whoever it was, was practically dragged to that bench by two of the monks.

They picked her up and laid her on it, but didn't tie her. They leaned down and spoke in her ear and even though I couldn't make out a word, it seemed to calm her down. She stopped shaking and moving and fighting. Soon, more monks stepped forward. The Chancellor stepped forward. The monks began chanting something.

"Is that Latin?" Will whispered.

"Yes," Wolf responded.

"Are they going to sacrifice a human being?" Mae asked behind Adam. "Like kill her? Because you know if they kill someone in front of us and we do nothing we're all complicit."

"And it's fucking murder, Mae." That was Nora. "It's no wonder Nolan can't get Scarlet to join The Eight. These are the things marring our reputations."

"That's not why she won't join and you know it," Nolan said, transfixed on the scene across from them. "Dude, should we do something now? If they kill her . . . "

"They're saying something about virtue and a trinity," Will said.

"You understand them?" Marcus whispered.

"A little. I studied Latin. Don't ask." Will frowned. "Now they're praying. I've never heard this prayer before though."

"What trinity? Like the holy trinity?" Mae whispered. "I don't understand."

I understood though. They were planning to sacrifice one of the three sisters. Maybe all three. I looked all around me. I was surrounded by people who would support whatever move I decided to make, at least that was what I hoped as I stepped toward the fire.

CHAPTER THIRTY-NINE

EVA

Dr. Thompson and Debbie should have been here with the police by now. Wendy had given them little information to go on, but it was enough for them to run to the police while Wendy, Stella, and I ran to The Manor. Dr. Thompson wasn't in agreement with our being here, but after we explained that our birth mother was also here and that we'd have back up from The Swords, he really couldn't stop us from coming.

Stella, Wendy, and I were standing together a few feet from the fire. We didn't know which one of us they'd pull in first, but I hadn't expected it to be Wendy. She turned to look at us, squeezing Stella's hand first and then placing both hands in mine. Even as the monk who was standing just steps away called her name again, she didn't budge. Her brown eyes looking into mine as if she was trying to convey something, but *what?* All of the things we had to say couldn't be said in the measly twenty-four hours we'd had together. The only thing I knew for sure was that Wendy didn't deserve this. None of us did, but unlike Stella and I, Wendy was pure.

"I don't want you to go," I whispered. "Let me take your place."

"This isn't your choice to make." She squeezed my hand again.

"I know what happens next, Wendy." I shook my head. "I don't want you to go."

"The chosen ones survive."

"What?"

"The chosen ones survive. Remember that." She smiled sadly. "It was the honor of my life to meet you and to call you my sister."

The monk closed the distance between us before I could ask her what she was talking about. She went willingly. I covered my mouth to keep from screaming as I watched her walk up to the bench and lay on it. The monks surrounded her quickly and chanted as they walked in a circle as if they were summoning God, or the devil himself to join us. My hands shook at either possibility. I'd spent so much of my life kneeling in a church pew, that you'd think I'd be excited, but all I felt was fear. I slipped a hand into the pocket of my robe and closed it over the covering of the small blade Wendy had provided.

She had tonight's ceremony down to a science. She'd never been to one like this, but she said she knew how it would go. She wasn't sure which one of us would be sacrificed, or how, whether we'd all be used for sex or actually murdered. The fact that we were talking about murder at all was enough to keep my knees shaking. That was what the knife was for though. Wendy told us that if the police still hadn't intervened by the time we were called, we should use the knives. I'd never used a knife before, not for anything outside of the dinner table, but if necessary, I'd definitely make use of this one. I felt jittery as I looked around, my adrenaline spiking with each word the monks spoke, each movement they made.

I watched as the priest stepped forward, as he lifted himself onto the bench in the middle of the monks. I shut my eyes momentarily. I couldn't stand by and just watch. Wendy's plea rang in my head once more. As if sensing my discomfort, Stella reached over and grabbed my hand.

"She said not to intervene."

"How can we not?" I looked at Stella beside me.

"She said not to. They outnumber us."

I looked back at the spectacle. Stella was right. They did outnumber us, but not if the nuns were on our side. Not if they chose us over them. It was something even Stella said she wasn't sure about. *Maybe they'd follow, maybe they won't,* she'd said. *We can't save them all. We're not God.* Stella's hand squeezed tighter when the priest disrobed and stood in yet another robe, this one brown like the one the monks wore. He spoke, said something about the trinity, about sacrifice again, turned his face to look at Stella and me. To seal our fates. *Only the chosen ones survive.* What did that even mean?

"Tonight is a long-awaited night," the priest announced, his voice floating throughout the forest. "Thirty years we've waited for this. Thirty years, and because we have a perfect trinity—three sisters, triplets—we are able to partake in this sacred ritual. Our sisters will raise their gowns tonight and let the men in. Our establishment . . . "

He continued on, but I couldn't make out his words past the ringing in my ears. I looked at Stella.

"Everyone?" I asked. "All of them, all of us, will be raped? Even the elders?"

"I've never . . . " Stella's tears trickled down her face.

"Had sex?" My heart stopped.

"Not like that." She shook her head.

Not with a man. That was what she meant. I knew it and

it killed me that she couldn't say it aloud. She'd just left The Institute. They'd probably done another round of that stupid conversion therapy on her. It killed me that they'd made her think her feelings weren't valid because they weren't for the sex they preferred a woman to be with.

"I won't let them touch you." I squeezed her hand.

Looking around, I wasn't sure what to think about the monks. Were they happy about this? Horrified? Their expressions were blank, completely bare of emotion. It occurred to me that I'd spent the last few weeks vilifying all of them. I hadn't realized how young they were or how coerced they must have felt. I kept saying the rape of that woman, the rape of all of these women today, but in a sense weren't they being raped as well? The ones being forced to participate anyway.

Suddenly, Wendy's kidnapping made sense. If that was the case, what were they so afraid of? We should have gone to them before this, told them they didn't have to do this, before we'd armed ourselves with knives and prepared ourselves to attack. In hindsight, I was beginning to regret a lot of things. At the top of the list—not looking for Adam and telling him what our plan was. I realized that the priest had stopped speaking. When I looked back in that direction, he was kneeling and Wendy was being disrobed.

It all happened fast after that. It wasn't like in the movies, where things played out in slow motion. The only thing I knew was that if I had to stand in front of a jury to explain what happened, I wouldn't be able to. My heart was in my throat as everyone ran past me in every which direction. This definitely wasn't part of the plan. It wasn't anything we'd discussed. What was happening? *Were the cops here? Had I not heard them announcing their arrival?* I looked beside me and realized Stella was no longer there. There were men and women with guns. There were nuns stabbing monks on the ground. There were groans and yells of pain, of remorse, all sounds I tried to block as I tried to listen for Stella's answer to my call.

"Stella?" I looked around frantically, pushing through the crowd. "Stella?"

I couldn't see her. My next instinct was to check on Wendy. As I ran over to the bench, shouldering past the monks running in the opposite direction, I was grabbed from behind. I kicked and screamed, jerking my body to try to free my arms to grab my blade, but it was no use, whoever grabbed me had a hold on me.

"Let go." I tried to fight them off.

"No." He growled, holding me tighter. "You're the sacrifice."

Tried to kick him again. I screamed as loud as I could, screamed again, but it was loud, everyone was screaming. Suddenly, I heard the loud bang of a gun. It was so close to my ears, my hearing was instantly replaced by loud ringing and muffled sounds. Something splatted on my face, covering my eyes, landing on my lips. I reached up and wiped it with the back of my hand and smelled the blood. This time, I screamed at the top of my lungs, but even that was muted to me. I couldn't hear anything. And when a new pair of arms wrapped around me from behind, I couldn't find the strength to fight, or scream, or cry.

"Eva. Eva." It was Adam's voice. He sounded so far away. "Hey. I got you."

"What happened? What's happening? I need to get Wendy." I was still flailing.

He turned me to face him. His face was also covered in blood. I looked down, my heart pounding, and saw a man lying in a pool of blood. When I looked at Adam again the realization of what he'd done sank in. We stared at each other for what felt like an eternity, as chaos continued to ensue around us, wordlessly conveying that there had been no other choice.

"We need to get out of here." He put his hands on my face so that I couldn't look away. "We need to get out now."

"I need to get Stella and Wendy."

"Stella's with Dr. Thompson."

"Wendy." I whipped my head in the direction of the bench and saw her still lying there, saw the blood running down her bare arm, saw the way her face was turned in an abnormal way, her neck bent. I took a deep breath and let it out in a loud shriek that seemed to quiet everything else, though no one stopped moving. "Wendy," I yelled.

"The paramedics are right there," Adam said. "They'll tend to her."

I saw the paramedics he was talking about, but I knew they wouldn't, couldn't tend to her. There was no way. Her neck. Oh my God, he'd killed her. The priest had killed her.

"I'm not leaving." I brought my hands up and knocked Adam's off my shoulders. "I am not leaving." I started running in Wendy's direction as fast as I could.

I was just a foot away when I saw, really saw. The blade was on the floor. The blood wasn't hers. It was the priest's, who was lying in a pile on the ground right beside the bench. Her eyes were wide open, staring at me, into me, through me. Her neck was so bent there was no way . . . there was no way . . . I fell to the ground, tears filling my eyes. Adam's arms were around me in a second.

"Wendy," I said. "She's dead. My sister's dead."

CHAPTER FORTY

ADAM

RAGE THREATENED TO TAKE OVER ME.
Rage because I hadn't been able to help Eva, not really anyway. Rage because things had gotten out of control on my watch. Rage because a place that held so much promise was deteriorating before my eyes and I wasn't sure I could help it. I watched the fire continue to burn and felt it as if it was on me, my own skin burning, my organs and muscles shrinking with it. I wasn't burning though, not physically, despite the way I felt inside. Eva was sitting just feet away, being questioned by Detective Barry and Riley.

They'd brought in strong outdoor lighting to shine on the entire scene. People were still scattered all over the place. Monks and nuns crying. There was blood everywhere, including my own hands. I'd killed that monk and felt sick about it. I saw him pull a knife on Eva though. I saw him grab her from behind, grab her breast as if he had any right to her body. It was happening all around me and when I saw it happening to her, I didn't think, I just acted. I took the gun from Officer Toby's holster and aimed it at the monk's head. I hadn't expected the gore, the pieces of flesh and the blood to splatter all over us. I should have, but those were things I'd only read on paper. I'd never experienced blowing a man's brains out and I definitely didn't want to experience it again. The mere thought of reliving it made me feel sick, but Eva was safe.

The rest of the nuns had also taken matters into their own hands. It seemed as though Wendy's outrage sparked outrage within the rest of them. There must have been at least nine stabbings tonight. None of the nuns were hurt, only Wendy, and she paid the ultimate price. I looked at the blood. Even though I knew it would wash away with the rain scheduled to fall in a couple of days, it didn't matter. Blood had been spilled on our turf. Eva's sister's blood was still spilling from the bench she'd been taken from. My eyes found Eva again. She was still crying, still shaking.

"I'll talk to you later," I said as I started to walk in her direction.

"I'll be next door," Nolan yelled out.

I continued walking. I should have thanked my brother, my friends, everyone who was present for this and would now be traumatized. I didn't stop walking until I reached Eva. When she looked up at me, she stood and threw her arms around me, sobbing into my neck. I lifted her into my arms and started to walk away from the scene. I didn't say anything. I didn't tell her everything was going to be all right because I didn't know. I held her though. I may not know what tomorrow would bring, but I knew that letting her go wasn't an option.

CHAPTER FORTY-ONE

GRIEF CAME IN WAVES.

There was the denial. I'd just met my sisters, just started getting to know them and under insane circumstances, and now I'd lost one. I'd never known a loss this great and some days it felt strange to admit that. She'd only been in my life, in front of my face, for a couple of days, but it was as though we'd known each other our entire lives. When you have a deep connection, regardless of length of time, the pain is magnified. I hated it, really hated it. Most of all, I hated that she was so close to getting out. So damn close.

The anger. The anger I could deal with. I relished when the anger came, like an old friend I hadn't spoken to in years but always seemed to find their way in my life. With the anger came the drinking, and in the past, the sex. I'd lost count as to how many times I'd picked up my phone to look for one of the apps I'd used for hooking up. Every single time, I thought of Adam, and I set it down. He'd allowed me to lose myself in him, but afterward, when I picked myself up and recoiled, the way I had in the past, with strangers, I could see the pain in his eyes. It was something I hadn't experienced with those other guys, since they didn't care about me the way Adam did. Seeing his pain was like inflicting it on myself, so I stopped using sex as a way to channel my anger and was on the path to learning to accept the love that came with it and him.

There was no bargaining in my grief. I knew it wouldn't get me anywhere. I had nothing to bargain with.

The acceptance wasn't coming at all. I just . . . I'd been looking for blood relatives for too long to just accept this loss.

It had been a week since the Manor Murders, as the members of The Eight were now calling it. It would have been a great headline in a paper, except, it wasn't publicized. Even with the police being there and breaking things up. Even with the paramedics who were called. Even with all of the recorded evidence of wrongdoing, nobody outside of the residence knew what happened. It was as if Wendy had been a ghost. As if everyone killed that day had been insignificant in life and now in death. It hurt.

Neil and Debbie had both been arrested, but were out on bail. We had enough videos to put them behind bars, but because they'd been acquired by hacking into their server, they may not hold up in court. This was how I found myself walking into The Institute. After meeting with The Swords and The Eight, my memory was refreshed on what happened last year, when Amelia Bastón's father had been arrested for murdering a girl. He'd been arrested and acquitted. Innocent men were placed behind bars and guilty ones walked every single day. I wasn't going to leave any of this to chance. And Debbie was still here, running the show as if she had nothing to worry about. I jotted my name down on the check-in sheet and waited for them to process my arrival.

"Eva?" Debbie's voice made me freeze.

I turned slowly. When I looked at her, I felt nothing but sadness. I should have felt anger. I would have welcomed anger, but that wasn't how the mind worked. She'd conditioned me to see her as an ally, a source of comfort, and so my treacherous emotions were at odds.

"I'll take her to her room, Candace," Dr. Maslow said to the nurse as she walked over to me. "Come."

I went. It was as if my feet weren't my own.

She took me to the room I'd come to know as my own and walked me over to the seating area, which was a bench in a little nook where I was surrounded by biographies, memoirs, and early education books.

"I should have reached out weeks ago. I'm sorry," she said. "I should have explained everything then. I'm sure you've heard awful things about us in the news, but you know how much they lie."

"Were they lying about you owning St. Nicolas' Orphanage?"

"Well, no, but to be fair, my great-great-grandfather was the owner and it fell upon us that way, otherwise we would have never sought it out."

"Did they lie about you specifically targeting women in need? Bringing them over here and paying for their medical bills, their food, their children's food, and then ripping the babies away from them?"

Debbie searched my eyes. I found no remorse in hers. No sign of discomfort. Nothing. My anger flared.

"Did they lie about you using my sisters and me in a study that's lasted twenty years? Did they lie about how you recorded each interaction we had? Or how you trained us to sit here like this with you without ripping your eyes out the way we should have? Or how you turned us against our own parents because you needed us to be on your side and not theirs?" My voice was hoarse from shouting, my cheeks wet with tears, but I couldn't seem to stop. "You tore families apart when you played God as if we were puppets for you to control and feed drugs to."

"You needed those drugs."

"No." I slammed my fist against the seat. "I needed my sisters. I needed real love."

"It wasn't fake," she said, her voice a whisper. "I didn't fake anything during our time together. I love you, Eva. I love all of you." Her eyes filled with tears.

"Wendy is dead."

"And I'm sorry about that. It should have never happened. We should have never trusted those sick, satanic monks." She glanced away briefly. "I am sorry. I tried to stop it years ago, once we realized there may be a link between all of your anger."

"And why didn't you? Why didn't you tell us about each other?"

"By then it was too late to tell you. The damage was done and . . ." She shook her head, wiping her face.

"And what? Your lawyers didn't approve of you coming clean?"

"What we did was entirely legal. Your parents signed a contractual agreement with us."

"Just because something is legal, doesn't mean it's ethical or morally right." I wiped my own face with both hands. "I hate you. I hate you and Neil and I hate what you've done to us. I hate that I took my anger out on Karen for so many years when most of it wasn't even her fault."

"Karen is a drunk."

"Because of me," I yelled, rearing forward. "She's a drunk because of me."

"She's a drunk because her mother was a drunk and her grandmother was as well. We've been watching her family for generations too. You think she's exempt from this? You think she's just a random person we chose to give you to?"

I gasped, covering my mouth and pulling away as if her words had slapped me. I wasn't sure what was worse, that this was written in the stars before I was even a blip on their radar, or that they'd given me to a person they knew was predisposed to becoming a drunk and were okay with that. Either way, my life felt like it had been a lie. Everything was a lie.

"What about having Stella here while I was at The Manor? What the fuck was up with that?"

"That wasn't my idea." She looked away. "Dr. Thompson caught wind of everything and didn't want his daughter involved with The Swords."

"So he was involved?"

"He didn't want either of you involved, but having you in The Manor meant his daughter wouldn't be."

"What are you not telling me?"

"Neil thought it would be a good idea to switch you. To tell you that you were Stella and tell her she was Eva. To see how you'd react to different socioeconomic backgrounds now that you were already developed by your own."

"So you, what, tried to erase my memory?"

"It didn't work. I hoped it wouldn't."

"I have no memory of those three days," I screamed.

"But you remembered who you were when you were at the station. You knew there was no Chris Ryan from Tinder. You knew and you went along with it and you agreed to go to The Manor in Stella's place. You're not innocent in all of this. You took their money, you used Stella's car, her clothes."

"Using my sister's car and clothes to try to find her is a

far cry from what you were doing for twenty years," I yelled. "Twenty years, Debbie."

"Like I said, I wish we hadn't."

"But you did. You stood by and watched."

I stood up and walked to the door.

"Where are you going?"

"Away from here. You're a monster. You're all monsters." I yanked on the door handle, but couldn't open it. I'd never been locked in. Not once. I looked at her over my shoulder.

"It's for your own good, Eva." She smiled sadly. "I'm sorry."

"No." I checked again, my heart thumping louder, faster, my hand slapping the door as I jiggled the doorknob. "Let me out. Let me out!"

"You need to stay a little while." I heard her come up behind me.

I knew she was close. I moved my elbow to jab her in the ribs with it and made contact. I heard her sharp intake of breath and shriek. The doors opened and two people walked in. I ran past them, even as they grabbed my arms I continued running, my feet lifted off the air, going nowhere.

"No," I screamed, thrashing against them. "No!"

They squeezed me harder, carried me back into the room. One of them grabbed my neck and squeezed, the pressure going to my head and making my vision instantly blur. They'd used this technique before. I knew it was only a matter of time before I blacked out. I knew they were seconds from tying me to the bed.

"I haven't signed the papers," I yelled at the top of my lungs. "I haven't signed the papers. You can't hold me here."

"Oh, Eva." Debbie walked over and set a hand on my forehead, her blue eyes all calm and caring. Fake. "I guess you forgot that I also have power of attorney over you while you're in here."

As the nurses settled me into the bed, one of their hands stopped moving and I knew. My heart launched into my throat. I started to sweat. The overhead light was nearly blinding me, but I kept blinking in hopes that I could see their faces clearly and remember them. They were all going down.

"She's wearing a recording device," one of them said.

"The little light is blinking," another said, the pressure on my neck tightening. My eyes began to roll. My limbs began to relax.

"Fuck." That was Debbie.

And then—nothing.

CHAPTER FORTY-TWO

ADAM

I GOT A CALL IN THE MIDDLE OF ASTRONOMY: INTRO TO GENERAL Relativity, a class I wasn't required to take, but chose as an elective because I figured there was no better place to learn about the subject than the place where Carl Sagan once taught. I grabbed my things and stepped out, answering Officer Riley's call before I reached the hall.

"You're not going to believe this, but Eva is in the hospital. She was found not far from The Institute."

"Found? What do you mean found?"

"She went to The Institute wearing a wire, something she'd set up with Detective Barry, and they threw her out when they realized they were being recorded."

"She . . . what? Where is she now?"

"Down at Cayuga."

I hung up the phone and rushed down the hall. The only reason I'd left Eva yesterday was because she'd been staying at Dr. Thompson's rental home with Stella and Karen. I figured she couldn't possibly not be safe there. As I was leaving Dr. Thompson's house, I made sure to speak to Karen so she'd keep an eye on Eva and not let her do anything stupid like go after Dr. Maslow. Somehow, I knew she'd try that. I knew she couldn't live without getting answers. It was what drove her to The Manor in the first place, but I had people working on it. I'd hired lawyers and investigators and promised her to stay on top of it. When I got to my car, I took a moment to close my eyes and take a breath. *Why did she have to be so stubborn?*

By the time I reached the hospital, all of the anxiety that I thought had been erased by The Swords had rushed back. I couldn't stop imagining the worst. Karen was walking out of the hospital room when I reached it. When she saw me she ran over and gave me a quick rundown.

"She's fine. I don't know what possessed her to go to The Institute after we had such a long conversation about it." She shook her head. "They're only allowing two visitors at a time. Stella's in there now. You can go ahead. I'm going to go get coffee."

"Thank you." I walked into the room and found Eva sitting in bed with an IV coming out of her arm. When she saw me, she smiled and I felt my annoyance diminish, just a little. "What the hell were you thinking?"

She sighed, lowering her head as I reached her and sat on the bed, holding her free-of-IV hand in mine.

"I just don't understand. What were you doing? Why would you go in there alone? Why were you wearing a wire? Why would you keep this from us?"

"I wasn't keeping it from you." She looked up again, meeting my gaze. "I just . . . didn't want anyone else to get hurt. Detective Barry and Officer Toby were outside, waiting for me. They even had an FBI lady with them. I was fine."

"You were fine?" My voice rose. "If you were fine then why are you here?" As I spoke, I spotted a bruise beneath the sleeve of her oversized hospital gown and lifted it. The anger rose again. I looked at her. "Fine? This is fine?"

"They tossed her out like she was a rag," Stella said behind him. I watched as she drew near and stood on the other side of the bed. "They tried to hold her there but when they realized she was wearing a wire, they tossed her out. Literally tossed her out into the woods behind the hospital."

"Are you fucking kidding me?" My voice trembled.

I'd been furious before, but this was the last straw. If those officers hadn't been there, waiting, surveilling, who knows what would have happened to Eva inside of those walls. I said that aloud and watched as Eva swallowed before shooting me a small smile.

"Nothing that hasn't happened before," she said.

"That doesn't make it any better."

"It's not meant to, but it's the truth. They've gotten away with so much already." She shrugged a shoulder.

"We can't let them keep getting away with it," Stella said.

"We won't." I stood and placed my hands on my hips, shutting my eyes briefly as I tried to gather my thoughts.

"That's why I went," Eva said. "All the evidence we have against them was stuff we'd gotten by hacking into their system. I spoke to Detective Barry about it and he said he'd been in contact with the FBI and they were making a case, but that if I wanted to add any information that would be helpful, they'd be glad to take it."

I shook my head. "Jesus, Eva. It wasn't enough that they fed you to the wolves once?"

"I don't want to talk about this anymore. I did what I did and it's over." She closed her eyes. "Can I rest now?"

Stella and I looked at each other and walked out of the room.

"The good news is, they fixed our prescriptions here," Stella said as soon as they'd closed the door behind them. "They were totally overmedicating us." She looked up at me.

"It's a start. Is Karen still staying at your house?"

"Yeah, Dad said he'd rather we all stay there until this is over."

"How's he doing?"

"After getting over the initial shock about him going missing and feared for dead? Fine. He just can't believe two esteemed doctors would turn on him and fabricate a story like that."

"I don't think we'll ever understand it."

The problem ran deep and was centuries old. I wasn't sure there was much we could do aside from sue the Maslows and The Institute. The orphanage was no longer standing, so we couldn't go after them. It wasn't like Stella needed the money, or Eva now, but who knew how many other patients they had like this.

"Are they done searching your premises?"

"No, they're still out there. I don't even know what they're looking for at this point."

"Maybe they're just being nosey and want to see what it is The Swords do for kicks."

"Well, they won't find much." I smiled. "We're not as creepy as people think we are."

"You call it hunting when you look for new members. That's pretty creepy."

I shrugged. Maybe it was creepy and I wasn't entirely sure where they could go from here. I'd set up a meeting about that later tonight, but first I had to make sure Eva wouldn't do anything else that would put her in danger and the only way I knew to do that was to stay at the hospital until they let her go home later.

"You could just have an open-invite policy," Mae suggested.

"That would take away the secret aspect of the society," I said.

"You have to change with the times, man," Logan added.

They weren't suggesting anything outlandish. Most of the other secret societies weren't very secretive at all. They'd shed their cloaks and invited outsiders, people who had no previous ties to the societies. They published their names in the school newspaper. Maybe that was the future of The Swords as well. Maybe they needed to hang up their cloaks. It could be a beginning, but it wouldn't solve the issue entirely. They all—The Swords, The Eight, The Seven, Skull and Bones, the Order of Gimghoul, Quill and Dagger—needed to adapt to the times. They needed to be more inclusive and work on minimizing the bad reputations they'd gained over the years because of their misconducts.

Those were things I would have to do from another position. I'd been giving it a lot of thought and decided that I'd be passing the baton to Will. I'd still be around to help out and attend major events, but it would be up to Will to report to whoever the next person in charge was. So far, the benefactors hadn't said. They did write everyone a letter stating that they cut ties with the church, and that bit of news helped ease the discomfort. According to the interim chancellor, the Byzantine priest as well as the monks and nuns had gone rogue over forty years ago and hadn't been backed by the archdiocese. Whether or not the newcomers knew that was a different story.

"Adam, are you listening?"

"What?" I blinked and pushed my thoughts aside.

"Is Eva okay?"

"Yeah, she'll be fine as long as she stops looking for trouble."

"Did her mom survive?" Nolan asked.

"All of the nuns did," I said, except for Wendy. She'd sacrificed herself, after all. "They're still in police custody."

"Jesus." Will exhaled. "Who would have thought?"

"I told you to join The Eight," Nora said, "but you're too stubborn."

"As if The Eight doesn't have its own issues," I responded. "You think a sex ring scandal like the one you guys have will just go away?"

"It's not a scandal," Logan said.

"Not yet." I shot him a look. "Until one of the girls decides to speak up and bring you all down."

"That won't happen," Mae said. "They all were there willingly and signed contracts, so unfortunately, even the ones who should speak out and be heard, probably won't."

"And it wasn't our society, it was the benefactors who created a separate entity," Nolan said. "We have nothing to do with it."

"I'm just saying, don't act surprised when those worlds collide and you're all screwed over."

"My father is no longer the president of The Eight and he was the main source of the problem, so I don't think that'll happen," Mae said.

"Rings aren't usually controlled by just one person. Look at what happened to us."

"What's still happening," Wolf said. He'd been oddly quiet this entire time, scrolling his phone, so when he turned it over to the rest of them and they saw the headline, all of their jaws collectively dropped.

Fetus Remains Found Buried in Yard of Rogue Priests' Homes

"So much for keeping secrets," Nora murmured.

"According to this article, the Catholic Church says they stopped funding or accrediting these people over thirty years ago," Mae said.

I knew that. It was what I'd heard from Riley, but fetuses? Disgust rolled through me. How long had these things been going on while I was there? While I waved at them. While I spoke to Father Becker and played the piano for him.

"I guess it's a good thing you're an atheist." Nolan punched Adam's shoulder playfully.

I rolled my eyes, shaking my head. I knew my brother was trying to lure me into going on a rant about religion, but I wouldn't give in. I was too busy trying to find ways to leave this organization better than I found it and in a sense, it would be, but it could always be better.

CHAPTER FORTY-THREE

HE KEPT ON COMING BACK. I DIDN'T KNOW WHY. I'D BEEN AWFUL the last few days. I was either not speaking at all or shouting all of my words. It was like I'd regressed to my teenage years and I couldn't find a way to control my anger for the injustices. Stella blamed my new medication. She said it would take a while to adjust to them. I imagined she was right. It still sucked to not feel like I was in control of my emotions though, especially around people who were being so kind to me.

"Adam's here." Karen's voice was soft.

I looked up at her from my place at the window bench I was perched on and nodded. We'd been staying at Dr. Thompson's rental, a mansion he'd been staying at for a while, since he started working at The Institute in the middle of last year. He'd invited us here and hired some private security ba-dasses to keep us safe. And yet, I felt unsafe. Of course, Dr. Thompson had apologized for dragging me into all of this. He'd been trying to protect his own daughter. He genuinely thought he'd be able to get me out of The Manor in a day, two days tops, once he got to the bottom of everything. He hadn't realized there was no bottom to this, no end. He hadn't expected The Maslows to go after him the way they did, to bully him into hiding out by using his daughter's safety against him, to plant stories about his mysterious disappearance. The entire thing was troubling, and now they'd found remains of unborn children and children born and killed right away. After interviewing the monks and nuns they had in custody, they found that the rapes had been happening for decades and because the women weren't allowed birth control, this was their way of covering them up.

I was sitting by the window today, perched upon the bench with a Billy Jensen book at my feet from my sister's collection, when Adam showed up. He was wearing dress pants, a light blue button-down, and a white lab coat. He kissed the top of my head and sat across from me; his hazel eyes searched mine momentarily before they fell on the book at my feet. He picked it up and turned it over to read the back.

"Have you started reading it?" He glanced up at me.

"Not yet."

"How long have you been sitting here?"

"What time is it?"

"Six thirty." He checked his watch and looked at me again.

"So, I guess . . . five hours?"

"Just staring outside?"

"Just thinking."

"What have you been thinking about?"

"Just life." I shrugged a shoulder.

"Why won't you come live with me, Eva?"

My bottom lip trembled. I could practically hear the heartache in his voice and it killed me. He'd asked me to go live with him as soon as I got out of the hospital a week ago and I'd said I'd think about it, as if there was so much to think about. My lease on my apartment would be up in a few weeks; they'd called me from the school saying there was an opening for a first-grade teacher that I would be perfect for. They'd even hire me while I waited to get my certification, since I was only two classes away from graduating. Adam was hot, smart, caring, ambitious, and I loved him. Really, what was there to think about? Nothing.

He set the book down and scooted forward, closing the distance between us. I lifted my legs and let him lift me onto his lap, setting my head on his chest. Closing my eyes, I listened to his heartbeat, took comfort in his scent.

"Tell me what to do," he said against my hair. "If you want me to stay here with you and hold your hand, I will. If you want me to carry you out of here, I will. You just need to tell me."

"I just need time," I whispered, tears rolling down my cheeks.

"Then I'll give you time." He kissed the top of my head and pulled away, wiping my tears with his thumbs. "I love you, you know that, right?"

"I know you do."

He smiled. He didn't even look hurt by the fact that I hadn't said it back. Instead, he leaned in, kissed me, and stood. He walked over to the box he brought and uncovered it on his way back over.

"Happy birthday, Eva." He walked over with it and set it between us on the bench.

I began to cry, and as the door opened and Karen, Stella, Dr. Thompson, Will, Mae, Logan, Nora, Wolf, and Nolan walked inside, I felt myself cry harder. When I looked at the cake, really looked at it, I realized it said *Happy Birthday, Eva,*

Stella & Wendy. Stella walked over and set a hand on my shoulder as they sang to us. We both wiped the tears from our faces, and as we blew out the candles, I wished Wendy was finally at peace, and that I'd have endless more birthdays just like this one, surrounded by these people.

EPILOGUE

EVA

MORE FAMILIES COME FORWARD IN A LAWSUIT AGAINST ESTEEMED *psychotherapists Debbie and Neil Maslow. After some sinister information about their famed Twins Study was brought to light, more families of multiples who had been ripped apart have come forward looking for justice.*

Switching off the news, I flung the remote control to the couch beside me. I was tired of following this news story. It was maddening enough that we were living it and the trial hadn't even started. Stella said she'd stopped watching it altogether. Since the whole ordeal, she'd started openly dating Cameron. She spent her entire life worried about coming out, because of church, and her father and brother, but when she finally told them, the only thing she received was support. Even Karen, who hadn't been accepting of things like that in the past was happy my sister felt safe enough to be herself around us and always invited Cameron over to her now weekly barbecues. I'd moved in with Adam the day after my birthday. It felt right.

Opening up my computer, I continued working on my paper. It was the last one of the semester before I graduated.

The last one until I started working on my master's in the fall. I hadn't planned on it originally. Originally, I thought I would just get a job in the small parish school, but I couldn't after everything. My phone rang with a 607 area code number. It was the fifth time this week they'd called and left no message, so I answered.

"Hello?"

There was silence on the other end.

"Hello?"

"Hi." It was a woman's voice.

"Um. Hi?"

"This is Penelope." She paused. "Your mother. Your birth mother."

"Oh." I shut my laptop. "Hi."

"I'm sorry it took so long for me to call."

"No. I mean, you were doing the mute thing."

"I was a coward," she said. "From the beginning. They brought us to this country the moment they found out I had triplets and then they ripped you away from me. And I let them." Her voice was calm, soothing, and very matter-of-fact. "I'm sorry. I should have stood up for you. For myself."

"Yeah. I mean, you should have, but it's fine. I mean, it's not fine, but it's over, what can we do?" I shrugged, all nonchalant, even though she couldn't see me through the phone line, but deep down I was angry. *My sister was dead and this woman was just now calling me?* "Why are you calling now?"

"I just needed to apologize. I didn't see it. Not until Wendy . . ." She let her words hang. "And by then it was too late."

"It was too late." My chest ached at the mention of her name.

"She made the ultimate sacrifice for us."

"She did," I said, my voice breaking before I cleared it. "I accept your apology."

"We're all just trying to survive, you know? We ignore the things that hurt us and box the ones we think will break us. I think that's what I was doing all those years."

"You were my daycare teacher," I said. "You were there and said nothing."

"I only took that job to be closer to you, but then I met Karen and I knew she loved you, so I stepped away. She did better than I could have."

I nodded, unable to say anything past the knot in my throat. Karen and I had many conversations about both of our past words and actions and agreed to let bygones be bygones. The only thing we could do now was move forward and do better.

"I'm sorry I called," she said.

"No, thank you for calling. It's . . . it's good to know you cared."

We said our goodbyes and hung up. I couldn't be sure how much time passed while I just held the phone in my hands and stared at the wall, thinking about that conversation, but I knew that by the time Adam got home, it was dark out.

"Hey." He set down his keys on the table by the door and slid off his shoes before walking over. He was holding a bouquet of wildflowers in one hand and a brown takeout bag in the other. When he reached me, he leaned in and kissed me. "How was your day?"

"It was . . . interesting." I sat up straighter. "I just got a call from my mom?"

"Oh? What'd she say? Yes to Christmas in Mykonos? Stella and Cameron just confirmed." He walked over to the kitchen and started unboxing our food.

"No. I mean, my birth mom." I stood up and walked over.

"What?" He froze, the wooden chopsticks in his hand as he stared at me.

"She just called and apologized. It was the weirdest freaking phone call of my life."

"It sounds intense." His brows rose. "Is she still a nun?"

"I didn't ask."

"Is she still at Ellis?"

"I didn't ask."

"Did you talk at all?"

"I . . . yeah." I helped him take our food to the table and sat down next to him. "It's crazy. All my life I wanted to know about my birth mother and it took everything that happened for me to realize that it wasn't really what I needed. I just needed family."

I thought about The Swords, Stella, Karen, Dr. Thompson, The Eight, and all the people I'd met throughout all of this. They weren't the family I'd been given. They weren't even necessarily the family I would have chosen for myself. But they were definitely the family I needed. The family I loved. That I'd do anything for. I put my hand on Adam's. He seemed to sense that I had a lot on my mind, because he stopped eating.

"What's up?"

"You know I love you, right?"

He dropped his chopsticks and laughed.

"Why are you laughing?" I slapped his hand, unable to stop my own smile.

"Because you finally achieved your full potential."

AFTERWORD

One of the most common questions I get is: where do you get your inspiration?

My answer is always the same: everywhere.

I listen to conversations, have conversations, and obsess over conversations. My favorite thing to do is take something and create a "what if".

This particular story stemmed from four things.

The first was a conversation I had with my friend's grandfather at brunch one day. Full disclosure, I was talking to my friend's girlfriend about weddings and my ears perked up when I heard the grandfather talking about all of the fetuses and babies found in a monastery in Cuba years back. That conversation has been at the forefront of my mind for over a year.

The second thing is this—I went to a private high school that was run by priests and nuns and monks. The monks were from Ukraine and were in our classes. My junior year, one of the monks (who was one of my classmates), killed a nun. He stabbed her 97 times. I will never, for as long as I live forget that number, or the faded bloody footprints we found days after the murder when the school went on as if nothing had happened.

The third thing, the triplet thing—I watched a documentary on Hulu and it's stayed with me. As a psychology student, I worked in the research lab my last few years there. I helped with a longevity study they were working on about the socioeconomic impact on people, in which they were following people from the time they were in elementary school until they were grandparent age. The Hulu documentary followed triplets who met during college. They were all adopted and had no idea the other existed before then. At some point after meeting they discovered they'd been part of a psychological experiment their entire lives. It was as riveting as it was devastating.

The fourth, the burials and caskets—my grandfather used to build caskets when my mother was a little girl. Her cousins have all sorts of stories about the caskets - hiding in them, burying them and hiding things in them, etc. I'm sure I'll incorporate more caskets in other stories because I have endless stories about them. Needless to say, my family get togethers are a bit strange ;)

So, this book is about a lot of things, as you just read, but more than anything it's about sacrifice. It's about our will to survive and find our place in the world, and I think that's extremely relatable.

Thank you for reading!
Xo,
Claire

Ps. Nolan's book is next.

Join my Facebook group, Claire Contreras' Crew, for exclusive content..

ClaireContrerasbooks.com

Twitter: @ClariCon

Insta: ClaireContreras

Facebook: www.facebook.com/groups/ClaireContrerasBooks

OTHER BOOKS

SECRET SOCIETY
Half Truths

NAUGHTY ROYALS
The Sinful King

The Trouble With Love
Fake Love
The Consequence of Falling
Because You're Mine

SECOND CHANCE DUET
Then There Was You
My Way Back to You

The Wilde One
The Player

THE HEART SERIES
Kaleidoscope Hearts
Torn Hearts
Paper Hearts
Elastic Hearts

DARKNESS SERIES
There is No Light in Darkness
Darkness Before Dawn